Legends and

Vows

Also by Greg Judge

Schea

Schea's Revenge

Voyages To Secrets

All are available on Amazon.com (Paperback or Kindle Formats)

GREG JUDGE

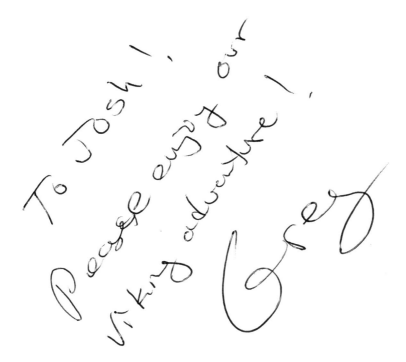

To Josh!,
Peasse enjoy our
viking adventure!,
Greg

Legends and

Vows

Legends and Vows

Cover Design by Jaclyn Judge, rothj3790@gmail.com

ISBN: 13: 978-1722200152

10: 1722200154

Fiction/Action & Adventure

To my brother, Mike, who has been an avid supporter of my efforts to become an author, and my most ardent and helpful critic. Thanks.

ACKNOWLEDGEMENTS

I would like to thank all of my family and friends who have supported and encouraged me through this entire process. They are so important to me in helping me to continue to feel motivated and excited about becoming an author.

I would also like to thank several people in particular. I would like to thank my brother, Mike, for his wonderfully helpful critical reviews of my work. They always help me to think more deeply about fresh ideas. I would like to thank my friends, Sandy, Pam and Deborah, who enthusiastically read my manuscript and provided excellent editorial suggestions for spelling, grammar and changes in the story. I would like to thank Claudia who I met by chance on one of my trips. She graciously agreed to apply her professional editing skills to my work.

I would like to thank Jaclyn for agreeing to lend her very talented artistic skills to the cover design. She not only did a wonderful job on the cover but also had a number of interesting ideas about the story.

Lastly, but certainly not least, I want to thank all of my readers. I am so happy that so many of you have also chosen to tell me your thoughts and feelings about my projects - it has all been extremely helpful to me. It also pleases me greatly when you tell me that you have enjoyed reading my stories. Thank you all so very, very much.

Chapters   Title

Chapters	Title
Prologue - 950 CE	Escape
One - Present Day	Going In
Two	Jason
Three	Discussion
Four	Erik
Five - (includes Present Day and 995 CE)	History
Six - Present Day	Missing
Seven - 1025 CE	Father and Son
Eight - 1055 CE	Final Burial
Nine - Present Day	Nicole
Ten	Caught
Eleven	Learning
Twelve	Changing
Thirteen	Off and Running
Fourteen	Following
Fifteen	Ingvill
Sixteen - 1605 CE	Yorkshire
Seventeen	To Oslo
Eighteen	Joana
Nineteen	Aki's Family - Hugin

Twenty	Nicole and Ingvill
Twenty-one	Plans and More Plans
Twenty-two	To Iceland
Twenty-three	All the Rest
Twenty-four	Planning the Hunt
Twenty-five	Iceland
Twenty-six	Team Building
Twenty-seven	Watching
Twenty-eight	Preparations
Twenty-nine	A Long Trek
Thirty	On the Move
Thirty-one	The Hunt
Thirty-two	On a Hike
Thirty-three	The Mountain
Thirty-four	Skjaldbreizzur
Thirty-five	Climbing a Mountain
Thirty-six	Treasure
Thirty-seven	Confrontation
Thirty-eight	Help
Thirty-nine	Decision Time

Forty   The Visit

Forty-one   The Next Day

Forty-two   The Meeting

Forty-three   One More Vow

Epilogue - Two Years Later   Final Vow

Legends and Vows

Prologue – 950 CE

Escape

Yngvarr stood beside his father, Ragnvadr, and grandfather, Aki. They watched the large, and growing, hoard of warriors gathering across the valley along the grassy hillside. The sun was behind the hillside and it shimmered off of the warriors' bright helmets, breastplates and swords. Their leader was Arild and he would win this battle; but Ragnvadr hoped that his son could eventually win the war.

Arild and his army had come to Ragnvadr's homeland of Hafrsfjord from Ytre Moa. Both areas were located along the coast of what is today known as Norway with access to the sea. Arild had long wanted access to ports in the south with better access to the lands of the Danes where he suspected there was great wealth to be had. He also wanted his kingdom to be farther from the wild Saami people on his land's northern border.

Ragnvadr turned to his father, Aki, who was already looking back at his son and grandson. He spoke what Ragnvadr was reluctant to say. "We need to save our men and their families, and our heritage. The disease that passed through our villages last year killed many of our people and reduced our number of young men and warriors. We cannot defeat Arild and his men. They are too many and we are a small force."

Ragnvadr nodded and looked at his son. "Yngvarr, go to the men and tell them to make ready to sail. Tell them to load all three of our ships with all the food, water and weapons they can find then place their families in two of the ships. You and the young men will take the third ship and grandfather will take the two ships with the families."

Yngvarr knew that his father was trying to be wise with this decision. They were vastly outnumbered by Arild's army of warriors and his people would be slaughtered if they stayed. Yngvarr's name meant "warrior of the god Ing", but he would have to accept that he would not be a warrior today.

Ragnvadr turned to his father, "You will go to the Yerke settlement to the south. And you, Yngvarr, will go to the settlement to the west in Thule. Your ship will carry our wealth and you will secure it there. Hopefully, the silver, gold and other precious items will allow you, or your sons, to come back some day and take back our lands and our rights. These precious items came from many generations of raids in the lands far to the east where the desert people live, and to the south where the wild painted people live."

"Where will you go, father?"

"I am staying." He saw the look on Yngvarr's face, and continued. "I cannot leave. I must stay and do what I can to bring honor to our name. I will also give you and father the time you will need to make your escape. I have my loyal oath-swearers along with many older warriors who have no one to start over with. They will all stay with me and we will all die here, in our land, near our homes. We will then dine and drink in Valhalla together. You two will join us in your own time." He paused and looked between his father and son. He truly loved them.

"Now, go! Go with Odin and tell your children and grandchildren all that has happened here."

Aki and Yngvarr each took and held Ragnvadr's arm then turned and left for the ships. When they arrived, they saw the men busily loading the two ships that would go with Aki to Yerke. Besides their families, they also took as many widows and orphaned children they could fit into the ships. The ships usually accommodated 80-90 warriors with all of their weapons and supplies, but this voyage would test their sailing and shipbuilding skills because they would be carrying over 100 people plus weapons and supplies.

Meanwhile, Yngvarr's men were loading the wealth of the land onto their ship.

While the men continued loading, Aki and Yngvarr moved off to have a private conversation. "Yngvarr, we need to keep your voyage secret in order to keep our wealth safe. You will also need to find a secure hiding place in Thule to hide it. Since only you will be hiding it, only you will be able to tell where it is located. We need to split the knowledge of its location between us. My secret will be where you went and your secret will be how to find it once there."

"But, grandfather, how will our sons know where to start? I have never been to Thule."

"I have been to Thule. It was a long time ago but I remember enough about the place to tell you where to start. It is a small island so it will not take you long to find this place. Sail in the direction of where the sun sets until you reach Thule. When you see the land, continue sailing along the coast with the land on your right. When the land turns away to the right of you, follow it. There is a good size inlet of sea, and the land will continue beyond it. Go into this inlet and continue sailing until you reach land again. Start there."

"I will do as you suggest. My father's brother is going with you to Yerke so his descendants will know that our wealth is located on Thule and mine will know the exact location but not where to start. I will tell my sons to go to Yerke in order to join forces with yours to recover our wealth. Hopefully, with that wealth, they will be able to build a new army, and come back to our land to reclaim it for our people."

They grasped each other's arms, hugged and departed for their ships.

XXXXX

Ragnvadr and his small band of loyal men were overrun by the invading army. They fought hard and killed many of the enemy, but there were just too many of them. They were killed and Arild's men did not bury their bodies. Instead, they were left where they fell to rot, and provide food for the birds and wild dogs.

Arild quickly dispatched men to search for the wealth but they found none. There were also no ships in the small harbor which meant that many of the people must have left in those ships. Unfortunately, Arild would have to wait a day for his own ships to sail into the harbor. Fortunately, one of Arild's men had seen the old man head south and the boy head to the west, and he told Arild. Arild decided he would send a ship after the son, figuring he had the wealth.

After three months had passed, and his ship had not yet returned, Arild sent another one. Two months later, that ship made it to Thule. There were few settlers there because much of the island had been covered with ash and debris when the Harkla Mountain erupted a generation ago.

The leader of the ship went onto the island with most of his men, leaving a handful to protect his ship. He found some settlers in a small inlet after two days of searching. They told him that a ship had been there several months ago, stayed for a few weeks resupplying then left.

The ship captain figured they had headed to the much larger island he knew to be in that direction, so he sailed for it and arrived after another three months of sailing. He sailed along its coastline looking for any evidence of people or safe harbors. He found none so he turned back for home.

One year after leaving, they pulled into their homeland's harbor and the ship captain immediately went to Arild to make his report. Arild was not happy but he had known it was a long shot to actually catch the son and find the treasure.

XXXXX

Yngvarr and his men stopped in Thule where they stayed for close to one month. He found very few people and many seemed to have only been there for a short time. Most of the men they met spoke the same language as they did but the woman spoke a language he could not begin to understand. The men told him that the women were mostly from the lands to the south and were brought to Thule after raids in those lands.

During that month, Yngvarr had part of his crew restock the ship while he and the rest of them loaded the wealth of his people onto rough made sleds then drag it all inland to find a good place to hide it. As they slowly trudged into the wilderness, Yngvarr made careful note of where they were, how long they had walked, and any landmarks he spotted.

After five days, they found a location to hide the wealth near a small settlement the locals called Thingvellir. They found a cave in a remote area with a small opening but a fairly large cavern. They loaded everything into the cave then sealed the entrance with stones and other debris from around the area.

When they arrived back at their ship it was fully loaded with supplies, and the rest of the crew was waiting. They set sail the following day. They bypassed the large island where the Greenlanders lived and continued to Vinland where the sun set. His grandfather had told him about its existence and suggested that it would be a good place for them to go after securing the wealth.

He had also heard stories from some of the travelers who had gone there then safely returned home. They told stories of the people there being very different in color and size from them. But they were fierce fighters, and should not be taken for granted in a battle. The stories also told of people who were friendly who had welcomed the new travelers to their land.

He was told them that there was good land as far as the eyes could see, and no matter how far you traveled into the land, it never seemed to end. There was also an abundance of fish and game to be taken.

Yngvarr and his men decided to head there.

One – Present Day

Going In

John called out excitedly. "Dr. McGuire, we've reached the chamber's wall."

Dr. James McGuire was the director of this archaeological dig, and taught History and Archaeology at the University of Cincinnati. McGuire had the look of a distinguished professor. He was nearly six feet tall, thin but not skinny, and had a mass of fluffy white hair. His hands were long and he seemed to always be looking for where they were going to go next. It was probably because the muscles in his arms and hands knew before his brain which tool or object needed to be handled next. He had a kind face with a ready smile.

McGuire left his conversation with Mike and moved down the narrow ramp to the wall of the mound's chamber. They had cut through the hard clay and layers of stone that had been used to construct the mound, and finally reached the chamber's wall. This mound's construction was an unusual type of mound construction for this area. It is more similar to the cairn style of mound construction found commonly in the British Isles. The cairn style involved a cist, or stone chamber, over which layers of stone and dirt were piled.

This mound was one of a group of mounds in southwest Ohio near the town of Peebles and its most famous mound is the Serpent Effigy Mound. The mound where they were working was located about 200 yards west of Serpent Effigy and unusually large for a cairn type of mound - 1200 feet in circumference at the base and almost fifteen feet high at the center. The chamber's floor sat five feet below ground level, which made the total height at the top of the mound nearly twenty feet.

McGuire chose this mound for a number of reasons but mainly for training purposes for his students. Not all of them could work at the mound for the whole summer season since they usually needed to work in the summer to help pay school bills. But some, like John, Tom, Mike, Doug, along with a couple others, could afford school without working due to scholarships or loans or parents, so they were at the site for the entire summer season. They were usually assigned as team leaders.

This mound is larger than most in the area with a similar shape, is relatively close to the university, and provides sufficient land area for parking, storage containers and tools. Plus, there are no fees involved since the area is owned by the county. McGuire was able to secure financial help from several area businesses as long as he uses their names in his recruiting material and progress reports.

Mounds exist all over the world and are built by people for many purposes - a spiritual one, a burial, or as a high place for the leaders of the tribe or group. The mounds in this area are part of an even larger group of mounds that stretch from Georgia to Minnesota. The largest representative group is from the Mississippian Culture group. The particular Native American group that built these mounds was probably the Lenni Lenape or the Shawnee, both part of the larger Algonquin cultural group.

McGuire fleetingly hoped that maybe this mound hid an artifact like the "Sandy" statue found outside of Knoxville, Tennessee. Sandy is a Mississippian culture object dating back to around 1300 CE that was found in 1939. It displays a kneeling man and is 18.5 inches tall. He had seen it in the McClung Museum of Natural History and Culture at the University of Tennessee in Knoxville when he was there fifteen years ago for a lecture series on the Mississippian Mound Culture. A find like that would certainly put his choice of this mound into the national spotlight.

Most mounds are almost indistinguishable when viewed at ground level. They simply look like small hills. Over time, they are often destroyed in order to flatten the area and make it easy for crop growth and cultivation.

This mound did not have the importance of the Serpent Effigy or most of the other nearby mounds, but it was large and had a stone chamber. Another unusual aspect, apart from being based on the cairn style from the British Isles, is that, based on test holes and ground-penetrating radar, it seems the chamber has a tightly spaced roof made of logs that appear to have been cut so that the roof is almost impervious. This certainly must mean that someone of importance was buried inside or that the mound was a tribute to something that that person had done for the tribe. The exact reason will lie inside the chamber.

Dr. McGuire examined the wall of the chamber trying to determine the best way to breach it and enter the chamber. He did not want to cause extensive damage, but they had to damage some parts of it in order to get inside. He took several pictures from different positions, which would be used later to verify the position and appearance of the stones that made up the wall.

"Okay, John. Let's try prying away one of the stones." He paused a moment and scanned the exposed wall. "Let's start with that one," and pointed to a stone to John's right. "It seems the most receptive to being pulled clear with no other damage."

"Understood," and John grabbed the smaller of the two pry bars he had, hoping it would do the job with the least damage. He began wedging it in about a half inch along the sides, top and bottom. Once he finished his first attempt, he began again, this time pushing it in about an inch. He then repeated this process two more times. After the last try, he stopped to let McGuire examine his work and make any additional recommendations about the process.

After viewing the stone and checking John's work closely, he stepped back and said, "Good job, John. Go at it twice more and we'll see where we are after that."

John started again, and about half way through his effort, the stone began to move inward. He looked back at McGuire and smiled.

McGuire nodded. John started again and it moved a little more but, so did several other stones. He stopped and turned toward McGuire.

McGuire moved up to the wall and lightly touched several stones. They each moved with only light pressure. He shook his head. "Okay, guys we are going to need to go into the chamber from the roof. I am afraid that if we proceed with this approach the whole wall will collapse which could destroy whatever is inside." He stepped away from the wall and moved back to the outside of the mound.

"Gentlemen, a famous archaeologist named Sara Bon-Harper once said, 'As an archaeologist, many problems are solved with a shovel'."

"We need to clear off all of the layers that cover the top of the chamber. But, we can't all climb up the sides of the mound and start digging. Our additional weight could collapse the mound and the chamber."

He walked around the mound, stopping occasionally. When he got back to his original starting point, he thought a moment more then said, "Let's try this. Mike, John, Tom and Doug will go up separately, work opposite each other from the top, and move down the side of the mound. Try to keep the same pace as each of you works downward. When all four of you reach the roof, we will decide how best to enter." They each nodded, grabbed shovels, spaced themselves an equal distance apart, and moved up to the top of the mound to begin digging.

It took two full days to get to the roof of the chamber since they had to remove stones as well as dirt. All of this debris had to be carefully moved from the mound to a special debris pile. In this way, it kept all of the removed material away from the work area at the mound. Later, it would be sifted and searched for any small artifacts.

When they finally reached the roof and brushed it as clean as they could, McGuire carefully climbed the side of the mound and took a close look at the roof. Once he decided where to begin, he took several pictures and called John over.

"Let's start from this end of the roof. We'll remove this log and wait to make sure the stones stay steady. If they do, then we'll remove the next two and stop."

John nodded and moved to one end of the log while Doc moved to the other end. They both grabbed their respective end of the log and began to slowly wiggle it. Once it felt loose, McGuire nodded to John and they both slowly lifted it up. The log came away and they paused with it about a foot above its former position. Once they were sure that the walls would not collapse, they handed the log to two other workers and began working on the next log. It also came away and they moved to the third.

After the third came off, they climbed off the mound and waited. It was almost dinner time, so McGuire suggested they cover the roof with tarps and begin again the next day.

XXXXX

The next morning they removed the rest of the roof logs, and the walls held steady. McGuire then asked for a ladder and gently slid it down inside the chamber. Once it was securely positioned on the floor and against the wall, he descended into the chamber.

The workers patiently waited for him to climb back out. After a few minutes, he slowly climbed up the ladder, and peered over the top of the wall. He turned to John and the others. "Men, we have truly an exciting find on our hands. This is going to involve a great deal of work but our work here will be extremely important to local and regional historians, anthropologists and archaeologists for years to come."

He smiled at the men. "You have all done a great job but we still have much more to do. John, please come into the chamber with me and we will figure out the best way to remove the objects and begin cataloguing them."

John and Tom went up the mound to the roof. McGuire climbed back down to the floor first then John and Tom began taking pictures. Once John was standing on the floor, McGuire began. He pulled his flashlight from his pocket and moved the beam around the floor. "As you can see we have a rather large chamber for this type of mound. It appears to be about fifteen feet square." The chamber was alive with what appeared to be hundreds of objects, and at times the light reflected back a collection of painted or plain objects, along with a number of metal items.

He looked at John and said, "Pretty cool, eh?" John nodded and smiled. They both then looked in the center of the chamber and McGuire moved the light over the strange burial box. "This is really unique. I mean, most burial mounds don't have a chamber, and certainly not a burial box. In those, the bones are usually just tossed inside a small hole or scattered on the floor, possibly with a few objects. This burial box and the many objects in here indicate that this person must have been extremely important to the tribe."

The specific objects they saw ranged from small bowls, goblets and vases, to military weapons and breastplates. There were also coins scattered on the floor, along with such items as jewelry and decorative pieces. Some were neatly arrayed around the chamber and a few were stacked on small platforms set against the wall.

As McGuire scanned the items, he kept coming back to the coins and metal objects. He knew that the tribes in this area and at that time did not have metal working skills, so these objects must have come from other tribes or areas where they may have had contact with travelers from far off lands. The other items he saw looked to be small pottery items that the tribe may have made or had been taken from other tribes or even gifted to this tribe. Lots of research would be required once they removed the items and began cataloguing them.

The large burial box occupied the center of the chamber. It was about three feet high, three feet wide, eight feet long, and sat on a stone platform about two feet high. The platform was created by stacked stones of similar size. The bottom, top and sides of the box all appeared to be cut from a very large tree, and each one was made from a single piece of wood. All of the pieces fit tightly together, and each piece looked to be about two inches thick.

McGuire carefully stepped towards it, constantly shining the flashlight onto the floor to make sure he didn't step on any of the objects. As he approached the box, he noticed that the sides were decorated with unique carved designs, probably done by a skilled craftsman. He stood to the side of it and peered at its top. It was also covered with strange characters and odd shapes. He thought that they looked Nordic in shape but they would definitely need an expert to help translate and explain the meaning of it all.

He moved the flashlight around the chamber again and smiled at the amount of objects they would be working to identify. He was looking forward to writing the final report and presenting their findings. Unfortunately, it would probably take several years to finish their work and write the final report because they could only work during the summer months.

He looked at John, "What do you think? Are we ready to start clearing out the chamber and identifying all of this?"

John smiled. "Boy, we certainly have a lot of work ahead of us, but our sponsors are going to be thrilled since we'll be producing numerous status reports and recruiting materials."

Two

Jason

It took several days to set up the lights around the top of the mound, and to secure the walls. Each light's location provided the most effective visual display of the interior in order to avoid stepping on objects or knocking something over. Once the lights were installed and the walls secured, they could begin to identify and catalogue all of the objects inside the chamber.

The day after the lights were installed, McGuire escorted Jason, his grandson, to the mound.

XXXXX

Jason was twenty, and had come to live with Dr. McGuire and his wife, Vicky, when he was ten years old. Erik, Jason's dad, had been a highly decorated police officer, who was killed in the line of duty when Jason was nine years old. Unfortunately, Jason's mom Tania, the McGuire's daughter, had not been able to handle the situation. The medications she had been given to control her anxiety had led to even more drugs and alcohol.

A year after Erik's death, she had tearfully asked her parents if they could watch Jason for a short time while she got her life sorted out. That was ten years ago. For a couple of years, she would come by every few months to say hello but never stayed more than a day or two. At present, they haven't seen her at all in three years and have given up trying to get her to settle down. Once a year, or longer, they might receive a postcard from her with only the word 'Okay' written on it, and of course, no return address.

Jason had been heartbroken when they came to his school and escorted him from the classroom to tell him about his dad in the privacy of the principal's office. He cried quietly all the way home and again in his mother's arms. He spent the next several days at home, most of it in his room looking at pictures of his dad.

Jason seemed to accept the situation sooner than anyone else. He recognized it for what it was. He would see his mother sometimes and his dad never again. His regrets centered on the things he would never do with his dad. They would never play catch or go hunting and fishing together. He would never get the chance to hear his stories and thoughts and instructions about living life and doing good. His dad had told Jason that on their next camping trip he would tell him all about his ancestors. Now, he would never hear or see his dad again.

Jason's personality and attitude gradually turned positive, and he became happy and fully engaged with life. His grandparents loved having him around; he was always helpful, never got into trouble, and did very well at school. He grew into a handsome young man with blue eyes, sandy colored hair and, at a sturdy six feet, he was tall for his age but not so much that he felt uncomfortable.

Jason loved history - ancient as well as modern. He was especially thrilled to read about the exploits of people like Alexander the Great, Genghis Khan, Napoleon and other famous, or infamous, characters throughout history.   He also enjoyed learning about the histories of the various peoples and cultural groups around the world. He was astute and felt that it was important to learn from history so that we can be better people going into the future. He eventually wanted to write about it, but wasn't sure in what capacity.

Their home was in Avondale, just outside of Cincinnati, Ohio. However, while he and his grandfather were at the dig site, they rented a small two bedroom house in the nearby town of Peebles, and used the living room of the small house as an office for the dig. Most of the workers at the dig are students from the university who stayed in their dorm rooms. The non-students find rooms to rent or commute to and from the site.

XXXXX

Jason and his grandfather climbed into the chamber and Jason gasped at all of the objects scattered around. But, the object that really caught his attention was the elaborately decorated burial box in the center. He seemed mesmerized by its size and the elaborate carvings on it.

He turned to his grandfather and smiled. His grandfather figured that he would enjoy being in the chamber, so he was already looking at him when he turned. "So, Jason, would you like to help me with the classification and identification of all of these objects?" Jason nodded vigorously.

"Good, because I am going to need lots of help with this," and swept his arm around the room.

Jason and his grandfather started moving around the chamber. They did not take notes or attempt to do any classifications or identifications. McGuire simply wanted to show Jason all that was there and to help him to understand the importance of not rushing through the process.

"The first important point is to not disturb any of the objects, meaning don't move or damage them in any way. To accomplish that, we all have to move very carefully, watching our steps, as well as the movement of our arms and the tools we carry. One brief look to the right and a clipboard held in the left hand could accidentally knock over a delicate vase."

"You have to be like a Ninja warrior - smooth, silent and invisible to your surroundings. You must be here physically, but act like a ghost." Jason smiled at the Ninja reference. His grandfather was funny that way. He always came up with unique ways to help others see what he saw.

"The next important thing for us is to be thorough. First, we have to photograph each object just as it sits in the chamber. Next, we have to describe it as we see it from as many views as we can without touching or moving it. Once that is done, we can finally move it while wearing soft, clean gloves, then take it out to be catalogued and entered into our computer database. Once all of this has been accomplished, we can move the object to the storage area and place it into one of the cargo containers."

It sounded like such a daunting task, but Jason knew that he would relish the whole process. I mean, how could he not love this work? It is what he has wanted to do since, well, he could remember. He couldn't wait to get started, but he had to be patient since that would have to happen later. Even though this was his third dig, he had always been just a helper. He was too busy with school to make it a full time vocation just yet.

He and his grandfather were walking back to the car as the sun was beginning to touch the tops of the trees to the west. It was nearing six pm and they had been looking at object after object for the past three hours. But, for Jason, it only seemed like three minutes.

The small house where they were staying was located next door to a local diner so they went there to eat burgers and fries before turning in for the night.

Three

Discoveries

At 7 am, after a hearty breakfast at the diner, Jason and his grandfather headed back to the dig site in his grandfather's old Ford pickup truck. When they arrived, McGuire asked Mike, John and the other team leaders to organize the workers into various groups.

One group was made up of more experienced volunteers. This group would help remove the objects from the mound and take them to the area for cleaning, cataloguing, and entering into the dig site's laptop. They'll enter data such as what it is, a description, where it was found, who removed it, and where it will be stored.

Another group would take the items that have been catalogued and place them into one of several storage containers at the site. These are refurbished steel cargo carriers that were once used on ocean-going transport vessels. The inside of these containers were fitted with shelves and small storage lockers that are labeled and numbered. The group doing the cataloguing will assign the location, enter it into the laptop, and print a tag to be attached to the item.

Jason followed his grandfather to the mound and found Mike standing near the side of the mound just below the opening at the top. "Good morning Dr. McGuire, Jason, it looks like we have a busy day ahead of us."

"Yes, we do," said Dr. McGuire. He turned to Jason, Mike and John. "Remember to be careful once we are in the chamber. We need to limit the number of people inside, as well as those who climb up the side of the mound. I don't want any objects to be damaged by a crowded chamber nor have the walls collapse because we have too many people climbing up the side. Once inside, I'll explain what we will do with each item. Any questions?" They all shook their heads. "Okay. Let's get started."

He turned and looked at Jason and smiled. Jason smiled back.

"Jason, Mike, let's go. John, please handle the work at the top of the mound. The objects will be handed out to you, and you will carefully take them down the side of the mound."

The four of them went up the side of the mound, and McGuire, Jason and Mike began to climb down into the chamber while John turned on the lights and stood at the top. Dr. McGuire was enjoying the sight of all of the wonderful artifacts located inside but, more importantly, he was also trying to determine the best place to start, and what approach to take in order to begin removing the items. He finally decided to start along the right side and move counter-clockwise around the chamber, leaving the burial box for last.

He turned to them to explain his approach. "I will select each item and Mike will photograph it exactly as it sits in the chamber. Then, I will carefully remove it from its location, and Mike and I will briefly discuss how and where it should be catalogued. Once that has been decided, Jason will take it up to John, and tell him the cataloging information and where it should be placed in the storage containers."

McGuire turned and pointed to the first item to remove. It was an ornate, hand painted vase that was about three inches tall. It had roughly drawn designs on its sides, along with a few red and blue stones lodged into a handle. Mike photographed it, he and McGuire discussed what it might be then McGuire carefully removed it from its position and handed it to Jason.

Before Jason turned to take it to John, McGuire said, "Please remind the next group to save whatever is inside of this, or any of the objects, in a separate bag and mark where it came from." He nodded and took the vase to John and repeated what McGuire had told him.

McGuire moved to the next item and the entire process repeated itself. It was slow and agonizing to watch. Not because it was boring, but because as each item was selected to be removed, all three of them grew tense with worry that it would break or fall or slip out of someone's hands, and no one wanted that to happen.

One of the surprises for McGuire was the fact that there were a number of coins and various metal objects scattered on the floor. McGuire bent down to get a closer look at them since he wasn't aware of the Mississippian cultural group having metal working skills at that time. When he shined his light at them he noticed that the coins seemed to be European. The other metal objects looked to be military arm bands or bracelets, and what looked to be pieces of various, military weaponry. He stood, smiled then turned to Mike and Jason, "This is getting more interesting by the moment."

XXXXX

They took a break at noon for lunch and, as usual, Joana's food truck was parked in the parking area near the other vehicles. She owned and operated a food delivery service and had started her business not long after the dig operation at the mound started. She also delivered to several small construction sites around the area. The volunteers and staff liked the service because it was prompt, the food was good, and Joana was friendly and pretty.

The young men probably liked it a little more because Joana was also young and, since it was summer, she often wore shorts and tank tops to the site, which helped to increase her tips. She was twenty-five years old, just over five feet tall, had dark, almost black, hair and large doe-like eyes. Her skin was naturally dark and her body was trim, fit, and sexy.

As Jason and McGuire came up to her small van, Joana said, "Hi Jason, Dr. McGuire. What would you like today? I made an apple pie last night so you can have a piece of that for dessert, if you like." She smiled and looked at Jason.

Dr. McGuire smiled. "We'll have two ham and cheese sandwiches and two colas." He smiled at Jason and said, "And one slice of your apple pie." Jason smiled and looked back at Joana. Like the other young men in the group, he found Joana hard to ignore.

"How is the dig going, Dr. McGuire?" Joana asked as she packed their items into a bag.

"Oh, it's going well, slow, but no problems have been encountered, at least so far."

Joana smiled and waved at them as they walked away. She watched them for several seconds longer before checking with the next customer. He was a young dig volunteer who wouldn't have minded if she had taken all day to fill his order. Joana smiled at him. "What would like today?" she asked, knowing full well what he might really like to ask her for.

After eating, Jason and his grandfather walked to the containers to see how things were shaping up in there. Each container had a number of items neatly stacked on shelves or inside more protective containers that usually contained straw or bubble wrap for protection.

Jason asked his grandfather, "What happens once everything has been removed?"

"Well, then the really difficult work begins. We will need to record a more detailed description and analysis of each and every item that we uncover. That includes the smallest shard to the largest breastplate. We will also need to do the same for the chamber itself. After all of that, we need to try to determine who is in the burial box and why. We also need to try to determine who built the mound, where they were from and anything else that will give us a comprehensive understanding of this site. And, finally, we will write a report about the dig, which will include all of the things I just mentioned."

"Grandfather, I think that is going to take a few years to complete because we only have enough funding for summers."

Dr. McGuire smiled. "Yes, it most likely will take two or three years. Heck, you'll probably graduate from college while we are still documenting it."

Four

Erik

Later that evening as Jason rested in his room, he thought of his father. He also dreamt about him sometimes, and those dreams were always full of fun. Those dreams often reflected things that they had enjoyed doing together - fishing, hiking and playing soccer in the backyard. His dad had been, and really still is, his hero. He was everyone's hero actually, if you believed what was said about him in the newspapers and at his funeral.

XXXXX – 11 Years Ago

Jason's mom and dad had lived in Glenville, Ohio, where Jason was born. Erik was a police officer in Cleveland, Ohio after spending twelve years in the Army right after high school. He had been in two different war zones during that time and the army had awarded Tech Sergeant Erik Swenson several commendation medals and the Bronze Star for bravery on his second tour, for helping to save the lives of three of his men.

He was very good at his job, and everyone had great respect for his honesty and fairness. He always tried to defuse situations rather than use force, and had only had to use his weapon twice. He felt that he could convince suspects to stay calm, which they usually did; at least until his last assignment eleven years ago.

He and his partner had gone out on a 911 call involving domestic violence. A neighbor had called it in because she was concerned about the violent nature that the yelling had taken on. These situations are always potentially dangerous because of the extreme feelings the people generally display.

He and his partner, Amanda Prator, discussed the approach they would take once they arrived at the scene, and decided that she would do the initial talking, while he stayed quietly behind her. Their plan was a good one, but unfortunately the couple having the disagreement didn't follow it.

Amanda and Erik stepped out of their patrol car and checked the area. The street was dark because several of the street lights were out. There were few cars along the street since most of them were parked in driveways. It had rained earlier and the lingering clouds added to the dark and dreary scene. The houses that lined the street were lower middle class in appearance with nothing fancy about them. However, they all seemed well maintained, except for the one they were visiting.

The house looked like it was abandoned. There were two old vehicles in the driveway that didn't appear to be capable of starting. There were toys scattered about, and the yard needed lots of yard-work, even just cutting the grass would have helped. The house was a single story clapboard house that needed lots of tender loving care.

They picked their way across the lawn and carefully went up the porch steps to the front door. They had been hearing nasty shouts and yelling from the time they stepped out of their vehicle. Amanda stood in front of the door, glanced at Erik to her right, and he nodded. She banged on the door and called out that they were the police, but the yelling inside continued at an even higher volume. They heard a man's voice yell, "See what you've done! The freakin' cops are here!"

Amanda reached for the door knob and Erik softly told her to be careful. She nodded, opened the door, yelled again that they were the police, and turned the knob. She pushed the door open and again yelled "Police". Erik was close behind her as she entered the ransacked living room. There was no one in sight but they could hear screaming from beyond the room. The couple appeared to be in the kitchen because they also heard the sounds of dishes and glass breaking.

Amanda loudly announced their presence again then started for the kitchen when suddenly, the screaming stopped and a man appeared around the corner heading toward Amanda and Erik. He was a big man with broad shoulders, but a fat belly. He hadn't shaved for a while and his hair was sticking out in all directions. Just as Amanda was ready to start questioning him, he pulled a gun from behind his back and started firing. As he fired, he kept yelling and cursing.

One of his first shots hit Amanda in the left shoulder and she fell onto her side. One of his next shots hit Erik in the chest, causing him to stagger backwards out onto the porch and fall backwards down the front steps.

Amanda was finally able to pull her own gun with her right hand and return fire. She hit the man three times before he went down. The woman suddenly appeared and started yelling at the cops to not shoot her husband, but she was obviously too late. Everyone was too late in their actions, except for the gunman. He had shot Erik and wounded Amanda.

Amanda painfully rose to her feet and stared at the scene. She moved to the gunman, checked that he was dead, and grabbed his weapon, while the woman continued to scream obscenities about the cops killing her husband.

Amanda looked around her but didn't see Erik anywhere. Her eyes scanned the floor and saw a blood trail leading out onto the porch. Her heart rate was already elevated, but she thought it might stop completely as the realization settled in that Erik might be severely wounded or, possibly... No, she wasn't going to think that.

She headed to the door while the woman kept up her ranting; but Amanda kept a wary eye on the woman as she moved. When she reached the porch, she saw Erik lying on his back at the bottom of the steps. She moved as quickly as she could to him and prayed that she would find a pulse.

But there was none. She applied pressure to the wound in order to stop the bleeding, hoping against all hope that she could somehow help him to survive.

Someone must have called 911 when the shooting started because several patrol cars arrived as Amanda continued trying to help Erik. One of the patrolmen immediately called for Emergency Medical while another patrolman took over from Amanda. Several other patrolmen went into the house.

The officer, who called for medical, calmly took Amanda's service revolver and the gunman's weapon away from her. She didn't resist. She knew that he was simply following proper police procedures. There would be an investigation into the circumstances surrounding the shooting, and she would be put on administrative leave at a desk job, which she would gladly take in order to decompress.

XXXXX

Amanda had been a new cop when she arrived three years earlier. She lived in Cleveland Heights and was married with a nine year old daughter, Nicole. She had spent eight years in the Navy as a Security Analyst after attending the Naval Academy in Annapolis, Maryland. When she arrived, she was assigned to work with Erik and, from their first day, she knew that she was working with one of the best. He was patient, knew how to do the job, and always took the time to explain what he was asking her to do. She had loved working with him.

Amanda also knew Erik's wife, Tania, and their son Jason, so she was the one who went with the Chief of Police to tell Tonia that Erik had been killed. She had held Tania while she cried and stayed with her while the Chief went to get Jason out of school. After Jason had been told and had arrived home, she had held the two of them and cried with them.

Once she healed from her wound, she helped Tania with the cooking and housework when she could. She also tried to spend as much time with Jason as she could, and often took him on short outings with Nicole so that Tania could have some time alone.

Unfortunately, Amanda also got to watch Tania fall apart. Within a year, Tania was drinking too much, never did anything for Jason, and never cooked. Jason either found something to eat on his own or Tania ordered pizza. Amanda tried to talk to her, but she rarely listened, and never changed her behavior. Amanda continued taking Jason on outings and helping him with his schoolwork, but she also had a job, and a husband, and a daughter, so she sometimes didn't see Jason for several weeks.

Amanda finally talked to Mr. and Mrs. McGuire when they came by to see Jason and told them what was going on. They tried to talk to Tania, and started taking Jason home with them each weekend to give her a break.

However, a few months later, Tania told her mom to just keep Jason with them then left. A month after that, Tania signed over the house to them, and a short time later, they received the paperwork for them to accept full custody of Jason. A year later, they sold the house and accepted the fact that Tania wasn't coming back for Jason.

About this time, Amanda received a great offer to be a detective in Dover, Delaware. She accepted it, and she and Nicole had a tearful departure from Jason. She kept in touch with Jason by phone, and always remembered his birthday and Christmas with money or a gift card. She had also married a lawyer a year after her first husband divorced her because of all of the time she spent away from him, and the dangers associated with her job. Nicole grew to love her step-dad, Brian Harper, and rarely saw her father, since he now lived in San Francisco.

Jason had missed Amanda and Nicole after they left, but was happy for them. Last year, he and his grandparents went on a road trip, and one of their stops was at Amanda's house. They met her new husband, who welcomed them like they had known each other for many years. They spent Saturday afternoon and evening with them and Jason spent much of that Saturday with Nicole.

Nicole was a bundle of energy, and turned out to be just as interested as Jason in history and science. She had grown to be a lovely young woman - caring, smart, and lots of fun. She had blue eyes, cute dimples when she smiled, lightly tanned skin, and dark hair that rested just a bit on her shoulders. She was of average height and weight for a woman, about five feet six inches and 115 pounds.

She was an avid runner and had already run three marathons. She regularly took martial arts training, and her instructor was impressed with how well she handled herself against any opponent, male or female. Nicole's mom had taken regular martial arts classes as part of her physical training for police work, and Nicole usually went with her when school and time permitted.

She and Jason were sad when the visit ended and promised each other to keep in touch.

Five

History

Recently, Jason had become more interested in his dad's personal history and genealogy. His dad's father had done a genealogy chart for the family, so it was a great source of information about his past. However, the chart only went back into the 1700s.

From it, Jason learned that his father came from a long line of men who served in the military before becoming policemen. His great grandfather had served in WWII and had been a policeman in Chicago. He died in the line-of-duty during a shootout with a couple of robbery suspects he'd been pursuing. His grandfather served in the Vietnam War and was a policeman in Springfield, Illinois. He died of cancer.

Jason also decided to have a DNA test done and learned that he was descended from Norsemen and Native Americans. With that combination, Jason figured the Norsemen must have come to North America well before the 1700s. He thought that was pretty cool, and spent a lot of time researching Nordic, specifically Viking, history in North America.

Based on what Jason read, he learned that groups of Vikings headed for North America from settlements in Greenland and Iceland around 900 CE. They landed on the coast of Labrador or New Brunswick where archaeological evidence indicates Viking settlements. Jason speculated that some may have even made their way down the St Lawrence River to somewhere in Quebec.

Jason further wondered if they may have entered Lake Ontario and stopped near Niagara Falls. Since they could not continue on their ships at that point, they may have decided to establish a small settlement nearby. Records from that time period indicate numerous Algonquin Native American settlements throughout the area. He wondered if the Vikings had eventually encountered one of them.

He reasoned that the probability was extremely high that, if they came across one of the Algonquin settlements, the encounter would likely lead to a battle. The outcome of the battle, he guessed, could have gone badly for the Vikings. They would have been vastly outnumbered; and even if they fought bravely, they would have eventually been overcome and beaten.

However, based on his ancestry, one or more of the Vikings must have survived the battle, and it was possible that if any had survived, and depending on their injuries, they might have been taken into a tribe as a slave. He just didn't have enough information to make an educated guess at the likelihood of any of these possibilities.

Jason smiled at the thought that his own ancestors may have been descended from those early Viking explorers. Jason had his DNA further analyzed to see if it matched other persons living or dead. A week after receiving this analysis, he and Nicole were talking on the phone and he mentioned what he had done. Nicole thought it was cool and said that she wanted to see his results when they next met.

After they ended the call, Nicole decided to send for the kit and get the same analysis done. Her mom had never had the time to learn any of her family's history, and there was no contact with the grandparents or any other relative. This made Nicole feel a little lost in the mass of humanity around her, except when she was with her mom, dad, the McGuire's, and Jason.

XXXXX – 995 CE

The old Viking, Yngvarr, now called Pajackok, sat on a rock outside his large hut. He was the tribe's chief, and his son would take over when he died and passed over to Valhalla. His son was a great warrior, would make a fine chief, and would likewise be called Pajackok when the Viking was gone.

Yngvarr and Alsoomse had had five beautiful daughters, who married well and now had fine families. Unfortunately, Alsoomse died of a fever several years after their last daughter was born. He eventually married a second time, and they produced one son. That son married a beautiful, strong woman, who produced a son a year later then two more over the next several years.

He recalled Megadagik's constant harassing behavior ever since the end of the battle that brought him into the tribe. Megadagik's hatred and anger continued, and he caused all sorts of mischief. The tribal elders had punished him for each offence they could prove but everyone knew he had done much more. It was believed, but unproven, that he even caused several warriors to die in a battle as he attempted to undermine Pajackok with the hope that he would be killed.

What Pajackok did not know was that Megadagik had overheard him telling his son the story of his homeland, his father's sacrifice, the wealth he had hidden, its location, and of his grandfather in Yerke. Megadagik, of course, passed this on to his sons along with the need for vengeance.

After Pajackok became chief, the elders suggested that Megadagik be banished, but Pajackok would not allow it. He reasoned that it was better to keep him close rather than letting him foment his hatred with another tribe. But, he felt no sympathy for Megadagik's children, and had them banished when it was proven that they had caused trouble.

Megadagik was eventually killed by an unknown person while he was out hunting. Pajackok and his son found the body while they were out hunting and buried it in a shallow grave, and never told anyone where it was. They didn't want any of his descendants to be able to worship him or help him into the afterlife.

As Pajackok sat on his rock and recalled his long life, his son came to him. "Father, how are you feeling today?"

"I am a little tired and feel like the time is near for me to go to my kinsmen waiting for me." He sighed tiredly. "I look forward to sitting with them in Valhalla and drinking beer from the udders of the Great Goat who lives there." He smiled at the old Viking legend.

He continued. "I want to remind you to remember all that I told you about my journey here and what happened along the way."

His son nodded. His father had started forgetting many things he had already said to him and others in the tribe. This had begun several years before and they all simply nodded and smiled when he did it.

"Now I need to tell you how I must be buried. My warrior ancestors usually wanted to die in battle then have their bodies burned on their ship." He smiled sadly. "But as I have no ship, I have decided on a new way for me. I remember as a boy on several adventures in the lands to the south countries and around my homeland seeing mounds. These mounds were places where people buried their chief or important elder or, in many cases, they were simply places of worship."

His son looked at him and shrugged. He had no idea how to build a mound. There were many in the area and he knew that people were sometimes buried in them, but he didn't know how it was done.

Pajackok saw his confusion, so he explained his idea. "People dig a hole and put a wooden box in it. They then put the body into the box and cover it with soil. But, they didn't stop with that. They continued until they had created a small hill above the grave. That is what I want you to do for me."

His son smiled. "I assure you, father, I will do exactly as you have asked, and I will then tell my son about your tale and your burial."

"Thank you. Now I am going into my hut to lie down. Please keep the little ones away for a few hours. I really need to rest."

"I will take the children to their cousins' hut to play."

At that, Pajackok went into his hut while his son wandered over to the children and herded them to another hut.

Three hours later, his son came back to check on his father. As he quietly entered the hut, and made his way to his father's resting place, he began to realize what he would find. As he looked down at his father he knew that he had gone to be with his fellow warriors in the place he called Valhalla.

Three days later, he buried Pajackok as he had wished, but he made one small change. He went into the forest and dug up the remains of Megadagik. He brought them back to the grave site in an old goat skin. When he was asked about it, he waved the questions aside. As the new chief, no one questioned him further.

When the hole was finished, but before the wooden box was placed in it, he dropped the goat skin and its contents into the hole. He then had the wooden box placed over them then placed his father into the box. He closed it, and the men covered it with dirt until the mound reached above the height of the tribe's tallest man.

He smiled at the result. *Now, Megadagik will lie below Pajackok forever, which is where he had always belonged.*

The son was now the Chief and he too was called Pajackok.

Six – Present Day

Missing

At the end of summer, the dig site closed and everyone returned to their studies or jobs or homes. Jason and his grandfather returned home, and Jason went back to school while his grandfather went back to the university to teach. McGuire still continued to drive out to the site to make sure it was secure, and to continue working with the objects.

Jason occasionally accompanied him on weekends and school breaks when he wasn't busy at school with studying, or participating on the track and wrestling teams. He ran the half-mile and mile, and often competed in state championships. He was an excellent wrestler, and made it to the championship level but never took first place.

His major at school was History and Archaeology. He had an Academic scholarship, a track scholarship, and worked part-time. His grandparents helped him, and would sometimes hand him a check telling him it was for incidentals.

His grandfather would be retiring from teaching in a year or two but Vicky planned to continue to teach at the local high school. He had a good pension and a Social Security check, while Vicky had an excellent health insurance plan for the three of them through the state's school system.

Jason tried to spend time with Nicole when each of them could get away from their studies or busy work schedules. They would go to the movies or plays or simply for walks at one of the many parks or trails in the area. They also took day trips to visit the many museums or historical sites in the area.

On one of these road trips, they stopped on the way back to have dinner, and finally arrived at Nicole's house around 11:00 pm. Jason walked her to the door and as they were saying goodbye, and talking about the next day, he suddenly leaned forward and kissed her. It was a short, sweet kiss, and they both blushed. But, as Jason began to turn away, Nicole quickly put her arms around his neck and pulled his mouth to hers. They executed a deep, passionate, full-on kiss.

As Nicole entered the house, she had a broad smile on her face. As Jason drove away, he also had a huge smile planted on his face. He called Nicole once he was home, and they started making plans to see each other on Nicole's next free weekend.

XXXXX

Two years later, Jason was about to graduate from the University of Cincinnati and the dig at the mound was still in progress. There had been so many items to retrieve and catalogue it just couldn't be done any faster with only the summer months to do all of the work.

They hadn't yet gotten to the burial box but that was about to change. All of the objects had been removed and catalogued or were in the process of being so. His grandfather planned to open the burial box that week and Jason, along with everyone else, was beside himself with excitement.

They had examined and photographed every square inch of the outside, and had rigged up a pulley system that they could use to lift the heavy carved wooden lid and sides up and out of the chamber. Once the lid and sides were off, they would remove it all to a storage container acquired just for the storage and examination of the special carvings and symbols.

The first task was finally about to commence. They wrapped several strong tie-down bands around the exterior of the box's sides and ends to make sure they stayed in place when the lid came off. They would then need to quickly place strong support slats across the inside of the walls to make sure they did not collapse inward. Once the bands were in place and the two workers were standing by ready to place the slats across the inside, they would use four strong volunteers to lift and maneuver the lid off.

Once the lid was off and the slats were in place, they would photograph the underside of the lid before attaching it to the pulley system for removal. Next, they would photograph the inside of the box and begin examining the contents.

John and Tom would place the slats on the inside while Jason and Mike, along with two other workers removed the lid. Dr. McGuire would handle the photography. There were also 2 other workers in the chamber if needed.

The process began at 9:00 am after reviewing the procedures. Everyone was ready. Jason, Mike and the two workers were at the four corners of the lid while Tom and John stood by with the slats. Jason and the others each grabbed a corner and started lifting the heavy lid. At first it didn't budge, but as they put more muscle into it, it began to move. With a great final effort, it came loose and they lifted it up far enough for the slats to be slipped against the inside walls. McGuire took pictures of the underside of the lid then it was secured to the pulley for lifting out of the chamber.

Dr. McGuire had taken pictures of the burial box after they first entered the chamber once the lights were set up, and had sent them to a friend of his at the University of Pennsylvania who was considered a leading expert on Viking History in North America. He was also capable of reading ancient Scandinavian languages, including runes.

His friend had responded a couple of months after McGuire had sent the pictures. He told McGuire that the writing is definitely ancient Nordic and he suspected it dated to the tenth or eleventh centuries. It told of a battle and a journey from what is now known today as Norway. It said that this group of Norseman made it to Ohio, battled with a tribe there, and only one of the Norsemen survived. He eventually became part of the tribe, a great warrior, and then chief. His name had been Pajackok.

McGuire had read and re-read this several times. He finally sat back in his chair and stared up at the ceiling. His mind churned over this until Vicky roused him to come for dinner. He couldn't wait to hear what the inside writing said, and he planned to send copies of the pictures they had taken to his friend. He would send any DNA they could secure from the bones or other material to a lab that specializes in DNA analysis. He decided to keep all of this to himself for the time being.

The lid was taken up and out for storage. Once all of that was accomplished, they moved to the box, positioned themselves around it and peered in. What they saw was, and was not, a surprise. They were not surprised to see a body since the mound had not been disturbed, and a burial box if not opened prior to this, would most assuredly have a body.

The surprise was that a trove of objects, like those they had found inside the chamber, was not found with the body. A box this large and ornate usually meant that the body inside was someone of great importance and significance. This almost always meant that they were elaborately dressed and adorned. This body was not adorned or elaborately dressed. It was dressed in the plain clothes that an average village person might wear, and there were no adornments at all. The only additional items with this person were a sword by his side and an amulet lying on his chest, which had probably been tied around his neck at one point.

Who was this person who was so magnificently buried but plainly attired? This was a real mystery for McGuire and the team to unravel but there was no sense trying to speculate on it now. They got to work taking pictures, removing items, and eventually taking the burial box pieces to the storage container. One thing he was convinced of was that this person was likely Nordic, or at least, had some contact with someone who was. The sword and amulet markings were almost assuredly Nordic, and certainly not local. He would send these pictures to his friend as well.

This find was getting more and more exciting with each new discovery.

XXXXX

Joana arrived, as usual, with the food truck at around 11:00 am and stayed until 2:00 pm. And, as usual, she had dressed for the task in tiny shorts and a low-cut, and very tight, tank top.

However, her real interest was in a volunteer named Matt.

She remembered their meeting years ago and wondered what he was doing here. He had only recently arrived and she needed to know if he knew more about what might be found on this dig than the rest of them.

XXXXX

Shortly before they planned to open the burial box Nicole contacted Jason and asked if he was going to be out at the dig site. He said he would be so she told him she'd come by when she had everything wrapped up at school. Her summer job was as an intern at a local Funeral Home, which she hoped would give her more experience in dealing with dead bodies. Several weeks later, she asked her boss at the funeral home for two days off so she could have a four day weekend, and headed for Peebles and the McGuire's.

Vicky McGuire always made sure the guest bedroom was available for Nicole. They looked on her as another grandchild and she loved them for treating her this way since she had never known her biological grandparents. Her mom's parents had divorced and went on to have their own lives with new families. Her dad's parents were never introduced to them and Brian's lived in Alaska, so she only met them at their wedding, and at his funeral.

She and Jason agreed to meet at the dig site, and when she got there, she was greeted by Dr. McGuire. "Nicky! It's so nice to see you.

You've come at an exciting time. We are going to open the burial box soon and Jason is helping to set up the process to do it without damaging the lid or box or its contents."

"Wow, Dr. McGuire, that's great."

"Nicky, will you ever start calling me James?"

She smiled. "Sorry, force of habit." But she still didn't call him James.

They walked to the mound and as they approached, Jason came out and grabbed a length of rope. When he looked up, he smiled, "Hey Nicky! Sorry, we've got to get this ready now."

She smiled and just waved off any worry about her. It was getting close to lunch so she wandered to the food truck she saw in the parking area. She stepped up to it in order to see what was available just as Joana came around the corner.

Joana greeted her and asked, "Are you a new volunteer at the dig?"

"Oh, no. I am a friend of Jason and his grandparents. I am just here for a visit." Nicole's eyes did a quick sweep of Joana's sexy outfit. She smiled inwardly and thought. *That should certainly increase the tips around all these young guys.*

Joana noticed the look and smiled sweetly at her. "What can I get you?"

"I'll just have a bottle of water, please." Joana handed her one, Nicole paid and said, "Thanks."

Later, after the pulley system had been set up, she and Jason had some time to hang out. When the day's work finally ended, they all went to the McGuire's home. While Nicole got settled into her room, Vicky finalized dinner preparations and Jason set the table.

After dinner they all sat in the living room and caught each other up on what Nicole and her mom had been doing.

Before Nicole left on Monday, she and Jason agreed that she would come back near the end of the summer. They hugged each other and shared a kiss. They were not boyfriend-girlfriend, they were just friends. But, Amanda and the McGuires were pretty sure that that may change at some point in the near future.

XXXXX

The removal and cataloguing of the burial box items would continue for a couple of weeks. Even though there wasn't much, the process was tedious because of the care that had to be taken when removing the items so that they did not damage the body. Only McGuire, Mike and John were assigned to do this work. They saw that, because the mound and box had been sealed since the body was placed here, there was little to no insect or animal damage. There was, however, the normal deterioration due to natural decay over time.

During this time period, Jason decided to try to research the native populations of this region to see if the identity or, at least, the tribe of this person could be determined. Each day it was the same thing, carefully remove an item, clean it, catalogue it and store it. It was boring, but Jason loved it and participated when he wasn't researching the body.

He also participated in the examination of the lid because it could possibly have information about who this person was. They had examined the outside of the box years before but he had not taken part in the analysis. Now, he felt very comfortable participating and actually working independently on it. However, as with the outside, the symbols meant nothing to him and he was looking forward to his grandfather's friend's translation. Everyone felt certain the symbols and carvings were Nordic but the translation would validate this and tell them their significance.

The clothes didn't tell them anything because they were so plain, and had no decorations of any kind. The sword was large, in fact, too large to be related to any Native American cultures that he knew of. There were no discernible designs on the blade but he could see designs on the handle, and suspected they were Nordic or northern European as well. He had seen charts showing runes in one of his textbooks and he was sure that some of the designs on the handle and amulet were runes. Runes are the old written letters in the alphabet of Nordic cultures. The objects needed more cleaning and restoration work to really have a chance at decoding any of it.

If the sword and amulet are Nordic in origin, then the questions would mount. Did this person find them, or did he take them from someone else, or travel to an area where there had been Nordic people at one time? The age of the body would help to provide a better picture of the circumstances surrounding the possible origin of the items since they would be able to date the time period of their burial, and help answer many of their questions. The best hope would be to be able to extract DNA from the body, but he was no expert in that area, and would have to leave that to others to investigate.

At one point, a volunteer started to place the amulet into a box to take it to the cataloguing area but Dr. McGuire asked him to wait. McGuire carefully took the amulet out and placed it on a flat surface area on the floor of the chamber. He pulled out his camera, and shot several close up photos of the amulet, focusing on the writing and symbols. He did the same with the sword.

During the middle of the 2nd week after opening the box, Dr. McGuire was ready to remove the rest of the box from the mound. This process would be the same as the lid. It all went without incident and they moved the sides and bottom into the container with the lid. While it was being secured, Jason wandered over to the mound, and went down into the chamber.

As he entered, the new volunteer looked up but turned back to his efforts to examine the space where the box had been. His name was Matt. McGuire had felt that there wasn't much to find under the box so he had assigned the work to several of the newest volunteers.

As items were found below the box's bottom in the pedestal area, they were photographed, removed, and placed in a small container to be taken to the catalogue and cleaning area. Jason watched the process and thought about joining but there wasn't room for another person, so he stood apart from them and watched, while trying to peek to see some of the items they found.

As he watched, he saw some small stones and bones that were probably animal, along with several pieces of pottery. At one point, Matt slowed, and seemed to look intently at something he had uncovered, but Jason's view was blocked by Matt's body. The others were intent on their efforts so they didn't pay much attention to Matt's work either.

Matt finally pulled something from the ground, and set it in the box. He then quickly placed several other items in the box, stood, and said, "Hey guys, I am going to take what we have over to the catalogue team so they can get started."

"I'll come with you. I'm really interested in what we might be finding since it could help me to date the site and the body." And Jason started to follow Matt out.

Matt called over his shoulder. "Oh, there really isn't anything significant here, so why don't you stay to see what might turn up."

"Nah, I need to head to the office to do some more research anyway so, as I said, maybe something in the box might help. If not, no harm done."

"Suit yourself." Matt proceeded toward the catalogue team, but then stopped abruptly. "Hey, Jason, would you mind going back to get my brush? I think I left it in the chamber. Thanks." He quickly turned and headed away.

Jason watched his back for a bit and thought he saw Matt glance back at him. He didn't remember seeing him with his brush, but he went back anyway.

The brush was not there so he headed back to the catalogue area. As he walked toward it, he saw Matt heading to the parking lot at a brisk pace. He didn't have the box so maybe he left it then remembered something he had to do that afternoon.

Jason walked to the team doing the work and asked, "Did Matt just drop off a box of finds with you"

"Yea", said one of the volunteers and pointed to it.

Jason went over and examined the box. He could see some of the stuff the workers placed in it, but as he looked more closely in the box, he saw a small piece of hide that looked quite old. He put gloves on then gently removed and examined it. He noticed that it was rigid with age but it seemed to have been wrapped around something. As he slowly examined it, he felt right away that something had been in it but had been removed or had fallen out. Maybe it was still in the chamber.

Jason took the hide and, before heading to the chamber, decided to head to the burial box storage area to talk to his grandfather. He also thought that if Matt had found this then he might be able to help identify what might have been wrapped in it.

XXXXX

Joana watched Matt slink away from the dig site, go into the storage container then rush out and jump into his car. He sped off like the cops were chasing him. Joana closed up the food truck, got in, and followed Matt at a discrete distance.

She smiled and thought, *No, it is not the cops, dumbass. It is me, Hantaywee, descendant of Megadagik. And, you have become my focus!* She watched Matt's car with a smile.

XXXXX

Unknown to both Matt and Joana, they were both being followed by another interested party. He was descended from Alsoomsa. His ancestor had been the brother of Alsoomsa and she had made him promise to always protect Pajackok and his descendants from the Megadagik family.

Seven - 1025 CE

Father and Son

The boy crouched in the tall grass and looked on quietly as his father moved through the bushes down toward the stream. The only sound he could hear was the soft rustle of the grass as a light breeze blew across it. The remains of a thin fog still hung in the trees and over the stream but a light breeze was working hard to carry it off.

They were hunting, as they often did, in an area about 200 paces from the village and nestled within forested countryside interspersed with grassy meadows and streams. He saw his father stop and give an almost unseen gesture with his head. This was his sign to move toward the stream and stop about fifty paces downstream from his father. He began moving slowly and, once in position, stopped and watched his father. They both waited quietly.

The boy had his knife strapped to his right thigh while his bow was held tightly in his left hand. He held an arrow loosely in his right hand with ten more in a quiver that lay diagonally across his back. His father was armed in the same way, except that each of his weapons was almost twice the size of his son's.

The boy knew his father was a great warrior and the tribe's chief. In fact, he was the most revered warrior in the tribe. He was also well known and feared by the other tribes in the region. So much so, no one from any of the tribes would ever think of attacking him, except if the tribes were at war, but that hasn't happened for many years. There was peace in the area and they could go where they wished without fear.

XXXXX

The tribe's story-tellers tell of his family's legend.

It tells of a small group of white men coming into the tribal lands many years ago. When the men of the tribe first saw them, they could not figure out whether they were actually men or some kind of new beast. All of the strange men had long unkempt hair and, on many of them, it was red. They also had long beards that obscured much of their face. They were huge men, and their bodies were covered with scars and strange paintings. Many of them wore a variety of bracelets and rings made of silver on their arms and hands.

A fierce battle soon erupted between the strangers and the men of the tribe when one of the tribe's warriors loosed an arrow at the strangers. This resulted in an immediate response from the strangers and a full-on battle raged far longer than any battle the tribe could remember. The white men never seemed to tire, even when severely wounded. Their bodies were punctured and sliced with numerous wounds, and the ground was slippery with spilled blood. As individuals, the tribe's men were no match, and when caught one-on-one, they were swiftly killed. The white men fought on and on and on until they simply fell over dead. Unfortunately, a great many of the tribe's seasoned warriors and young men lay dead or dying as well.

The battle was fought in a large grassy-field bordered by a forest of poplar, oak and other woodland trees. It didn't move into the trees, which was lucky for the tribe's warriors. For if it had, it would have made it very difficult for the tribe to prevail. The white men would have been able to use the trees as cover which would have severely limited the tribe's warriors from getting clear shots or strikes at them with their arrows and spears. But, since it was fought in the field between the stream and the ancient snake structure that many of the people worshipped but others feared, the invaders were completely exposed to the warriors' spears and arrows.

The tribe's chief finally held his warriors at bay and stared at the one white warrior left. He stood tall and strong as though he had only just arrived at the battle. He was at least one or two hands taller than the tallest member of the tribe. His arms and legs were muscled and his chest was massive behind his strange chest covering.

He faced the tribe without expression or fear. He simply looked at them and waited. After a moment, he touched an object around his neck, closed his eyes, and stood silently. The tribe's men didn't know what to make of this. *Was he praying? Was he deciding something? Would he now leave or charge them?* They decided to wait and let their chief decide what to do next.

The white man had been wounded several times and blood ran down his left arm and both legs. His right arm, with his sword in his hand, seemed completely unmolested by the battle. The tribe knew without mutual discussion that this warrior was truly favored by the gods, all the gods. He truly had the spirits, both good and evil, on his side.

The white man finally opened his eyes, looked at the tribe again, and seemed ready to continue the fight. The chief made his decision. He walked forward from the center of the front line of his tribe's warriors then stopped and stood about three paces in front of the white man. They stared at each other for what seemed to be an eternity, seemingly to be conversing with each other without words.

Slowly, they each lowered their weapons and moved cautiously toward one another. When they were almost within arm's reach, they slowly switched their weapons to their opposite hand, reached out with their weapon's hand, and grasped each other's arms just near the elbow. Once the silent agreement was confirmed between the two men, the chief stepped away and said something to his warriors. At that, each warrior in turn stepped forward and grasped the white warrior's arm. That is, except one angry warrior.

Megadagik held back. His name means 'kills many' in the Algonquin language and he seemed to want at least one more kill. He was jealous of his chief, and had long felt that he himself would make a better leader. He definitely did not agree with this action. But, the chief was adamant and demanded that Megadagik follow his lead. When he continued to refuse, the chief raised his war club as though to strike

Megadagik. As the chief was about to strike, he heard a loud grunt behind him and stopped.

The white warrior had said something which, of course, no one but the white warrior could understand. However, the message seemed clear, and the chief moved away from Megadagik. As he did so, the white warrior slowly moved towards Megadagik. Once close enough, he reached out his arm to Megadagik, who now realized that he was trapped. If he killed the white warrior, it would be seen as a cowardly act, and he would be killed or banished by the tribe. If he took his arm, then he would feel personally humiliated. He looked with hatred at the white warrior.

A moment passed and the tension amongst the tribe's warriors rose. None of them wanted to disobey their chief, and certainly none wanted to take on the stranger. Finally, Megadagik decided to take the warrior's arm and seek his revenge some other time.

Once Megadagik stepped away from the white warrior, the chief led the white man and the warriors back to the tribe's camp. He called all of the tribe together and spoke to them. He told them of the white man's fearsome warrior skills, of the stranger's decision to seek peace, and of his own acceptance of the warrior's peace offering.

The white warrior watched the tribe's reaction to whatever the chief was saying. He figured that he was telling his people about the fight and the decision to seek peace with him. He noticed that many nodded as he spoke and he assumed that they were agreeing. However, he did notice that some seemed to disagree, and still others simply stared at the chief then wandered off when he was done talking to them.

Yngvarr was unsure about how his future was going to play out. He had come to his decision to try to seek peace as he thought about what his father had said before he sent the ships off. He had told Aki and him to hide the treasure then build up a new army to come back to take their land back from Arild. He could not do that if he let himself die, so he chose to live and see what the future held for him.

Would I become a slave to one or more of the tribe's members? Would I be killed by one of the warriors as I slept, especially the one who didn't want to acknowledge me? Should I sneak off at night or at a time when no one was watching me? He decided to stay at least until he could heal from his wounds and gain back his strength. At that time, he would make a decision.

XXXXX

After months of rest and the care he received from the tribe's medical man, his wounds healed and he gained back his strength. He did the chores assigned to him and was never abused or mistreated.

Yngvarr decided to stay with the tribe. After another year, he was allowed to fight and hunt. He proved himself many times in battles and on hunts, and was then adopted into the tribe. He became one of the fiercest warriors they ever had, which of course, did not make Megadagik very happy.

Yngvarr eventually learned the Algonquin language and customs, and was given the name Pajackok, which means thunder in the Algonquin language, after he explained the meaning of the strange amulet hanging around his neck. He told them that the amulet was a symbol of his religion and his god, Thor. He said Thor brought the thunder using his great war-hammer.

Pajackok later took a wife named Alsoomse, which means independent. She was taller than the other women but still shorter than Pajackok. She was strong, a skilled hunter, and an excellent tracker. She had long black hair and smooth light brown skin, as soft as beaver fur. After a tentative year of getting to know each other and learning how to better communicate, they became inseparable, madly in love, and had a daughter.

She later explained that her father named her Alsoomse because she was always off in the woods running with the boys. She would readily get into fights with them if they pushed her around or tried to get fresh with her. After winning a few of these fights, she never had to worry about the boys getting fresh with her.

Over time, the tribe learned that the white men were sometimes called Vikings, and often went to other lands seeking to steal and do harm. They learned that these particular men constantly staged mock battles during their travels so that they could keep their fighting skills fresh. The white men came from far across the big waters, and had followed several rivers and the stream near the tribe's settlement, to end up in the area. Yngvarr also told them that the white men became warriors when in foreign lands, but farmers when they were in their own homeland.

Not surprisingly, Megadagik told his descendants a very different legend concerning the white warrior. His story involved the white man's cowardice, his own betrayal by the chief, and the humiliation perpetrated on him by the white man's shifty actions. His descendants believed every word of his version of the events, and vowed to seek revenge on the white man and his descendants.

XXXXX

The boy's name was Kitchi, which means 'brave', and the white warrior in the legend is the boy's great grandfather. As the chief, Kitchi's father's name was also Pajackok. All of the oldest sons in his family's line of descendants took that name when they became warriors, and Kitchi would take it once he achieved warrior status. Kitchi smiled as he glanced over at his father, and his heart swelled with love and pride, especially when they were out hunting together like this.

Suddenly, his father turned and faced Kitchi. He motioned for him to follow and Kitchi did, staying well behind. Soon, he too saw the group of deer silently munching grass in a small group of trees on the other side of the stream.

His father gave him another silent sign and Kitchi moved into position at the edge of the stream down from the group of deer. His father slowly moved down to the stream a little way up from the group. Once in position, his father quickly rose, took aim, and shot an old buck standing off to the side of the group. The arrow hit the old buck, and the group immediately took off in Kitchi's direction. It was now Kitchi's job to finish the hunt.

He knew that his father would try to take the weakest of the group since they would be the ones that would likely die in a drought or during the long winter months when food was scarce. In this way, a hunter's actions saved food for the herd that would otherwise have been eaten by their weakest members, who would probably die anyway.

Kitchi watched the old buck, took aim, shot, and hit the buck in the right side of his chest. It was an excellent shot and would kill the old buck swiftly.

The buck ran a short distance, slowed then fell over in the tall grass about 100 paces down from Kitchi. He and his father ran to the buck, arriving just as it took its last breath. His dad smiled at him, ruffled his hair, and told him, "Well done, son." Kitchi's chest expanded with pride.

A few hours later, they began to drag the deer carcass to the tribe's camp. It would provide enough food for the tribe for many days. Its hide would also help to provide material to replace several of the old hides used on many of their shelters, while its antlers could be used as tools or as simple weapons for the younger warriors.

It had been a good day.

XXXXX

The man pulled back on his bow and took aim at Kitchi. This man was Megadagik's great grandson and he was about to let loose a killing shot at the Viking's great grandson. As he readied his shot, he was struck in the back with an arrow and fell forward into the wet grass and leaves.

His older brother, who was kneeling quietly by his side ready to shoot Pajackok, turned quickly. He never saw the arrow that entered his skull through his left eye.

Quietly, the man in the grass not far behind them made his way toward the forest not far behind them. He didn't smile. He simply congratulated himself on two fine shots.

Eight – 1055 CE

Final Burial

Kitchi was now chief of the tribe. He had grown to be tall like his father but not as big across the shoulders. He was still strong and brave, and had proven himself in several battles. As a result, he was now officially known as Pajackok. However, after giving it some thought, he decided to keep his given name and only use the name Pajackok in formal ceremonies.

One of his first decisions was to re-bury his great-great grandfather. His father had told him about the journey and wealth hidden by the old Viking, so he wanted to show greater reverence for his ancestor. And, that required a more grand burial and mound. However, he also had another reason for the reburial.

He called his tribe's elders together and informed them of his plan to re-bury the Viking warrior and tribe's most revered chief. They were in full agreement and helped put together a group of skilled carvers and builders to accomplish the task.

The plan was to build the new burial mound ten paces to the south of the old one. This would make it easier to move the remains from the old to the new. Kitchi knew about the bones of the traitor Megadagik and he wanted them transferred as well to be placed below the new burial box they planned to build.

The burial box was to be made of the best wood they could find in the nearby forests, so Kitchi sent out several of his ablest woodsmen to search for the perfect tree. The plan was to cut the tree into pieces large enough to create a lid, bottom and sides for the box. The lid was also going to have designs carved into it that told of the Viking's legend but, of course, not the secret. That would be placed placed in the mound by Kitchi when no one was around.

The mound would be twice the size of the old mound, and have a room inside it to house the burial box. They would need to dig down first and create a circular pit roughly ten hands deep. They would build a pedestal of stones to hold the burial box once Kitchi had tossed Megadagik's remains into it. The burial box would be placed on the pedestal, Pajackok's remains would be placed inside, and the lid would be placed on top after they apply a sealing compound around the edge. The sealing compound would be made of the same material they used to water-proof their canoes.

Kitchi also planned to ask each member of the tribe to choose one of their most valuable possessions to place inside the burial chamber, which should amount to quite a few items. The tribe had grown in size over the last couple of generations due to the relative peace with the nearby tribes. They had also absorbed into the tribe several of the smaller tribes in the area who wished to take advantage of their prosperity and protection.

Kitchi and his father had begun to have frequent conversations over the last couple of years of his life. They talked about many things, including leadership of the tribe, being a good father and husband, and relationships with the nearby tribes. One of the additional topics had been the Viking story and legend.

Kitchi promised to continue to pass the story on to his sons and encourage them to do the same. But, he and his father had also agreed that it was growing considerably unlikely that any of the descendants would want to muster up the manpower and resources to sail all the way across the ocean to find a trove of wealth that may not even be there anymore. So, they had developed a plan.

The woodsmen found two trees that were large enough and sturdy enough to use to construct the large burial box. They cut the pieces, and would begin carving the lid as soon as Kitchi gave them the design to use as a guide. The builders had already created the pit, and had gathered the material they would use for the construction of the mound and the roof of the chamber.

The design for the top was being created by Kitchi's great-aunt. She was very old, maybe close to 100 summers. She was Kitchi's grandfather's eldest sister and was descended from the same line as Pajackok's first wife, Alsoomse. She had actually learned the meaning of the Viking signs and language directly from the old Viking when she was a small child.

Kitchi went to her and asked her to write out the story of the Viking's arrival, the battle, the peace and the great chief Pajackok. This would be sculpted onto the burial box lid. He also asked her to write out the name of the location of the treasure of wealth and the directions to find it. He had her write the location on the old amulet which he would then tie around the Viking's neck. The directions to find it would be on a small copper sheet that Kitchi had been given by his father when he died. Kitchi had been told that it was something that the Vikings had brought with them. Once she had finished creating the location and directions on the items, Kitchi hid them in his hut. He gave the carving design for the lid to his carvers.

At the end of each day, Kitchi wandered around the burial place to check on the progress of the work. Once the goat skin with Megadagik's bones was placed in the pit, and all of the workers had left, Kitchi took the copper sheet with the directions, wrapped it in a piece of bear hide, and hid it within the bones and other debris.

Later, when the Viking's remains were placed in the burial box, he placed the amulet's lanyard around the neck as best as he could, then he rested the amulet on the Viking's chest where, hopefully, it would remain undisturbed. At that, he stepped back to let the workers apply the sealing compound, then the lid onto the box. The donated items from the tribe's members were placed all around the chamber.

The log roof was then put over the chamber and the doorway was closed up with a wall of stones similar to the rest of the walls. The chamber was covered with a mix of dirt and stones up to a height of three times the tallest tribal member.

When all was completed, Kitchi stood to the side, smiled, and whispered a prayer to the old Viking. He told him to have fun with all of his ancestors and friends at the legendary beer party in Valhalla.

Nine - Present Day

Nicole

Nicole walked the short distance from her dormitory to the library along a tree shaded path on the campus of Ohio University. Even with her heavy backpack, her pace quickened as she got closer to the building. The books in her major area of study were always big and heavy. But, other than easing the burden on her back, she couldn't wait to get into the next three chapters of her forensic science text in preparation for the exam she had in two days.

She had been at Ohio University for two years now and loved it. It was only her second year but she already knew she would become a Forensic Scientist. Her mother, Amanda, was a detective with the Cleveland police department and Nicole had become very familiar with the type of work that needed to be done in order to find someone involved in a crime. She had heard her mother discuss the basics of crime solving, and especially enjoyed hearing her mother discuss how they solved it. When it was time to choose a college, she looked for one with the best Forensic Science program.

She settled on Ohio University for a number of reasons. It was a great school with an excellent reputation, especially in her major area of study. It was not too far from her home and her mom in Cleveland Heights. And, it was also not far from her friend, Jason. However, one of the best doctorate programs in Forensic Science was at Sam Houston State University, so she may be going there once she graduated from Ohio University. But, she didn't want to think about that now.

After her dad, Chad, had left years ago when she was eleven, she and her mom moved to Dover, Delaware where her mom eventually met and married her step-dad, Brian. Life was great there. Her mom enjoyed her new job as a detective and her step-dad was a wonderful father to her. She never saw her biological dad after he left and had forgotten much about him, especially because of the kindness that Brian showed her, and the fun he always tried to create for the family.

She had missed her school friends from Cleveland at first but then started making new friends at her school in Dover. The only friend she truly missed from Cleveland was Jason. They had only known each other for a few years when his father died but it still seemed to her that they had grown up together. They kept in touch through social media, and saw each other a few times on family trips but, unfortunately, with several years in between.

Sadly, after only having Brian in their lives for a short four years he passed away from pancreatic cancer. It was diagnosed too late and he only lasted six months. Her mom was heartbroken but knew she had to remain strong for Nicole, and Nicole had felt the same way, so in reality, they took care of each other.

When it came time for Nicole to head for Ohio University, Amanda immediately applied for a job back in her old precinct. They responded quickly and offered her a detective position. Dover was sorry to see her go but understood, and threw her a large going-away party.

They found a house about three miles from the same community where they had lived just seven years before and Nicole immediately called Jason to tell him the news about their move, and her enrollment at Ohio University. He sounded so happy over the phone. Nicole smiled and told him, "I am also excited about seeing all of my old friends." After hanging up she thought. *And, being able to spend more time with Jason.*

XXXXX

A few weeks before she had to return to school and after her internship ended, Nicole drove over to the dig site.

When she arrived, she parked and walked up to the site. She could tell right away that something was wrong because she saw Jason and Dr. McGuire talking very seriously to the group of volunteers. John and the other site leader were franticly moving in and out of a storage container rooting through boxes on a table, returning it to the container, and then rooting through another box. They were also looking over their catalogue of items, which made it seem like they were looking for something in particular.

Everyone knew her by now so as she walked to the table where John was looking through a box, he merely said, "Hey, Nicky." He then went to get another box. He left the box he had been looking into so she took a peek at what was inside.

Like Jason, she had a love of history and archaeology, probably more because of Jason's interest than her own. As she looked into the box she noticed that it was rather uninspiring. She was used to seeing vases, cups, shards and other unique items, but this box looked like it contained some old scraps of animal hide, a few stones, and a collection of human bones.

John returned with a new box and she stepped away to give him room. He left shortly after with both boxes.

She decided to just sit and wait for whatever was happening to settle down, so she moved off to one of the picnic tables. After about thirty minutes, Jason separated from the volunteers, saw her, and came over.

"Hey, Nicky. Sorry to keep you waiting. We might be missing an item and we think that one of the volunteers may know more about it, but he had to leave early today. We are trying to find out what it was and where it might have gone." He spoke rapidly.

"No problem, Jason. I can come back later."

"No! No! Pease stay. I am glad you are here. We're almost finished here today, so we can go home and get you settled. I know that grandma is looking forward to seeing you again."

"I'm excited to see her too."

XXXXX

That evening after dinner, they were all sitting on the deck enjoying coffee and tea.

Nicole asked, "Other than what happened today, how is the dig coming along?"

Dr. McGuire looked at Jason and smiled. Jason took the hint.

"Well, as you know we removed the lid a couple of weeks ago, and have examined it pretty closely. We have also examined the body we found inside the box. There wasn't much to see in terms of artifacts, just a sword and an amulet. The clothes were pretty plain and had deteriorated a good bit."

"I glanced into one of the boxes John was examining while I was waiting. Don't worry I didn't touch anything." She smiled as did Jason.

"Which one was it?"

"I think it was one from inside the burial box." She told him the catalogue number. "It had some scraps of material and human bones which must be from the body."

Jason looked at her then at Dr. McGuire then back at Nicky. She was staring at him like she had said the world was flat. "What's wrong? Should I not have looked at it?"

"No. No. I'm just surprised because that box came from underneath the burial box. Those were not items from inside the burial box. Are you sure the bones are human?"

"I suppose, to be fair, since I am only a student, I could be wrong but I would still say that I am ninety percent sure."

Jason looked at his grandfather and asked, "How in the world did a body get under the burial box? Maybe it was someone who worked on preparing the site for the box. But that doesn't sound right either. If he somehow died before the box was placed there, then they would have simply removed him before setting the burial box in place."

Dr. McGuire was thoughtful for a moment. He glanced away then back at Jason. "That's a good point. But, what if the dead person was placed there on purpose before the box was put there?"

They all looked at each other, stayed quiet, then Jason said, "That probably means they were put there on purpose by the people who built the chamber. Maybe they are somehow connected to the hide we found as well as the missing item."

Jason saw Nicky's confused look. He explained. "Earlier, one of the volunteers suddenly left in a hurry. We didn't think much about it but still decided to check the last box he handled. It was the one you saw. Anyway, I found a small piece of rigid animal hide that had dried out and was folded in a way that looked like it had held an item about the size of your hand."

"We asked several other volunteers who had been working with Matt, and one of them remembered that he had seen the edge of something protruding from the hide when Matt picked it up. He said it had a coppery look to it." He stopped, glanced at Dr. McGuire and looked at Nicole.

She said, "I think you need to take a look at that box again."

Ten

Caught

Joana followed Matt to his rented room in an apartment building outside of Hillsboro, Ohio. She didn't live too far away, and hoped Matt would take at least thirty minutes to pack whatever he was going to take with him. She drove to her apartment, changed, packed a few things quickly, and switched to her sedan. She locked her food truck and headed to Matt's. He was pulling out of the apartment parking lot just as she drove around the corner.

Joana followed Matt at a distance. He stopped once for gas just outside of Zanesville, Ohio, grabbed a soda and a snack then started again. Joana filled her tank at a station within sight of Matt then lingered until she saw Matt begin to leave.

Matt finally pulled off of Interstate 70 south of Pittsburgh near Washington, Pennsylvania and checked into a cheap motel. Joana stopped down the street then, once Matt entered his room and she saw the lights go out, she drove into the motel's parking lot. She parked around back of the motel where there were only two other vehicles.

She sat in her car and debated what she should do. She could continue following him, but that was taking her farther away from the dig where she was sure there would be some kind of evidence of the old Viking that would help her in her quest. She wasn't even positive Matt had any evidence or even an item that led to 'a whole lot of money'.

She had to decide, and decide quickly. She had left most of her belongings back in her apartment, and needed to get back before anyone became curious about her absence. *I don't even know where he is going or what he has or why he is in such a hurry*, she thought. After a minute or two, she made her decision.

She exited her car and walked around to Matt's room. She was dressed in black with her hair pinned up under a stocking cap. It was close to 2:00 am so there was no one around. One of her former 'clients' taught her how to pick locks so she pulled out her tools, and was in Matt's room within ten seconds.

Joana watched Matt sleep, and debated what she should do with him. While she debated, she moved to a chair where his clothes had been thrown. She found nothing in his pockets of interest so she moved to his small suitcase and began rifling through it.

She suddenly saw stars and slammed into the wall. Before Matt could hit her again, she ducked to the right, and slammed a hard punch to his kidney. He bent over, and as he did, she hit him twice with uppercuts to his throat.

Matt went down on his hands and knees and shook his head as he tried to recover. When he started to stand, she came down with her elbow on the back off his head. He went flat and fell unconscious.

Joana sat on the edge of the bed to catch her breath. She placed her hand on the spot on her head that Matt had hit. She felt a lump growing but there was no blood on her hand. She slowly rose and peeked between the curtains to see if anyone heard the scuffle, and had become curious about what was going on in the room.

She didn't see anyone and turned away smiling. She figured people who stayed in this motel were probably used to noises coming from the rooms at all hours of the night. She went back to her search while glancing cautiously back at Matt to make sure he stayed down.

As she slipped her hand into a small side pocket inside the suitcase, she felt a hard object there and pulled it out. It was wrapped in a soft white cloth. She moved to a small table and carefully removed the cloth. As she pulled the last fold away, she saw a thin, 3 by 4 inch piece of copper metal with strange writing on it. She picked it up carefully and turned it over. There was more of the strange writing on that side too.

She laid the object aside and continued searching. She found a large clasp envelope that was thick with papers. She undid the clasp and saw, perhaps, twenty or thirty pages with writing and drawings. She also found a small thumb drive. She decided to leave and peruse the items back at her place. She dropped the copper piece in the envelope then set it aside.

She repacked his suitcase and restored the room as best she could. As she backed toward the door, she paused, and glanced at Matt.

Should I leave him as is? He might come to and chase me or turn me in. He may only know me as the lunch girl but that was enough. I have killed once before when that jerk I brought back to my room tried to rob me and started to strangle me when I fought back. It was an accident, but the interesting thing is that I felt no remorse.

She made her decision. She grabbed the pillow that Matt had been using and gently laid it under his face as he laid face-down. She sat on his back and pressed her legs tightly into his sides. She leaned into him, grabbed the edges of the pillow on both sides of his head and pulled up and back.

He didn't move at first. But, as his lungs began wondering where the oxygen was, his body started jerking up and down while his legs kicked wildly. He also tried to claw her off his back but he couldn't reach her. As she tightened her grip and continued to pull back, he finally passed out again.

Joana pulled the pillow away but continued to sit on his back. She stared down and thought. *What am I doing? He is an ass and he would probably kill me if given the chance. But, his death would complicate my situation.*

Joana reached down and gently felt his neck for a pulse. After a second or two she found one. It was slow and shallow but it was there.

She carefully climbed off of Matt and collected the envelope. She went to the door then turned to make sure she hadn't left anything of hers. Once she was satisfied, she slowly opened the door and peeked out. She saw no one, so she quietly exited and closed the door. She walked quickly around to her car and climbed in.

She drove out a back entrance without her lights on until she reached the entrance to the Interstate. She had a 4 hour drive and would arrive at her place around 8:00 am. This would give her time to shower and change before heading to the dig site.

When she reached her place, she tossed her stuff on the bed, striped and went to the bathroom. She smiled as she showered. She slowly moved her hands all over her body. As she did so, she thought. *I am so glad that I have this body. It has supported me very well over the years providing income and protection*!

After dressing, she took the envelope and hid it under her mattress. She needed to get going right away in order to restock her truck, and drive to the dig site by lunch time.

She would have to wait until this evening to search through the envelope to determine what she had found. Well, truth be told, she hadn't found anything, Matt actually had done all of the work. However, she intended to take over from here.

XXXXX

An hour or so after he passed out, Matt stirred and opened one eye. He couldn't see very well but his sense of smell worked fine. This was unfortunate because he was lying face down on the raunchy carpet which smelled of urine and other aromas that he didn't want to think about.

Suddenly, his mind kicked in and he remembered how he had gotten there. He swung his arm back hoping to land a punch on his attacker. But his arm merely moved the air around and he hit nothing harder or more substantial than it.

He made it to his knees and looked around the room. He saw no one, and the room didn't look like there had been a fight in it. Chairs were in their upright and normal position, the bed covers were a little messed but not tossed about, and he saw nothing broken.

Did I imagine a scuffle? Had there really been some guy in here rooting through my stuff? The guy was probably a drug addict looking for something valuable to steal and sell.

Matt shook his head and slowly rose to his feet, but then sat quickly back on the edge of the bed. He dropped his head down onto his hands and closed his eyes until the wooziness went away. As he began to feel better, he suddenly remembered the envelope and piece of copper. He checked his suitcase side pocket. The piece of copper was gone.

He moved his hand around the inside of the suitcase then simply dumped all of its contents on the floor. He scrambled around on his knees rooting through its contents. No piece of copper and no envelope. They were gone. He rose and walked around the room.

Matt sat on the bed again. *Why would a druggie steal an envelope and a piece of copper?* Then it hit him! *'He wouldn't. He couldn't sell any of it. Maybe the copper, but it wouldn't be worth his trouble.*

Then he quietly said, "But, I know who might want the items. Someone at the dig came here and took the items."

He thought he had been careful, and no one had followed him, but he was wrong. Someone had followed him here then snuck in while he was asleep and stole the items after beating him up. *But, who at the dig is clever enough to follow me without being seen and strong enough to beat me up even after I had given him a pretty good knock on the back of the head?*

Matt lay back on the bed and closed his yes. He needed to think.

Eleven

Learning

McGuire, Jason and Nicole arrived at the dig site early and headed for the storage locker where the burial box was stored. They found the container with the items from under the burial box and Nicole put on a pair of gloves. McGuire and Jason watched as she carefully picked out one of the smaller bones from the container.

She held it in the palm of her hand and showed it to McGuire and Jason. "This, I am almost positive, is a finger bone. You can still see the shape of the knuckle to which it was attached." She replaced it and pulled out another bone that was shaped like a quarter moon. "This one I believe is part of a rib bone. I also think there is a pelvic bone and part of the cranium. There may even be enough bones in here to reconstruct the person who owned them. Once you do that, you might be able to determine the cause of death, and you should certainly be able to get DNA."

Jason looked at his grandfather. "Do you know anyone at the university who can do that for us?"

"Not here but I know someone at Sam Houston State who can. She is one of the most famous skeletal reconstruction artists in the country. I'll call her later today to see if she has time to help us. In the meantime, I'll have someone come out from the university to get DNA from the body in the burial box and the one under it." He smiled and shook his head as he finished that statement. *What next?*

"By the way, I received the translation of the burial box and the amulet's writings." He paused, smiled and looked sheepishly at the two of them. "I actually received it three days ago but with all of the excitement of the bodies and the missing item, it slipped my mind to tell you about it."

"The professor I sent it to originally, Dr. Frank Michaels, was not familiar with the runes and symbols used on the box but he was able to translate the amulet. Its message was simple. It only said 'Iceland'. Well, it actually said 'Thule' which is an early Norse name for Iceland. Unfortunately, that is all it said and with only that we probably would never know what it was trying to convey."

Then he winked and put on a mischievous grin. "He couldn't translate the box writings but he felt that he knew someone who could. He met her at a conference on ancient Norse languages and runes he attended in Amsterdam a couple of years ago. She teaches at the University of Oslo and is a guest lecturer at the Universities of Copenhagen and Iceland on Norse languages, writings and culture."

Dr. McGuire continued. "Anyway, she translated the box and sent her conclusions to my friend and he has passed it on to me." By now, both Jason and Nicole were shifting from foot to foot hoping that Jason's grandfather would get on with the translation. He did.

"The designs on the exterior sides of the box appear to be random symbols of various animals and things, which is also what Frank had thought. He will check with a friend who is familiar with Northeast Native American languages and cultures to see if they have some Native American significance. The top of the box was definitely a Norse language and it actually tells the story of the body inside the burial box."

Jason and Nicole smiled and looked at each other. They both thought. *Now we are getting somewhere.*

However, Jason was also thinking that maybe this could be the Norse heritage he had found out about in his DNA and his other research into the origin of the person, box and burial site.

They waited expectantly for McGuire to start again.

"The story tells of a battle in the man's homeland which was lost to a rival king. This man's father was the losing king, and he sent this man and the king's father away in order to save the wealth of the tribe and many of its people in the hope that they might be able to eventually get revenge."

"This man..." and McGuire pointed to the body in the burial box, "carried the wealth and his loyal men to Iceland to hide it. After hiding it, they continued to Vinland, which is now North America. They traveled to this area, had a battle with the tribe located nearby, and all the Norsemen were killed except this man in the box."

McGuire paused to catch his breath, collect his thoughts and drink some water. This only took about fifteen seconds but Jason and Nicole were anxious to hear more.

"Okay, okay I'll get to the rest of the story. Just let me take another sip of water." They did but not without grimacing at him. "This man and the tribe decided to seek peace rather than have him and more warriors die. He eventually assimilated into the tribe, learned the language and customs, became a great warrior, and finally chief of the tribe. He also took a wife and they had several female children, but she died so he married again and had a son." McGuire stopped and smiled at the two young people but they continued to look at him like they were puzzled by something he said. "What?"

Jason was first. "What happened to the wealth? Where did the grandfather go? Where are his descendants?"

"How did he die and who is this person?" Nicole held up the bone she had shown them at the start of this whole conversation.

"Whoa! Take it easy on me. I'm just the messenger." He sighed then said. "We know that the wealth is in Iceland somewhere. The writing says the grandfather went to Yerke, which is now York, England. That person's descendants are not mentioned so maybe the DNA will help with that question. I'd give the same answer about the person under the box. How they died may become clear for both of them once you are able to reconstruct the skeletal remains."

"Grandpa, you didn't tell us that the grandfather went to Yerke."

"Oh. I guess I forgot that bit of information."

At about this time, the other workers started arriving, and work commenced at the site in earnest so Jason and McGuire also started working. Nicole left to go back to the McGuire's, and research whatever she could find on the internet related to what she had just heard.

XXXXX

Joana arrived with her food truck a little before noon just like it was any normal day. She was tired but she hoped it didn't show since she used a little extra eye shadow and makeup to hide her tired look. Of course, she also dressed the part since it was another hot day and figured none of them would care about her eyes or anything else above her neck.

Shortly after she was ready to start serving-up drinks and sandwiches, her first few customers arrived. They greeted her like any normal day, stared at her body like any normal red-blooded guy, and engaged in several standard delaying tactics in order to see her just a bit longer.

About a half hour after the first few people arrived, Jason and Nicole stopped by to get something to eat and drink.

"Hey Jason. Hi Nicole. What can I get you today?"

Jason and Nicole had been talking so they stopped and smiled at Joana. "I'll take a turkey club and an orange juice. Nicole?"

"Oh, um, I'll have the same."

As Joana rooted in her frig and cabinets for their stuff, Jason and Nicole continued their conversation. "So, do you really think there is a treasure hidden somewhere in Iceland?"

Jason thought a moment then said, "Well, it says it on the top of the burial box so maybe it's true. Actually, I think it is true. I mean the translator in Oslo, or was it Copenhagen, anyway, was very confident of her translation, and just the way the story talks about a battle, fleeing with the wealth, getting to America, and ending up here just sounds pretty definitive. So, yes, I believe there is some kind of treasure hidden away somewhere in Iceland."

Nicole smiled. "Yea, too bad we don't know where."

As they walked away, Joana smiled. *Well, I think I know where it is, or will as soon as I get a translation of the writing on that piece of metal. Maybe the translator can help me with the task.*

XXXXX

That evening Joana thought about what she heard Jason and Nicole talking about. This was a concern for her. She already figured that Matt knew more about all of this, and maybe even about Iceland. Now, Jason and Nicole and McGuire and who knows how many others know about Iceland. She needed to get moving before there was suddenly a crowd heading for the same goal. Her only hope was that none of them knew where to look in Iceland.

She had to go to wherever this translator lived and convince her to translate the hunk of metal.

She rooted through the envelope that she had found in Matt's hotel room. She found receipts for hotels, gas and various other purposes. She also found notes he had been making and what looked like a plan for how to find this treasure. She also found a map of York, England that he had made notes on but she had no idea why he had it and didn't care.

She put the stuff back in the envelope, which she planned to burn at some point. But now, she had to find out where the translator was and book a trip there.

She pulled out her laptop and began working on her own plan.

Twelve

Changing

It was a good thing the mound was no longer an active project because several storm systems had moved through during the past week with heavy rain, thunderstorms and tornadoes. The site of the mound had been covered with a wooden structure and they had built several drainage systems to keep the pit from filling with water.

Unfortunately, one of the storms passed close enough to do damage. The winds were stronger than the structure, and parts of it were blown away. The drainage system was overpowered by the heavy rain, and the volunteers had to keep bailing out the pit. But, it survived, and nothing was damaged beyond repair. Fortunately, all of the artifacts were inside the storage containers and well protected from the elements.

Matt arrived back at the site two days after he left. He explained to McGuire that he had gotten a text message about his brother relapsing into his opium addiction and being in the hospital, so he had gone to see him and to learn what he could do for him.

Everyone was sympathetic, except for one person. Joana saw Matt the day he arrived back. He acted normal around her so she still figured that he didn't recognize her from years ago and the night she knocked him out.

She didn't do much business during the storms because she often had to close up her truck to protect her supplies. On several occasions she just packed up everything and left, hoping the next day would be a better day. It didn't really matter to her because she was making plans for her next task.

Joana found a Dr. Bergstrom who taught at the University of Oslo but was currently in Copenhagen teaching in their summer program. Her credentials were impressive so she was a likely candidate to have been the translator. Joana also noted that she would only be there until the end of summer, which was a couple of weeks from now, so Joana had to either move fast and get to Copenhagen or wait until Bergstrom was back in Oslo. She decided not to wait, and began planning a trip to Denmark.

One of the college guys she had been with while she worked as a bartender taught her all about computers and, more importantly, hacking. She was pretty smart and had learned quickly how to get into most systems. So, as soon as she felt comfortable with her skills, she dumped the creep.

She now used those skills to hack into a couple of bank accounts in Texas to acquire the money she needed for her trip to Denmark, and eventually Iceland. She never cleaned out the accounts she hacked, and never took more than a thousand dollars. Whenever she needed more, she would find an account in another city and state.

Once she had accumulated a little over ten thousand dollars, she stopped, and began planning her trip. She had some credit cards that she stole from several men while they were sleeping or busy in the bathroom but she had to be careful using them. You usually needed IDs and they almost always had cameras in the area. But, she figured that she might be able to use one or two in Europe if needed.

She was getting excited because she was getting close to her goal and appeared to be far ahead of everyone else.

XXXXX

McGuire and Jason were sitting on the deck drinking coffee one evening. Nicole had made a quick trip back to school to get mail and check on her upcoming class schedules since she would be back in two days. Vicky was taking a nap after a long day as a volunteer at the local Senior Center.

"Oh grandpa, I forgot to tell you that I received the second set of results from my DNA analysis. I had them take the earlier results and search their database for any people who might actually match my DNA in a way that would show that we are related. Isn't that cool?"

McGuire was staring off into the distance and didn't say anything when Jason finished. Jason asked again. "Grandpa, isn't it cool that I am getting a list of possible relatives based on matching DNA?"

"Huh, oh yes. That is wonderful." He said it matter-of-factly and began staring into the distance again.

"Grandpa, please tell me. Are you okay? Is everything okay? Is grandma okay?" He waited.

McGuire sighed and turned to Jason. He looked sad and serious, which only made Jason more worried. It was like his grandfather had something awful to tell him but was struggling for the right words to do it.

"Yes, everything is okay with grandma. But, I need to talk with you about your father." He stopped then seemed to remember something and quickly said, "And about me."

"What is it?" He sat a little forward in his chair.

"Your father had a secret that he wanted me to tell you if something happened to him. He knew that in his line of business, life could be with you one day and gone the next. Sometimes it is others – maybe a co-worker, maybe and innocent civilian and worse, a family member. He was worried that he might be hurt or killed and didn't want to take the secret with him."

"So, he told me what it was and made me promise to tell you when I felt you were ready. I believe you are ready to hear it now, especially because of the recent events."

Jason looked into his grandfather's eyes and nodded.

"This is not a bad thing, it is a good thing. And, when I saw the translation of the burial box's top, I knew that now was the time. You see, you are a descendant of that man in the burial box and I know lots about him. He is the son that left Norway. His father was Ragnvadr and his grandfather was Aki. Aki went to Yerke, now York, and saved as many people as he could. Ragnvadr stayed and died with the remaining men at the hands of Arild."

"The son is the one who hid the wealth on Iceland. He is the one who led his men here, and fought the native American tribe. He is the one who survived the battle, became a member of the tribe, a great warrior and the tribe's chief. He married two women and had children. His name was originally Ingvarr but was later changed to Pajackok when he became chief. This legacy has been passed down for over a thousand years from son to son. Aki also passed down the same secrets to his descendants."

McGuire stopped and watched Jason for a reaction. What he saw made him smile. Jason was smiling like he already knew the story. He continued.

"The man under the box is named Megadagik. He refused to accept Ingvarr into the tribe but the chief at the time was ready to kill him until Ingvarr stopped him, and shook arms with Megadagik. Later, this Megadagik was killed by someone so Pajackok and his son buried him in a secret place. Unfortunately, he had already passed on his hatred for Ingvarr and his descendants to his own children. So, that hate is still out there but I don't know who might have it."

Jason was about to say something when McGuire held up his hand to forestall him. Jason waited.

"I also needed to tell you that I am in the early stages of dementia." Jason's face fell and he looked like he was going to burst. "Jason, please don't react to this yet. Vicky knows and she has adjusted to it." He smiled. "As you know, she is the strong one in this family."

"We have great medical coverage, so when the time comes, I will be well cared for. And, I want you be strong, and to help your grandma deal with this when she has to. It could happen next year or in two years, no one knows. Until then, I plan to work and enjoy the time I have. Do you understand?"

Jason took a deep breath and let it out slowly, calming himself. "Yes, I understand. Do not worry. I will always be here for you and grandma."

McGuire chuckled. "Well, I hope that is not true. You need to live your life. You need to start a family when you are ready. I want to see my great-grandchildren someday, but if not, I want Vicky to see them so she can tell me all about them when we are together again."

"Yes, grandpa. I want that too, but I will always be close by."

"Good. Now, let's get down to 'brass-tacks'. A map to the treasure was with the Megadagik body and I think that it is what was stolen. We need to find out by whom and where it is now."

Thirteen

Off and Running

Joana arrived at the site over the next three days on time and ready with food and drinks. On the fourth day, Friday, she sought out Dr. McGuire as she was about to leave, "Dr. McGuire, this will be my last visit to the site. I am not sure if another food truck will take over but I'll ask around and try to find one for you."

"Oh, okay. Is everything alright? I hope no one has done anything wrong here."

"No. No. I have decided to head back to California. I have a cousin there and she has been talking to me about opening a restaurant. I like her ideas and think it would be a great opportunity for me."

"Okay. Well, we will all miss you around here. Your truck has always been a welcome sight when it pulls into the parking area. And, you have always been pleasant and easy going with us, especially with all these young men around here."

Joana smiled shyly. "And, I have enjoyed coming here this summer. I will miss everyone and they have also been very sweet to me."

McGuire gave her a grandfatherly hug and held her hands in his.

Joana turned once and smiled as she climbed in her truck. He waved as she drove off.

He made his way back to the group as they finished their lunches or sat chatting. He told them that Joana would not be returning and that she was heading to California to start a restaurant with her cousin. They all moaned about where were they going to get their lunches, and that it was so convenient having her food truck come to them. Many of them didn't verbalize their other thoughts about her looks and sex appeal, but their smiles told their buddies exactly what they were thinking.

XXXXX

Kevin Rivers had been watching Joana and Matt since Joana had arrived at the dig. Kevin's Algonquin name is Keme, which means secret and he had two of those. The first was his true identity and the second was his task. His true identity was, of course, Keme, and his task was to continue his family's vow, which was to protect all of Pajackok's male descendants.

Keme was in the direct line of descendants from one of Alsoomse's daughters. At one point the male line from Alsoomse's brother disappeared so the task was shifted to the existing male line from one of Alsoomse's daughters. Over the centuries he was told that it had shifted again but was now back.

The family lines had stayed close, and had started several businesses that prospered. The one that really made them rich was oil. They had been part of the investors in the oil wells that started in Pennsylvania and Ohio in the mid-1800s.

Over time it became more difficult to keep switching the role of the 'keeper of the vow'. So, several prominent family members decided to keep it in one line, assign the task to one person in that line, and make it their only job. The family had plenty of money to fund the 'keeper' and a 'watcher'. They finally decided in the early 20th Century to assign someone to keep track of the Megadagik descendants to see which one was going to take on their 'revenge vow', and this someone is the 'watcher'. At several points over the centuries some members of the family wanted to give up this 'vow role', but the majority always won out and kept it alive.

For many years the revenge role assignment seemed to just go away, but then it might suddenly return as it had with Joana. The fifty years prior to Joana had been quiet and the 'keeper' had nothing to do but stay alert and wait for the 'watcher' to tell him or her that someone looked to be going active in the revenge role again. Joana certainly seems to have become very active in the role.

Keme had noticed that this Matt fellow seemed to also be very interested in Joana's activities over the years. He had first noticed Matt when he and Joana met a few years ago, and started spending a good amount of time together. Keme had asked the 'watcher' to see what she could find out about him.

The 'watcher' didn't physically wander about watching someone but used the various social media and search sites to find out as much as possible about the revenge role target. Sometimes it proved to be a dead end and nothing needed to be done. They had actually failed in their roles with Jason's father and great grandfather.

Keme, now Kevin, would not fail. His uncle had been assigned the 'keeper' role when Erik was in high school. He had followed him into the military and actually served in the same unit when Erik won the Bronze Star. The military and policeman's jobs were tough ones to be successful in the 'keeper' role. The descendants were often murdered by a stranger and not a revenge role person.

This time, Jason did not seem inclined to become a policeman or go into the military so Kevin had to be vigilant, and he now really hoped the 'watcher' would soon have information on who this Matt fellow is. He had asked the 'watcher' to dig deeper.

XXXXX

Matt's ancestors had lived in an area not far from where the battle of Hafrsfjord, Norway was fought over 1000 years ago. There was a family legend which told that the battle was won by a king who had come from somewhere to the north, and that an ancestor had been an oath-swearer to this king. An oath-swearer swore to defend the person they were sworn to, even at the expense of his own and his family's lives.

The legend said that their ancestor witnessed the escape of the defeated enemy's father and son on three ships. The son went to the west and the father went to lands on the wild islands to the south. One of the new king's ships had followed the son's ship because the king believed that he possessed the wealth of the people, but that ship never returned, so he sent a second ship and Matt's ancestor had been on that one.

A year later, when the second ship returned, the ancestor went with the ship's commander to report what they had found back to the king.

Over time, a family legend evolved which believed that the son and his men continued to America either with the wealth or they had hidden it in Iceland because that appeared to be the only place he had stopped before going to Vinland, or North America as it is now known. Matt figured that even if it was hidden in Iceland and not in America, the defeated king's descendants probably left clues about its location.

Knowing this Matt had decided to go back to America and continue his study of history and archaeology, hoping to learn where the Vikings may have settled.

XXXXX

Many years before, Matt had come to America initially with his mom and dad when he was 5 years old. He grew up in a strict Lutheran home. His dad beat him when he was bad, and never praised him when he was good or won awards at school. He finally decided to do what he could to get out as soon as possible.

He studied hard at school in Mankato, Minnesota then went back to Norway in order to attend the University of Oslo to study history and archaeology. He lived on campus but often visited his grandfather who lived in the small village of Hamar just north of Oslo. His grandfather was as mean as his son but Matt ignored that stuff and politely listened to all his stories. He was glad that he had.

On one occasion, Matt's grandfather told him, "Your great-great grandfather was a military diver for the Swedish Navy. He also enjoyed diving with friends. On one of his dives with his friends in the waters just outside of Stockholm Harbor, he found himself staring at the 250 year-old

Swedish ship, the Vasa. It was beautiful and too tempting to ignore. So, he moved into the ship very carefully, trying to make sure he didn't tangle or damage his breathing and safety lines. He couldn't go far but he did manage to get into the captain's quarters." His grandfather paused to sip some of his tea.

Matt waited patiently, at least on the outside. On the inside he was trying to keep from yelling at his grandfather to get on with the story. He finally did and Matt became transfixed on his every word.

"He couldn't stay long so he meticulously and slowly moved around the cabin looking in trunks and places where valuables might have been stowed. When he felt two tugs in quick succession on his safety line, he knew he only had a few more minutes to search. That is when he saw it. It was a small box wedged tightly between some large books in a trunk. The books were of no use because of the water and worm damage, but the box looked fine. It was elaborately designed and had the royal seal of Sweden engraved on it. He guessed that whatever was inside must be valuable."

"Diving suits at that time were heavy, rigid bulky things with extremely limited movement so he noted the box but didn't tell his friends about it. Instead, he related his secret to his son, but the son wasn't interested in diving, and ignored the idea of retrieving it. He was going to go back himself, but he was just too old and weak to undergo the rigors of a dive in the bulky suit."

"Years later, when my grandfather was approaching his 85th birthday, he decided to tell me about the secret. I was fascinated and swore to him that I would get it. I became an amateur diver, joined the Swedish Navy to learn more, and to have access to the latest and best equipment. They had the new and recently developed autonomous diving suit with independent air tanks."

He smiled at Matt. "I secretly dove onto the Vasa, retrieved the box, and hid it away. Later that evening in my small barracks room I pulled out the box to examine it, but I couldn't read it because it was written in a very old form of the Swedish language. I opened it very carefully to see what was inside and found a small object that looked like a coin with a different style of writing on it. I knew I would have to get the two items translated, but who could I take it to that I trusted?"

"Then, I remembered an elderly uncle who lived alone about 200 kilometers west of Stockholm in a town called Karlstad. He had been a Professor at some university I didn't remember. But, I did remember that he had specialized in ancient languages."

"I left for my uncle's place a month later on a weekend pass from my commander. When I got there, I showed him the box and the object, and asked him if he could translate it. My uncle gave it a cursory look and said, 'Maybe'. He also told me that he didn't have time now and to come back next month, so I left the items with him."

"I couldn't get a pass from my commander until three months had passed. Once I had it, I went immediately to my uncle's home but he was not there. I thought maybe he had gone hunting or was visiting a friend, so I waited. As I sat and waited, I looked around at the interior of his place. It was only two rooms with an outside toilet. I began to notice that it didn't look like anyone had lived there for quite a while."

"I got up and started searching the rooms, and noticed that clothes and personal effects were missing. It didn't look like there had been any kind of struggle so my only conclusion was that my uncle had simply left. And, my small box was nowhere to be found. He had obviously taken off with it, but where to and why, I had no idea?"

"A year later, I was out of the military and was still angry at that uncle for taking my box. I had tried to find him on a couple of weekends when I had the time but had no luck. Once I settled into a new job at a marina and found a place to live, I decided to try to find him again."

"Two months later I found him by accident. I was out on a Sunday afternoon enjoying some free time by wandering around Gamla Stan. I grabbed some coffee and sat on a bench in the Gamla Town Square near the Obelisk. As I scanned the crowd, I saw my uncle walking out of the square at the opposite end of it."

"I followed him. He crossed the narrow land bridge and headed to the Stockholm City Museum. I had to act or he would be lost to me in the museum crowds. I reached him before he entered and steered him down behind the train station. He didn't resist. He seemed to accept that I had finally found him."

"When we reached an isolated area, I spun him around to face me and asked where my box was. He said that he had sold it because he needed money. But, he said that he did get it translated by a friend in York, England. He told me that he had read part of the outside of the box and noticed it said Yerke, which is the old name for York, so he went there to see a friend from his Navy days. His friend had settled there with relatives from here, and told me what happened."

"There was a huge migration of tens of thousands from Scandinavia into northern Anglo-Saxon England back in the mid-ninth century. His ancestors were part of it. The Vikings that arrived first were warriors but the majority of the rest of those early invaders were settlers - farmers, tradesmen and families. My uncle's friend's ancestors were in this second group, and became prosperous farmers and landowners."

"I went to him and he welcomed me to his huge estate about a day's ride outside of York. After a couple of days of visiting, and when we were alone in his study, I told him about the box and object inside. He asked to see it so I retrieved it from my bag and handed it to him. He looked at it for a long while but didn't open it. He finally set it on the small table between us. He leaned back in the large leather chair and closed his eyes. I didn't know what to think and almost rose to leave in order to give him some privacy."

"He suddenly opened his eyes and smiled. Then, he proceeded to tell me this extraordinary tale of a group of Vikings arriving a hundred years after his, of their joining together as one large family, of a battle lost, and a treasure hidden then lost. Apparently, an ancestor five hundred years after this group's initial arrival decided to give up the secret and sent it to the king of Sweden for safe keeping. The secret was hidden in this box, and this box was on the Vasa when it sank and now I had brought the box back to its rightful owners." He stopped.

"I waited for him to continue but when he did not, I asked, "Well, what did it say? What did he do? Tell me!"

"He told me that these ancestors only knew where to look but not the exact location. He said it was in Iceland but that was all he knew."

"Well, I had no money and certainly no interest in going to Iceland to find some treasure that may or may not still exist. So I asked him if he would like to buy it from me and he agreed. We haggled briefly and I sold it to him. It was enough for me to come back here, buy a small apartment, and live until the end of my days."

"I got so mad at him and yelled that he had sold my box, not his, and that I wanted the money that he had gotten. He said no. He needed it to live. I became enraged and shoved him, his foot slipped, and he fell backwards onto the train tracks below just as a train was coming. He was killed and now I knew nothing, again. Not who this person was in York. Not where my uncle lived. Not where he kept his money."

"So, I snuck away and came back here."

Matt listened to all of this and found it absurd, but feasible too. He left his grandfather's, went into the city, and decided to do some research into his tale. The mass migration did happen, and there was a battle near Hafrsfjord around the time he said, and there was a rumor of a number of the former king's family escaping. It seemed also true that the conquering king found no wealth anywhere from the former king.

XXXXX

Matt eventually moved back to the United States and lived in several cities around the country taking various courses in history and archaeology. He also started volunteering at digs just to get more experience, and of course, information about other digs, what the dig's goals were, and what was being found at them. He figured that if these Vikings made it to America then evidence of their existence should turn up at an archaeological dig somewhere.

Six months ago he ended up at the University of Cincinnati. He knew that Dr. McGuire was planning a dig nearby but the goals were primarily to help give students first-hand experience and training. He didn't need any of that.

One evening a month ago while out at a local bar, he sat with several other students from the archaeology program. After two hours of random talk, he was bored and decided to leave after his beer was finished. When he was about ready to get his check, one of the students started talking excitedly about the dig being directed by Dr. McGuire. He said that during previous summers they had dug into the mound, found a stone chamber, cleared off the roof, and went in. They had found a large number of objects that they had been cataloguing since then.

Matt was just getting ready to gulp down his last bit of beer when the guy stopped him short by saying, "And, now we are getting ready to open a burial box with, what looks to be, ancient Nordic carvings on the top."

Matt quickly called a waitress over and asked for another round of drinks for all of them. As the guy went on about what they were doing, Matt became convinced that this was definitely worth a look.

The next day he took his application to Dr. McGuire to join the dig. McGuire said sure. "We can always use some extra help and you appear to have some very good experiences. Come by the dig site tomorrow and we'll get you started."

Matt planned to take the item he was looking for, if found, from the storage location when he was there alone. He knew how the process worked so he could easily cover its theft. Besides, he wasn't planning to stick around for very long after he had it. His story was going to be that his mother had suddenly taken ill back in Norway and he had to return there. He just hoped that they found it soon, but regardless he would not leave until he had it in his possession.

When Matt's parents died in a car crash several years ago, he was happy to be rid of his dad. He was sorry about his mom, but only a little since she rarely came to his defense when his dad was yelling at him. He was particularly happy after they died because he received the payout of the insurance policy on them. It was over $25,000 and had set him up nicely to keep searching for what he really wanted.

XXXXX

The 'watcher' found out most of this by hacking Matt's computer and his social media information, which most people thought kept their data well protected and safe. Nope.

She passed the information on Matt to Kevin. The important part for Kevin was that Matt was not a Megadagik descendant. But, the part that required Kevin to continue watching Matt was that he was also pursuing the secret location of the wealth. This, Kevin feared, could result in Matt doing something drastic which could include murder.

His role was to watch Joana no matter what. He asked the 'watcher' to keep an eye on Matt and to let him know if Matt diverts his attention to Jason or Nicole.

Nicole didn't know it yet, but she was in the direct line of descendants from Alsoomse. So, she was family and Kevin was not about to let anything happen to her either. She was also the 'watcher's' family and the 'watcher' promised to keep a very close eye on her.

Fourteen

Following

"She is flying to Copenhagen in two days and has booked a room at the Hotel Astoria for one week."

The 'watcher' hung up. Kevin thought about this event for a minute or so then called the 'watcher' back. "Can you book me on the same flight and in the same hotel?"

"For the same time period?"

"Yes. But, please keep an eye on Matt, Jason and Nicole. Send regular updates to me if things appear to change. Thanks." He put his phone away, and went to his hiding spot near the dig.

The hiding spot was literally an old hunter's hide that he must have used to watch for deer. It didn't appear to have been used in quite a while so Kevin figured maybe the hunter passed away or moved or stopped hunting. No problem. He used it because he was not finished hunting.

XXXXX

Matt arrived at the dig late, as usual. He immediately went to McGuire and apologized but told him that he had been on the phone that morning getting an update on his brother. McGuire nodded and went to find Jason.

Matt had denied knowing anything about the object they were looking for, and denied that he had even seen what was wrapped in that old piece of hide. He was believed because everyone seemed to believe his story about his brother. He didn't really care one way or the other because he was planning to leave in a few days since, after all, the item he needed was now gone.

But, he carefully watched the rest of the volunteers to see if he might be able to determine which one may have followed him to the motel and taken that piece of copper. It had to be someone here. No one from outside the dig would know or even care about that cheap piece of copper.

He sat every day with the group to have lunch. Now, they usually sent someone to buy two large pizzas from a nearby pizza shop. He had asked why the food truck stopped coming and was told the story about Joana going to help a cousin start a restaurant. He was disappointed, not because of the food, but because she was definitely easy on the eyes and really 'hot'!

After two days of interacting with the other volunteers he still had no idea who might have followed him to the hotel. He even hung out with a few of the college student volunteers at a bar near the site to see if he could learn anything there. But, he learned nothing and just wasted his money buying them drinks to try to loosen up their tongues.

By then he had heard the news about the translation of the top of the burial box but not the amulet. He already knew about the treasure because that is why he was here in the first place. He also knew it was somewhere in Iceland but not where exactly to find it. He needed a map, and he was thinking that maybe that is what was on the copper sheet. After all, it had a bunch of weird writing on both sides of it.

He needed that copper sheet. But, first he needed to find out who took it, and where they were now.

XXXXX

Kevin was now in Copenhagen staying at the Hotel Astoria. He had followed Joana for two days now and she seemed to be just wandering around randomly. Yesterday she had gone to the University and wandered the campus for a short time then entered one of the buildings. She lingered a bit outside of one of the offices then exited and went to a restaurant for lunch.

He noted the name of the professor on the door and passed it along to the 'watcher'. He was still waiting for her to get back to him about the professor, and an update on Matt, Jason and Nicole.

He was now outside the hotel looking into the window of a nearby shop. He was not looking at the objects in the window but the reflection on the window. He was waiting to see if Joana came out and went somewhere again today.

He saw her exit and go around the corner from the hotel. He followed her to the university again and watched her go into the same building as before. She was likely meeting the professor.

XXXXX

Joana called the University shortly after arriving in Copenhagen, and asked for Dr. Ingvill Bergstrom. When she came on the line Joana told her the story she had created.

"Hello. This is Dr. Bergstrom."

"Hello, Dr. Bergstrom. My name is Pamela Larsen and, as you can tell, I am from America. I am very sorry to bother you but would you have some time tomorrow to see me? I know this is a strange request but my ancestors are from Scandinavia and I have long been interested in knowing more about our family history. I learned a great deal through the internet and certain genealogy sites, but that is not why I am calling."

"I have a very old object that has some strange writing on it. Someone told me that it looks like an old Nordic language. I searched online for an expert to translate it and your name came up. So, I came here to see you, and ask if you could translate it for me. I'd be happy to pay you for your time."

"Well that is a very interesting sounding object to me. I cannot meet you tomorrow because I have students all day but I can make time the next day for you. Would 10 o'clock in the morning work for you Ms. Larsen?"

"Thank you so much. That works perfectly for me. I'll see you in two days at 10:00 am. And, thank you again Dr. Bergstrom. It is very kind of you to make time for me."

"Think nothing of it. See you soon. Bye."

Joana was now on her way to her meeting with Bergstrom. She had wrapped the copper piece very carefully and stuffed it into her backpack. She had worried about it during the flight because she had to pack it into her checked luggage. She couldn't take it through security because it would have set off the scanner, and they may have asked questions about the artifact which might end up being confiscated. But, it made it and she had it and she was going to learn what it said. She truly hoped it was the exact route and location of the treasure.

She arrived at Dr. Ingvill's office and knocked lightly on the door. She waited for someone to call her from the other side and tell her to come in. But suddenly, the door opened, and there stood this beautiful young woman in front of Joana. She had lovely blond hair that cascaded down her back, a pretty smile on her smooth slightly tanned face, and a very cute sundress that hugged her shapely body. The Dr. couldn't have been much older than she was. Joana was also surprised because she was looking straight into her eyes, not up.

"Hi. You must be Ms. Larsen. I am not sure what etiquette to follow upon meeting you for the first time but you may call me Ingvill, if you like."

"Thank you and you may call me Pamela. I am so happy to meet you Dr. ... ah, Ingvill." She put out her hand.

Ingvill grabbed it, gave it a nice soft squeeze, and smiled at Joana. "Please, come in. We do not need to stand out here."

Joana entered the nicely furnished office and Ingvill led her to a small sitting area where they could sit opposite each other with a small rectangular table in between. "Would you like some coffee or tea or water perhaps?" asked Ingvill.

"Water would be fine for me, thank you."

Ingvill moved to her desk and picked up the phone. She spoke softly in Norwegian and hung up.

She sat back down opposite Joana again and began, "I am very excited to see this object, Pamela. Was it passed down from generation to generation or was it simply found with some other old possessions?"

"Well, I am not sure if it was found or simply handed down all of these years. I received it from a very elderly uncle who had no living relatives, and wanted someone from the younger generation to have it. I was the only one that he knew, and we had kept in close touch. He said that as far as he remembered, it had passed through family hands for many generations but he wasn't sure how far back it went, and no one has ever tried to have it translated."

Just then there was a soft knock and another young woman came in with a tray and set it on the table. The tray had two glasses with ice, a water pitcher, and a small plate with several types of cookies on it. Ingvill thanked her, and poured water into the two glasses. When she finished, she handed one to Joana and took the other for herself. She took a sip from hers while waiting for Joana to drink some of hers.

Joana began again. "Anyway, I decided that I had the time and the resources to research the item so, well, here I am." She smiled.

"Great. May I see it, please?"

Joana reached into her backpack, pulled it out then took the wrapping off of it. She placed it on the table in front of Ingvill.

Ingvill didn't touch it but moved to her desk and retrieved a pair of white gloves along with what looked like a jeweler's eyepiece. She then moved back to the table, placed the eyepiece on, and carefully picked up the small copper sheet. She turned it over then back over again. She moved it from side to side and turned it around several times. She then placed it back on the table, removed the eyepiece and gloves.

She sat quietly for a few seconds then looked at Joana. She smiled. "This appears to be a very old item, I would think from the 11th or 12th century. It has Nordic writing as well as runes, which is an even more ancient writing style. I am sure I can make sense of it but it might take a week or so to finish it. Will you be able to stay in the area that long? And, more importantly, may I keep it until I have a translation for you? You see, my schedule is very busy now with classes finishing here in a little over a week. I must then return to Oslo to begin preparing for my next semester's classes there."

Joana didn't like giving up the object but what else could she do. If she kept it, and tried to keep coming back here when Ingvill was free, then the whole process might take even longer. And, what if it takes so long that Ingvill must leave for Oslo. Joana would then have to go there, and do the same thing. No. She felt comfortable leaving it with her.

"Yes, I am comfortable leaving it with you, Ingvill. Will it be secured when it is out of your direct possession?"

"Oh yes. I handle many valuable and rare objects so I have a very state-of-the-art safe in my workroom next door where I lock everything when I am not here."

"Well, okay. That sounds fine with me. I am at the Hotel Astoria in room 212. Please call me if you have any questions for me, and definitely when you have a translation. I am very excited to know what it says."

"I will call you as soon as I have something for you." She rose, put the gloves on again, re-wrapped the copper sheet, and took it into her work room. She waved for Joana to follow so that she could be assured that the item would be safe. She opened an impressive looking safe in the wall, placed the item inside, closed the door, and turned to Joana with raised eyebrows.

Joana smiled and nodded.

They walked together to the door, and Joana exited the office and building. She was hungry so she headed for a restaurant.

And, Kevin followed. After she entered the restaurant, Kevin sat on a bench in a small park nearby. He had bought a local paper earlier so he pulled it out, and pretended to read it. A couple of minutes later he received a text message. He read it and immediately called the 'watcher'.

"Get me on a flight from here as soon as possible. You can keep tabs on Joana. Call when you have my reservation. And, hurry."

He put his phone away and stared into space. *Please don't let me be too late.*

Fifteen

Ingvill

After Pamela left Ingvill's office, she sat at her desk and tried to reason out what had just happened. The girl's story was certainly plausible. She could have ancestors that were descended from Viking settlers in North America. Or, it could be something that one of her more recent relatives found and kept for many years not knowing what it was or how to learn about it.

The story was believable. But, the girl wasn't. Ingvill had a funny feeling about her. She sensed that even though the girl said she was comfortable leaving it with her, she really wasn't. The means by which she came into possession of it was believable. However, she didn't believe that this girl acquired it that way. There was just something about her demeanor and voice and eyes that made Ingvill wary.

Ingvill had been very lucky throughout her life. She had had the opportunity to travel a great deal with her family because her father was in the diplomatic corps for Norway and her mother was a well-known expert in Viking and Scandinavian history. As a matter of fact, Ingvill had taken over her mother's position at the university when her mother decided to take a sabbatical to write. Ingvill had only been twenty-five at the time, and was by far the youngest faculty member the school ever had.

As an only child, her parents were very generous with her, not by spoiling her, but by giving her various pathways to grow in knowledge, and any other area she desired. She was an accomplished concert pianist. She had already written several children's books. Her name was on three respected research studies, and she already has won a handful of awards for her teaching style.

She has studied abroad, including America, the United Kingdom and Germany. Her two years as an exchange student in America were, by far, her fondest memory of her time abroad.

Her host family was the Harpers. They were composed of a father, Brian, and a mother, Amanda, and a daughter, Nicole. Ingvill had, and still does love this family. They had made her feel as if she were actually a part of them. She still kept in touch with Nicole and had been saddened when she heard that Brian had passed away a year after she had gone back to Oslo.

She had also met Nicole's friend, Jason. She had thought that they were a couple but Nicole insisted that they were not. Ingvill smiled at the memory because she didn't believe for a minute that they were 'just friends'. Regardless, she bet that they were a couple now.

She had attended the same high school as Nicole but was two years older and two grades ahead. It didn't make any difference to either of them. They hung out together, did sports, went to dances, and had lunch together anytime they had a chance. She hasn't seen Nicole in several years because they have both gotten so busy with college and work.

Ingvill had learned a great deal about people, especially girls, and especially young girls while in school in America and in Europe. But, she probably has learned the most while teaching. Students often have reasons for not doing assignments or being late to class or doing poorly on an exam. She has become quite adept at reading between the lines of these 'excuses'.

And that is what she was doing with Pamela's story, she was reading between the lines. Pamela had said almost nothing about her so called ancestors. Why? Was it because she really didn't know anything? Well, then what was all this talk about learning her family's history and what this object had to do with it.

Why did it seem that Ingvill was the first person she had thought of to take it to for a translation? There were many qualified people in the United States who could provide a translation, or at least, a preliminary one. Why did she pick her?

The only recent item she had translated was the top of the burial box for a dig director in Ohio. It had also been of Norse origin. Did this object have anything to do with the burial box?

She decided to send a message to the professor who had asked her to do the translation.

In the meantime, she would translate the item but delay telling Pamela. She wanted to think about the translation to determine if it had anything to do with the burial box translation, and she wanted to wait until she heard from the professor in America.

XXXXX

Jason and Nicole finally had some time for fun.

It had rained all night and was forecast to continue all day, so McGuire called off any work for the day. He told Jason that he was going to spend the day working on the dig report while it was fresh on his mind.

Jason knew what that meant. It meant that he wanted to write down as much as he could now while he still had his memory. He hadn't told Nicole, and planned not to until it was obvious to her and everyone else. He hoped that that day was well into the future.

He and Nicole decided to spend the day at the library researching the burial box story. He also planned to tell her what his grandfather had told him about his ancestors.

Nicole had recently told him that she had received her results from the DNA analysis along with the relative search. They planned to bring both sets of data to discuss what it might mean for each of them.

They were in the library now and had taken a table well off to the side so that their discussions would not disturb anyone.

Nicole started with a smile. "Hey, Jason. I wonder if Ingvill is the person they went to in order to get the box translated? I mean, I know she finished her Doctorate and has been hired as a professor at only twenty-five years old. On its own, that is an amazing feat. But, to be asked by a much more senior professor to do a translation would be amazing."

"Oh definitely. I didn't know her as well as you, of course, but I did always think she was smart, and hot, I might add." He smiled at Nicole.

"Hey, get your mind back on our work here." She grimaced at him but he knew she was just teasing him.

Nicole suddenly stopped and grabbed her phone. "As a matter of fact, I am going to send her a message right now to ask her about it. Besides, I'd like to know what she has been up to." She started typing a mile-a-minute.

Jason, in the meantime, headed to the book racks and began checking spines to find some material on medieval England, Vikings and settlements.

XXXXX

Ingvill worked on the copper sheet translation that first evening and planned to work on it each evening if necessary. She hadn't planned on doing it this way but she really wanted to see the translation and to try to determine if there was something else going on here.

She had made good progress the evening before and actually hoped she could finish it this evening. She had classes all day so she wouldn't have a chance to start until around 6:00 pm.

Classes were over and Ingvill was eating a quick dinner of a slice of pizza and a soda in the work shop off of her office. She put the wrappers in a trash bin, the aluminum can in a recycle bin, and was about the start working on the copper sheet when her phone began beeping at her.

She had no intention of answering until she glanced at the sender. It was Nicole. She immediately grabbed her phone and read the lengthy message.

Nicole had written, *Hey Ingvill. Long time no talk. Jason and I are in the library studying. We are wondering if you are the expert who translated the burial box writing that was found at the dig where Jason's grandfather is working. Wow, that would be pretty cool, right? By the way, Jason and I have found out that we might be related to Vikings from the past through our DNA, but who knows. Jason and his grandfather are very concerned because some object from the dig is missing. It is some kind of metal piece with writing on it. Anyway, don't want to bore you. We are well and I just wanted to touch base to congratulate you on your new position at the university. Take care. Love, Nicky.*

Ingvill sat stock still staring at the message. She read it again and then a third time. The copper sheet absolutely has to be what they are searching for. She dialed Nicole's number.

XXXXX

Nicole and Jason had started comparing their DNA results and noted that they both had Scandinavian ancestry but the amount was significantly different. Jason had about sixty percent Scandinavian DNA while Nicole only had ten percent. Nicole, on the other hand, had sixty percent Native American DNA while Jason only had ten percent.

Nicole was about to say something to Jason when her phone rang. The librarian looked at her with a look that said, *You will die if you answer that phone in here.* Nicole looked at Jason and mouthed Ingvill as she quickly headed out the door.

Once through the door she answered. "Hi Ingvill. Wow this is wonderful. I am so …"

Ingvill immediately interrupted her. "Nicky, I think I have your copper sheet. Go someplace where we can Skype and talk. Okay?"

Nicole said, "Yes, sure. Give me about twenty minutes while Jason and I get to his grandfather's house where we can use their computer. I'll call soon." They both ended the call.

Nicole hurried back inside and started packing up her things. Jason asked, "What's wrong?"

"Ingvill said she might have the copper sheet and we need to go to your grandfather's place to Skype with her. Hurry up. We gotta go."

Jason packed up his stuff and they both headed out to the car. As Jason drove back to his grandfather's, they both sat silently thinking about what all this might mean. *How did Ingvill end up with it? Who gave it to her? What did it say?*

Sixteen – 1605 CE

Yorkshire

Henric sat at his small writing table in his spacious room reading and taking notes. His family had amassed great wealth over the centuries as merchants. He had never wanted for anything, and had received one of the finest educations available at Oxford University.

He loved his father and his step-mother. His real mother passed away from one of the many diseases that seemed to pass through York every few years. He was born in 1575 shortly before she passed, had four brothers and six sisters, and at thirty, he is the oldest son. His family is descended from the old Viking, Aki, and Henric knew the secrets.

But, Henric didn't want to seek revenge. He wanted to pursue peace and to seek God. He had converted to England's version of Protestantism and wanted to eventually join the teaching staff at Oxford University someday. However, he was terrified of telling his father about his desire. He barely tolerates his son's conversion to Protestantism, and this would surely be seen as a betrayal.

God works in strange ways. When Henric turned thirty-five years old and felt he had studied enough to successfully be admitted into Oxford to join the staff, he didn't have to worry about telling his father. His father died suddenly 3 months prior.

He prayed for his father's immortal soul. He dutifully followed protocol. He handled the details of the estate, and taught his brother all he needed to know about the estate and their businesses. Then, he went to a lawyer, and drew up a will leaving his entire portion of the inheritance in equal portions to his brothers and sisters while naming the brother he had trained as the manager of the family's businesses. But, he told no one about the treasure story.

In 1610, he sent his application for a teaching position at Oxford, was accepted, and said good-bye to his mother and siblings. He left everything of value that was his to his mother to do with as she pleased. He then headed to the south of England and the career he really wanted.

But, he did take one thing with him. It was a small gold platted box with another small item inside of it. The box had various designs that made it look beautiful. But, the small gold item inside had writing that intended to start a war, and create death and destruction. On it was written the location of the wealth, the need to join with the family in the New World then take back their land and power in their ancient homeland. He did not want his brothers to find it.

He thought about destroying it, but he didn't feel that the box deserved that fate. Being an educated man, he knew about the history and politics of the region. He knew his ancestors came from the old Nordic lands on the west coast of the Kingdom of Sweden and he knew that the current king was a benevolent king, at least as much as a king could be.

So, with a gift of money from his step-mother he ventured to Sweden in 1612 and secured a brief audience with the king. After the usual formalities, he quickly told the king the basic story of their emigration, and why, and gave him the box with its contents. Then he left.

XXXXX – 1628

The new king of Sweden had a large warship built in the waters of Stockholm harbor. It was massive. Some said it was the largest of its type ever built, and it was named the Vasa. When the ship was ready for its maiden test in the harbor, it was loaded with soldiers and supplies. The king sent his personal belongings and some of his favorite treasures onto the ship. One of the items was a small gold box that the king favored. He planned to join the ship after the maiden voyage.

The Vasa set sail with much fanfare and celebrations. Twenty-eight minutes later it tipped over and sank to the bottom of the bay. Almost all on board lost their lives and all of them, along with the king's possessions, were now sitting at the bottom of the cold waters of Stockholm Harbor.

Henric heard about the sinking one year later, and was saddened by the loss of so many lives. He also felt remorse now for giving the box to the king in 1612. He assumed that the box was one of the new king's possessions that now sat in the Vasa at the bottom of the harbor. He probably should have kept it in the family and just not told anyone what the markings meant.

He eventually decided to retire from teaching in 1635, and took a serving position at the small Church of Saint Magnus the Martyr in London. He was appointed as an assistant to the Rector of the church. The church sits at the very end of London Bridge as it rests on the London side of the Thames.

Henric enjoyed his time at the church as he worked quietly to support the parish church members. He died quietly and happy in 1640 and was buried in the cemetery at his family's estate.

XXXXX – Present Day

Lord Wilkinson called a meeting at the estate house. His three sons and six grandsons were in attendance. They were sitting around a large ornate dark oak table in the library. The library is located in the west wing of the house, and contains over 5000 volumes. The Lord and his ancestors were lovers of books and knowledge.

The estate lands have grown a bit smaller over the centuries but the house has grown larger since it was built in the fifteenth century. Construction had started back then but the current house was not completed until the nineteenth century. It has fifteen bedrooms each with its own bath, two dining halls, several meeting rooms, and three TV rooms. There are also five cottages on the property for servants or guests as the need arises. The house has a staff that can vary but usually runs about ten, all living in nearby towns. More staff can be brought in when they have special events or guests.

The family business moved on from agriculture to mercantile to manufacturing and was currently into technology, specifically software design. Each of his three sons are directors of one of the arms of the businesses and the six grandsons all have had various jobs over the years in each business in order to prepare for their eventual directorship roles.

"I have asked all of you here today because, as most of you know, I have been poking around lately in our family's ancestral history. Today, I would like to explain why and give you some additional background on why I even started down this path. You see, a little over 400 years ago, our family was betrayed by one of our own."

He paused there and watched their reactions. One of his sons had no visible reaction but the other two raised an eyebrow. The grandsons all looked puzzled, and glanced to and from each other's faces.

"You see our family roots go back to the mid ninth century. We were part of a mass migration from Scandinavia into northern England and are descended from Vikings." He smiled as did the grandsons. They probably thought it was cool. "The first wave was a large group of warriors who killed and chased out the Anglo-Saxons. The second and subsequent waves were all families with merchants, laborers, and craftsmen, and they numbered in the tens of thousands. I actually do not know which wave we were in. But, approximately one hundred years later a small group of actual Vikings came into our lands from what is now Norway. They represented a larger group of people from a kingdom there. Unfortunately for them, they were raided by a more powerful king with a much larger group of warriors."

"This group eventually became assimilated into the families located around the north of England. So, essentially we are also descended from them. They brought with them a vengeance legacy which they wanted to fulfill. They wanted to eventually go back to their lands and take them back from the other king. They also had two secrets. The first secret was that a second group of Vikings from their land had gone to another place to hide the wealth of their tribe."

"The second secret is that they knew where that group had gone but not the exact location of the wealth. However, they passed the name of the place they had gone to down through the descendants from father to son."

"The group that hid the treasure continued on to what is now America. Their plan was that someday the descendants would contact each other, and share the knowledge of where the wealth was located. The American group would never be able to gather enough warriors because they were living in the wilds of that country. However, the group in the north of England would have direct contact with many warriors from many locations, and could muster a large force with enough money."

"Well, none of that happened. I do not know what happened to the group in America but I do know what happened to our ancestors. They were betrayed by a direct descendant who decided on his own to not share where the treasure was but to get rid of the message of its location and then join the Oxford University teaching staff. I am a direct descendant of that traitor's younger brother who knew some of the story but had never learned where the treasure was located."

"Well, almost 40 years ago, a man came to me who, by way of military service, became friends with one of my cousins. He needed help. He needed money. He asked me to buy a gold box that he had found on the sunken Swedish ship, the Vasa. He had been a diver and an old relative told him about the box."

"I have the box because I bought it from him. It is a nice box and is gold plated. The outside simply says that it is a present to the King of Sweden. But, I bought it for one reason only. It contained the secret location of where the treasure is located. The traitor had given to the King of Sweden. So, gentlemen we know where the treasure is located but, sadly, not exactly where it is once anyone gets there."

"Throughout the history of this plan, the secrets were passed from father to oldest son. If there was no son then it was passed to the oldest nearest male relative. This method kept the secret safe from being accidentally spread to others who might take advantage of that knowledge right away. Well that method failed 400 years ago. So, I am telling all of my sons and their sons."

His youngest grandson asked, "So, grandfather, what is the location?"

"Well, my dear Hugin. It is located in Iceland. What do we do now?"

Seventeen

To Oslo

Jason and Nicole arrived at the McGuire's house and moved straight to the bedroom they had converted to an office. Vicky watched them hustle past her and wondered what was going on so she followed them.

When she entered the room, Nicole was already on the computer and her fingers were moving quickly across the keyboard. In less than a minute, a lovely young woman appeared on the screen and said hello to Nicole. Vicky turned to Jason and whispered, "What's going on?"

He smiled at her reassuringly and said, "I'll tell you after. I need to hear what Dr. Bergstrom has to tell us." Vicky nodded and watched the two begin their Skype session.

"Hey,Ingvill."

"Hi, Nicky. It's so good to see you again. Oh. Hello, Jason."

"Hi, Ingvill." He turned to his grandmother and said, "Ingvill, this is my grandmother, Vicky."

Vicky smiled and waved while Ingvill said, "Hello."

"So, Ingvill, you said that you might have the copper sheet that we have been searching for. What makes you believe that?"

"Well, a few days ago, I received a phone call from someone asking if I had time to do a translation. By the way, I am in Copenhangen teaching for the summer and I leave for Oslo next week. Anyway, the woman told me a story about her ancestors and an object with strange writing on it that appeared to be Viking in origin. I had some free time two days later, so I told her to come over around two o'clock in the afternoon. She arrived and we sat in my office."

"Who was she? What did she look like? Have you done the translation yet? What ...."

"Whoa, Nicky. One question at a time." She smiled at her on the screen.

Nicky nodded. "Sorry. Go ahead."

"First, the reason I even contacted you was because of your text message wondering if I may have translated the box lid which I did. But, then you mentioned the lost item. As I thought about the translation, and the missing item being part of the material under the box, and the story she told me, I figured that the two must be connected somehow. That is why I contacted you."

"Now, as for the girl, she said her name was Pamela Larsen. She was young looking, so maybe in her twenty's. She was pretty, had long dark hair pulled back into a ponytail, pretty eyes, and a cute round face. She is petite but has a tough disposition. Not mean or threatening, just someone who got her way."

Nicole looked at Jason and he said what they were both thinking. "She sounds like Joana. She left last week and told Dr. McGuire that she was heading to California to help her cousin open a restaurant. Maybe that wasn't exactly the truth."

Ingvill went on. "Well, whoever she was, she related the story and then showed me the copper sheet." At that point, Ingvill reached over and gently brought to the screen the copper sheet. She turned it over and held it in that position a few seconds then set it back down on her desk. "So, is this the piece you are looking for?"

Jason shrugged. "Actually, no one has seen it. It was wrapped in an old piece of animal hide when we found it under the burial box we had recently removed. That's the box with the lid that you translated for Dr. McGuire. The copper sheet was removed from its position on the ground under the box, and placed into a box with some other items to be taken to the cataloguing group then placed in our large storage containers. Somewhere during that process it was removed and stolen."

"Do you think this Pamela or Joana woman could have done it?"

"I don't see how. She is never near any of our objects, and would be questioned if she tried to gain access to them. I am almost sure she couldn't have taken it. Even if she came by at night after the site was shut down she would have had to break into one of the containers in order to get it. If she did that, then there would be evidence of a break-in the next morning. No, it had to be someone here at the dig."

"Well, she is the one who brought the item to me so if she didn't steal it then someone else must have. And, by the way, to answer your last question, Nicky, I have not translated it yet. I told her that I would try to get it done before I left for Oslo and then call her. But, I am guessing that you would prefer I not do that. Right?"

Nicole spoke right away as she looked at Jason. "No, please try to put her off. Is there any way you can wait until you get to Oslo to translate it?"

"Of course, but I also assume that when I do, you do not want me to give it to her."

"No. I want you to give it to me. And, I am coming to Oslo to personally receive it, and of course, to see my dear friend." She smiled.

"Wonderful. I have missed you and I'll plan some fun things for us to do. We can also talk about old times, and new times, and the handsome man sitting next to you." She winked at Jason.

Nicole laughed and said, "Yes, we can do all of that and more. I'll send you my arrival information as soon as I can book the trip. Bye, love you!"

"Love you too. Bye Jason. It was nice to meet you Mrs. McGuire." Then, her image disappeared.

"Nicole, you can't go off to Oslo now and by yourself. What about your mom? What about school? And, we don't know enough about what is really going on here. I am worried. Grandma, tell her she can't go."

"Oh no, Jason. This is her decision. Come on. She is what, twenty-four? She can talk to her mom and to the school."

"Jason, my mom will understand. She remembers Ingvill when she stayed with us for two years as an exchange student. She loves Ingvill, and will be happy that I am getting a chance to see her again. As for school, I can tell them that I want to take the next semester off. I am doing well, and have great relationships with my instructors. It will be fine. And as for you, you need to stay here, and help your grandfather finish up with the dig and cataloguing. You know how much he needs your help right now." She looked at him sternly.

"I know. I just worry because we know nothing about who is doing this, maybe it's Joana, maybe it is she and others. What is their goal? All of this is unknown." Jason had not told Nicole about his family history regarding the old Viking and the treasure.

"I'll be fine. Now, I need to get home so that I can tell my mother, and talk to the school, and book my flights."

Jason walked her to her car. As she turned to say goodbye, Jason pulled her into a tight embrace and kissed her softly. He could taste the mint she had sucked on early.

Before he could even think about pulling away, Nicole stood on her toes, put her arms around his neck, and pulled him to her even tighter than he had. As she kissed him, she started rubbing her hands down the sides of his back gently kneading his tight muscles.

Jason responded by dropping his hands down to the top of her butt and felt the tight muscles as they strained to keep her on her toes.

Before it could go any farther, Nicole slowly settled onto her heals and pulled her mouth from his. He followed her, and they stood looking at each other while she held her hands in front of her chest.

Finally, Jason softly told her, "Please be careful, and call me when you get there, and every day after. Please."

"Of course." Nicole smiled and dropped into the seat of her car.

As she drove off, Jason watched until the car was no longer visible. Then, he turned and made his way into the house. When he came in, Vicky put a comforting hand on his shoulder and said, "She'll be fine, don't worry."

Later that day, after Nicole talked to her mom, and to the school, she made her flight reservation.

The following day after McGuire had talked about the day's work to the few remaining volunteers who hadn't left for school or home, Jason briefed his grandfather about the copper sheet, and Ingvill, and Joana, and Nicole's trip.

Matt was nearby talking to one of the other volunteers about where Joana had gone, and the volunteer related what McGuire had told him. He also asked Matt why he didn't remember that. But Matt wasn't listening to him anymore. He had only asked because he wanted to stay close enough to Jason and McGuire to hear if there had been any progress on the search for the copper sheet. That is when he heard Jason mention the sheet and Joana and Ingvill. After the other volunteer wandered off and Jason went to the container with the burial box, Matt followed.

"Hey Jason, I heard you mention Joana and I have been wondering where she is?"

"Don't you remember when Dr. McGuire explained about her trip to California?"

"Well, yes. But, just now I heard you mention her to Dr. McGuire and I was worried that something happened to her."

"Oh. No. She showed up in Copenhagen, Denmark asking about the object that we lost last week. Nicole knows the professor who will translate it so she is going to Oslo, Norway to see her and to check on it."

"Oh. Good. Okay, let me get back to work." He smiled and wandered off.

Jason continued on his way to the container.

That evening, Matt also booked a flight to Oslo. He didn't know when Nicole was going so he decided to simply take the next available flight which was two days away. He planned to call McGuire tonight and tell him he would no longer be coming to the dig because his brother had taken a turn for the worse.

The 'watcher' passed Matt's and Nicole's plans on to Kevin. After she told him, he told her to book a flight and room for him there as well, and the sooner the better.

Eighteen

Joana

Joana was getting nervous. It had been three days since she had given the copper sheet to Dr. Bergstrom and she had not heard anything yet. She decided to call.

"Hello. This is Dr. Bergstrom."

"Yes. Hi. This is Pamela Larsen. I hate to bother you but I am wondering if you have made any progress on the translation of the copper sheet?"

"Oh. Yes. Hi Pamela. I have made a little progress but because my classes will be ending in a few days and I must return to Oslo next week, I am afraid that I will not be able to finish the translation until I get to Oslo and settled into my new class schedule. I really do apologize but this cannot be helped. If you like, I can finish the translation then send it to you along with the object."

Joana had to pause a moment. She was getting angry and she knew that she could not let her annoyance get in the way of her goal. Once she settled herself, she spoke calmly to Ingvill. "Oh my. I am so very sorry to have placed this burden on you. I should have realized that you have many more important tasks to accomplish than my little piece of copper. I can ..."

Before she said more, Ingvill spoke quickly. "No. No. Please Pamela. I really do want to work on this, and absolutely promise to finish the translation within no more than three days after I am in Oslo. The translation work can be done in the evenings once I am there. I would do it here but my evenings are full with grading exams and research papers. Please, Pamela, let me complete the task for you. You will not be disappointed with my work. And, again, I promise to have it for you within two or three days of my return to Oslo."

Joana had to think quickly. She didn't like this delay, and she really didn't like that Ingvill would be taking the sheet with her to Oslo. However, what choice did she have? She needed this translation as soon as possible. If she took the sheet back and tried to find someone else then that could take much longer than letting Bergstrom do it.

She sighed and said. "Yes. I appreciate your efforts, and I will be happy to wait a little longer. I will actually head to Oslo myself when you do, and check into a hotel near you so we can communicate with each other more easily."

"Yes, that would be wonderful, Pamela. I will let you know the day of my return to Oslo as soon as I have it. Goodbye, and thank you so much for your patience."

Joana simply commented, "Thank you and I will see you in Oslo very soon, I hope."

She placed her phone in her pocket and sighed. She thought about her Native American name's meaning – faithful, and her journey to this point. She was placing her faith in Bergstom to do the translation then send her the results. Her past didn't seem to indicate that being faithful made any difference in what people did.

XXXXX

Her father had named her Hantaywee, which means faithful, not because he cared whether she was faithful to a husband or anyone else, but because he wanted her to be faithful to the family's need for revenge on Pajackok's descendants.

They had lived in Bellevue, Nebraska, just outside of Omaha and close to Offutt Air Force Base when she was growing up. Unfortunately for her, when she turned fifteen, her father noticed her maturity and began raping her. Joana's mom had left six months before, probably because he was such an ass and regularly beat her. This left Joana on her own to deal with it.

Joana had noticed him staring at her when she was thirteen and fourteen, especially if she were wearing shorts or her bathing suit. When she caught him, he would quickly look away.

The morning after the rape, he apologized and didn't touch her again until three weeks had gone by. One night, as she slept, he snuck into her room, as he had done before, and raped her again. The next day he did not apologize, and his nighttime visits became a regular nightmare for her.

She didn't know what to do. She was too scared and embarrassed to tell anyone so she kept it in and just turned herself 'off' when he visited her room. She felt alone, lonely, and sick inside. She began hating herself, him, and every man she saw.

However, when his friends started raping her, and then men she didn't even know, she knew she had to get out. One of the men told her that her father was selling her body to men where he worked or to men he met in a bar.

When she turned sixteen, her sweet sixteen birthday present from her father had been a foursome with her father and three strangers. Had she had a gun, she would have killed all three of the strange men then shot her father with all of the remaining bullets. As a final touch, she would have castrated each of them.

Instead, after they finished, she quietly dressed, stole over a $1000 from the passed out men, and took the first bus out of town.

She began working odd jobs to make as much money as she could in order to head to another town even farther away. After a couple of years, she started to work in bars where the tips were usually better than in a restaurant. She also occasionally turned tricks with guys she met while working at the bar.

Joana already knew what her body was worth, and how to use it with men, but she felt she needed to learn more than the quick stuff her father and his friends did with her. She was a quick learner and some of the men were good teachers.

She never went back to school. Besides her body and its uses, she felt she needed to learn more about technology and social media. Math, science, history, and the other stuff bored her in school and were a waste of time. None of that stuff would help her get rich and out of this miserable existence.

She began to search for a young, smart guy, who could teach her about tech stuff and social media. She knew that she would have to pay for this knowledge, but she had learned that her body was worth alot to men.

She found just the right guy at a bar in Colorado where college students liked to hang out. She gave him what he wanted, and he taught her lots about technology, smart devices, and social media. Once she felt she had learned enough, she dumped him then moved to San Diego.

The next area where she wanted more knowledge was in self-defense. She had had to fight off a couple of guys several times, and it had gone badly for her. She didn't want that to happen again. She searched and found a self-defense class at a local gym, and signed up for it.

After a couple of classes, one of the guys approached as they were leaving. He praised her for her hard work, and suggested that he could work with her one-on-one to help her to get better. She of course heard, 'Hey if you sleep with me regularly, I'll teach you stuff that I know'. She smiled and said that she would love to work with him. She soon found out that he was an MMA fighter and had only taken the self-defense class to help hone some of his skills.

Eighteen months later, she moved to Phoenix. The MMA stuff had proved its worth several times over the past few months when a couple of guys started getting a little rough with her, and she had taught them what rough really felt like.

Phoenix is where she met Matt.

XXXXX

Men are so stupid and easily manipulated. When she met Matt he was attending Arizona State University working on an MA in History. He had only stayed for one semester before leaving, but she had learned a great deal from him during their short relationship.

Joana had been a waitress at a local bar and restaurant that the university students liked to frequent. The bar hired mostly pretty young girls as bartenders and servers, and she had been one of them. The tips were good at the bar, and there were plenty of teachers and students to flatter in order to earn even more.

Matt had taken an interest in her the first time he saw her. She was okay with that since he tipped well. Besides, she sensed something was not quite on the up-and-up with him. This usually meant that he would be an easy mark for extra money, and whatever else she might want from him.

But first, she would probably have to give him something. She became even more motivated to hang with him when, on one evening shift at the bar, she heard Matt bragging to a friend that he was going to become wealthy very soon. This really caught her attention. She figured that she would need lots of money to continue her search for the wealth the traitors stole. Her dad had told her about the Viking, and that the treasure was probably somewhere in Ohio, or maybe Iceland. Her father only remembered a small part of the conversation between the Viking and his son that was passed down to him.

Maybe Matt was searching for something from his past or knew of a friend or random person with money. It didn't matter. If she could find out more about his wealth tale then steal it, she would be able to fund her efforts. Her father had also taught her to be hardened to anyone else's feelings or needs. Those were the only lessons from him that were worth anything.

She started cozying up to Matt and overtly flirting with him at the bar. She would even occasionally plan an accidental meeting on the campus. He couldn't resist her and they began dating. They started with movies and drinks, but soon they began meeting at his apartment.

On one of those meetings, she decided if she couldn't get him to talk about this supposed wealth, then she was going to move on. She was tired of him and his bragging. If he didn't break this evening then she was going to drop him.

They were sitting on the couch kissing. She had already fed him several drinks made with grain alcohol, even though he had asked for a gin and tonic, and she could tell it was having the desired effect. His speech was more slurred than usual, and he had started talking about his secret plan to become wealthy.

"Hey baby, let me get you a fresh one. I need one too because I am getting so hot." She smiled, kissed him and stuck her tongue in to make it more lascivious for him.

"Oh yea, baby. I'm hot too and I know you want me." He smacked his lips and grabbed her butt as she got up. "I can tell you this. In a few years, you are really gonna want me. I'll have soooo mush money I could buy a whole harm, harme, whatever them A-rabs call their bunch of women."

As she stood at the counter, facing away from him, she rolled her eyes, and made a quiet gagging sound. She fixed his 9 parts alcohol and 1 part tonic water, and took it back to him.

"Here you go sweetie. Wow, that sounds really cool and hot. Could I join your Haram and be one of your regulars?"

"Oh baby. You'll be my number one." He sucked down most of his drink. "I got this plan."

And, although it took a long time, and she had to prod him to keep him going using a little rub on his thighs, and some other practiced moves with her hands and mouth to keep him talking, she eventually learned his plan. Once she knew, she left, and never saw him again.

That is, until at this dig. The funny thing was that he didn't seem to recognize her at all. Not even a double-take or two. Maybe the grain alcohol erased the memory of her from his rattled brain. Even if he did, she had prepared a story about having a twin sister.

She had used her tech knowledge over the next few years to follow Matt around, and learn what he was up to. She had set up a couple of fake social media accounts on several sites using made up names and biographies. She even posted some hot pictures of her body, not face, in order to attract his attention. The pictures were more PG13 than R rated, but she showed enough to do the job. It worked and he signed on to her sites.

She learned that, although he wasn't one of the traitors to her ancestor, Megadagik, he still knew about a treasure and where to find it. That was good enough for her, and she kept track of Matt as he moved from schools and digs.

Two years ago, she moved to Hillsboro, Ohio. She figured that since the treasure she wanted was possibly somewhere in Ohio then she wanted to be closer to it. Who knows, maybe she'll hear something in a bar while working. She had saved a good deal of money over the years because guys often gave her stuff that she would have had to buy otherwise. One guy even gave her a used car, but it was in great shape, and she didn't care about the model, color or other fancy stuff. She used some of her money to buy a food truck, start a lunch service at several local construction sites, and McGuire's archaeology dig.

Then, a month ago, she learned from one of her media sites, that Matt was going to a dig in Ohio near the town of Peebles. She figured it was Dr. McGuire's so she went online to check more closely what they were finding. She found out that the dig had uncovered what they thought were Nordic objects and a rather elaborate burial chamber. She immediately reasoned that this must be what she had been looking for.

And now, she figured that Matt was after the same thing. Ever since he had arrived she had been waiting for him to make his move. And, he had.

Nineteen

Aki's Family - Hugin

Hugin had listened to his grandfather talk about the family history and legend with fascination. He loved it. He didn't really enjoy his job within the family business. He didn't hate it – it paid very well and it gave him all sorts of perks. But, truth be known, it was boring. He was a technology guru and all he did was sit at a computer, analyze data, create software to protect against hacking, and deal with other geeks. Well, maybe he did hate it at times.

However, this new role of protecting their legacy and possibly joining with another branch of the family to restore their lands and wealth, now that sounded like great fun. He definitely wanted to be involved with that task. He decided to approach his grandfather, and ask if he could take up the mantle to make the connection with the American branch of the Viking family.

Hugin knocked softly on his grandfather's office door in the estate house. After half a minute, he knocked again. As he waited, one of the staff came by and told him that Lord Wilkinson was not in. "He is meeting several friends at the Black Swan in Burn Bridge."

Their estate was located just south of Harrogate near the small town of Burn Bridge. It was a great location for the family business because there were several auto manufacturing facilities nearby – including a BMW plant. The Pannal rail station was only a short distance away and there were several quaint accommodation facilities in the area if there proved to be insufficient room at the estate.

Hugin was anxious to get his grandfather's approval for the task of fulfilling the family legacy so he decided to risk interrupting his grandfather's time with his friends and their drafts at the pub. He hopped into his own BMW and headed to the Black Swan. The pub was located at the south end of Burn Bridge about 100 meters from the River Crimple and not far from the Pannal Cricket Club.

He was lucky because there was an open parking space in front of the pub, otherwise he would have had to find a space along one of the residential streets which could have placed him a kilometer or more from the pub. The pub had recently been purchased by a new owner, and they had done some extensive renovation to upgrade the electrical and plumbing systems, plus they added new kitchen facilities. They also painted and updated the décor and furniture but kept the look and feel of the exterior and interior as original as possible.

Hugin entered and found his grandfather sitting alone at his favorite table near the window at the front of the pub which gave him the afternoon sun. This was very good because if he had been with his friends then Hugin would have had to wait until evening to talk with him.

He approached the table, and his Grandfather looked up and smiled. By an unseen signal, the bartender brought Hugin a pint of Notorious F.I.G. from Ilkley Breweries. His grandfather was having the same so, of course, Hugin needed one too. He thanked the man and turned to his grandfather. They tipped their pints to each other and had a sip.

Hugin set his pint back down on the table and started. "It's a lovely day. I hope your pals are not late, grandfather. I know you're not accustomed to being left waiting."

Lord Wilkinson smiled at his grandson. "They are not late and I am a bit early. I was hoping that it would be you who came to me."

"What do you mean? You were expecting me to show today? I don't understand."

Wilkinson smiled. "Of course you understand. You know exactly why you are here just as I do. And, I repeat myself, I am glad that it is you who has come to me."

Hugin was still unsure what his grandfather meant so he just plowed on into his request. "Oh, well, um, I wanted to ask your permission to pursue our family Viking legacy."

Wilkinson smiled indulgently. "Yes, I know and you have it. Now, how do we begin?"

Hugin stared a bit then plowed on with his thoughts. "Since we know nothing of our American side of the family, I was thinking that we will need to take a larger view of the story and zoom in as we get better information. By that I mean, since you acquired the box forty years ago, and a quick search shows no recent findings of ancient Viking artifacts in Iceland, it seems to me that we can assume nothing has changed regarding the status of the supposed treasure in Iceland."

Wilkinson took a long swallow of his beer and nodded at Hugin. He was really enjoying this young man's enthusiasm. If he himself had been younger when the box came into his possession, he might have charged into the search.

"So, I am proposing to create a search program that will search all airline reservations for anyone from America or Canada making a trip to Iceland or a Scandinavian country. I will also create a search program to look for any of those making a trip to a Scandinavian country and then a trip onward to Iceland. I am guessing that if someone in the American family, which could include parts of eastern Canada, decides to try to pursue the treasure story then they may or may not know it is in Iceland. If they are in possession of the route details to the treasure, your information tells us that they will not know where the route is located. In which case, they might decide to go to a Scandinavian destination to search for a clue to the location."

"I agree, Hugin. I think that is a very perceptive assessment and I approve. If you identify someone making the proper trip or trips, what will you do next?"

"I suspect that I will get many matches to this itinerary. Many folks from the United States and Canada have roots in those countries and might want to visit them. I think I will focus first on anyone from the north eastern part of the states and far eastern Canada since history tells us that Viking settlements only exist in far eastern Canada. But, my guess is that it is quite possible that some of those adventurous explorers may have wandered down into the eastern United States."

I will look at the matches and toss any that do not seem to fit the profile of someone who might be following an old Viking legend. One thing we need to keep in mind is that the current generation may have no information about a legend or, even if they do, they may have no desire to acknowledge it as being real."

"And, even if they have the information and the desire, they may not pursue the story now because they may not have the resources to do so." Wilkinson took another swig of his Notorious.

Hugin smiled and did the same. "You are correct, grandfather, and, if I identify any possibilities, I will need to keep that in mind when I attempt to make contact with them. They may have no idea what I am talking about or they may be hostile because they may think I am trying to beat them to it."

Lord Wilkinson and Hugin toasted each other and finished their beers. Hugin left to begin his search and Wilkinson nodded at the bartender who immediately brought another Notorious to him. He watched through the window and smiled as his grandson drove off. He was truly glad that it had been Hugin who had come to him about this legend. He felt that only he, of his sons and other grandchildren, had the brains and tenacity to be successful.

As he continued to look out the window, the first of his friends arrived, sat at his table, and the bombastic conversations began.

XXXXX

Hugin went directly to his office in York. It was located in the southern part of the city near the Clifford Tower, but still inside of the old city wall. As a matter of fact, he had a good view of the tower from his window. He had asked his grandfather, when he was in his pre-teen years, why the office was located so far from the center of the city.

His grandfather's response was surprising to him. He had said they were in the southern part of the city because it was the farthest point from the York Minister he could get and still be in the city. He learned that his grandfather disliked the Church of England, and until now, he had no idea why. He suspected that it was because of what the traitor had done by joining the church all those years ago. Hugin, himself, was a member of the church and believed in God and Christ. As he thought about it now, he was happy that his grandfather never forbade him to pursue his faith in-spite of his own feelings and beliefs.

He sat at his desk and fired up his computer. He had gone to school for a degree in technology so that he could help manage the various aspects of the family business. In his free time, he learned the latest programming languages and techniques. At first, it was just a hobby but he loved it so much he began working side-by-side with the people in the programing department. He was always willing to learn and enthusiastic about new ways to program, and this made him a welcome guest in the work areas.

He began writing the code to track the air travel from the eastern United States and Canada to Scandinavia and Iceland. Of course, technically what he was doing was illegal because he was essentially hacking into multiple airline databases in order to track their data and capture it in his own database. But, his code would be well hidden and almost impossible to find.

Once it was written, he tested it on one air carrier to see what results he would receive. After checking the results and making a few tweaks to the program, he tried it again several more times. When he was satisfied with the results he received, he launched it onto all travel sites.

Since he also had a regular job, he set the treasure pursuit thoughts aside and started working on his company job.

Twenty

Nicole and Ingvill

Kevin arrived at the Oslo Central Train Station early in the morning by train from Copenhagen. He checked into the Comfort Hotel Grand Central which is actually connected to the station. The 'watcher' told him that Matt and Nicole would be arriving in two days, and that Matt would be the first to arrive. She had given him both of their flight details, and told him that Matt was staying at the Clarion Hotel. However, she had no information for Nicole regarding her accommodations. Kevin assumed that she may be staying with Dr. Bergstrom and asked the 'watcher' for her address.

When Matt arrived at his hotel, Kevin was across the street at a small coffee shop. He planned to keep a careful watch on him, especially once Nicole arrived the next day. Kevin also wanted to check out the area around Ingvill's residence before she arrived.

Ingvill lived in a small house in the community of Lofthus, which is about twenty kilometers north of Oslo central. Kevin had rented a car and would drive out this afternoon if it looked like Matt was simply getting settled into his hotel and not up to some mischief. The watcher had told Kevin that Dr. Bergstrom would be arriving by train at 4:00 pm. Kevin wanted to check out her house and the surrounding area before she arrived home.

Kevin knew that as soon as Joana realized that Dr. Bergstrom had left Copenhagen, she would likely follow her here. He wasn't looking forward to shadowing both Joana and Matt but there was no one else to help. The 'watcher' would let him know when she arrived.

XXXXX

Hugin's search program turned up hundreds of travelers from America flying into Scandinavia, and each day there were more and more. He decided to adjust the program to include each person's departure point. He hoped that this would allow him to analyze trends and to narrow his likely candidates. Once finished he re-ran the program against what he had so far in his database. It didn't reduce the numbers but he could now check to see if there might be a connection between the departure point and the people leaving there. He was reviewing the data when his grandfather came into the room.

"How is the search progressing?

"Well, grandfather, I have adjusted it again to see if that helps me to narrow the candidates for the American side of the family."

"That sounds promising. Maybe this piece of information might help. I was recently reviewing several of my usual online news feeds and came across an article that talked about an ongoing archaeological dig in the state of Ohio."

Hugin was half listening and merely mumbled, "Uh huh."

Wilkinson smiled and continued. "The article spoke about the dig's director, a Dr. McGuire, finding numerous Norse and Viking artifacts at this location. This is very interesting because Viking artifacts have never been found in the United States." Hugin mumbled again. "The other fascinating find was a burial mound with an elaborate wooden coffin inside a chamber."

Wilkinson cleared his throat. "And, this coffin had elaborate carvings on it that no one could read. So, they sent a photo of the carvings to an expert in Oslo."

Hugin looked up now. "Did he translate them?"

"Yes. It appears that *she* did. The article did not provide the translation and I could not find it in any of my searches. But, I did find another interesting piece of information in a medical journal. That story talked about the increased effectiveness of extracting and analyzing DNA from very old bones. In the article it referenced a recent success story that involved extracting DNA from bones found in a burial box in a small archaeological dig in south eastern Ohio." Wilkinson stopped and smiled at Hugin.

"Yes, grandfather." He waited but Wilkinson continued to smile. "Grandfather, what did they find?"

"They found that the DNA from the bones was almost 100% Nordic. And, I believe, my dear Hugin, that we have found our ancestor."

Hugin immediately searched for the dig site that Dr. McGuire was operating. He then searched for the nearest departure airport with flights to Scandinavian countries, non-stop or connecting. He found the two most likely candidates were Cincinnati and Columbus. He quickly adjusted the search program to look for people departing those two cities with destinations in any Scandinavian country.

The new search turned up a list of twenty-four names. He searched online for the dig data again and made a list of any names that appeared to have had even a small association with the dig. He added those names to the search program and adjusted it to only look at these names for travel to Scandinavia. Two names appeared – Matt Williams and Nicole Prator had gone to Oslo. He showed the results to Wilkinson.

"Well. We know that the location of the treasure is in Iceland and that the translator lives in Oslo. Perhaps they are heading there to meet with her to find out what the burial box had to say about it. Maybe McGuire didn't share it with all dig participants and they want to know what it said for some unknown reason. One reason might be because they are related to our American ancestors and want to continue following their family's legacy."

"I think I should go to Oslo and try to meet one of them. I'll do a search on them to try to find out where they are staying in Oslo. Once I know, I will book a flight there."

"I agree and please be careful, Hugin. We can't be sure these are the right people."

"I will." Hugin began typing.

XXXXX

Jason was worried about Nicole going to Oslo alone. They didn't know much of anything but he was sure that Joana could be a big problem if she did indeed steal the copper sheet. And, add that to the fact that Matt had suddenly left, also worried him. After all, Matt was probably the last person to hold the copper sheet before it disappeared. He and Joana could be working together.

He had been staring off in the distance when he felt a hand on his shoulder. Dr. McGuire gently squeezed and sat next to him at the picnic table where they were eating their lunch before continuing to catalogue more items with any additional detail they had gathered after their initial assessment.

"Jason. There isn't much here to do and I still have John here to help me. You go home, and give Nicole a call, and ask her if all is well. That will make you feel much better."

"Thanks, grandpa. Are you sure you will be okay here?"

"I will be fine and I will call Vicky to come get me if you have not returned. Now go." And, he gently pushed him away.

Jason smiled and headed for the car.

XXXXX

Nicole arrived, exited the arrivals hall, and saw Ingvill waiting for her. She waved at Ingvill, and rolled her bag to where she was standing behind the mass of others waiting for loved ones or those here for a tour.

When she got to Ingvill, the two young women hugged then pulled back to assess each other. They both smiled at what they saw.

"I am so happy to see you, Nicky. It has been so long since we were in school together."

"I know and I have missed you terribly much. And, look at you, a Doctor already!"

"Yes, well, I am not a Doctor doctor. I am just a scientist doctor. But, enough of this, let's get to my house so we can relax over some tea and catch up on each other." Ingvill grabbed Nicole's bag before she could protest, so she simply followed Ingvill out to the car.

It was a long stroll to the parking area and they chatted all the way, occasionally laughing at something said.

Ingvill suddenly stopped at a bright red Peugeot. Nicole smiled. "Wow, a hot little car for a hot young lady. Nice!"

"Yes, well, you notice that this young lady has no ring and probably never will. But, who knows, with your help now, maybe I can catch one of your rejects."

They both laughed. As they drove to Ingvill's house, Nicole jumped right to the reason for being here. "I don't really know who Joana is or much about her but, if she stole that copper sheet and made her way all the way here to see you, then she must have some idea about the treasure and its background story. And, if that is true, then she may know about Jason's role in all this."

She filled in Ingvill on Jason's family history and legacy. She had debated telling Ingvill this on the long flight to Oslo but ended up deciding to do so. Nicole felt that Ingvill was caught up in all this now because of the burial box and the copper sheet. If Joana is as serious as she thought she might be, then Ingvill needed to know all of it. Who knows, maybe she might have some insight into this legacy thing.

XXXXX

Matt had arrived at Ingvill's house a short time ago. He hid in his car just up the street from her house.

What Matt didn't know was that Kevin had seen him, and was waiting in his car on a side street. He had been shadowing Matt since he arrived in Oslo, and had followed him here then parked out of his view. By the way Matt was moving about in the open on this trip, Kevin was sure that he still didn't know he was being followed and, therefore, didn't know who Kevin was.

About an hour after Matt and Kevin arrived, Ingvill and Nicole pulled into Ingvill's driveway. The women exited the car and Ingvill pulled the suitcase from the trunk. They entered the house through a side door which led to the kitchen.

Matt remained in his rental, as did Kevin.

XXXXX

Ingvill showed Nicole to the spare bedroom then went to the kitchen to make some tea. Nicole had looked around as they drove up to the house. The exterior could have been found in many American suburbs. There was a small, well-kept lawn with a few flower beds. The house was a single story, boxed shape home painted an off-white shade. The interior was very neat and tidy with what appeared to be well made but inexpensive furnishings.

Ingvill told her on the drive over that she had inherited it from her grandparents when the grandmother passed away four years ago. She had been very close to her grandparents. When she graduated from college, she rented an apartment but spent much of her free time with them.

As Nicole was pulling stuff from her suitcase, her phone rang. It was Jason. She picked it up and said, "Hey Jason. This is a nice surprise."

Jason smiled then opened with a more serious tone. "Hey Nicole. I am glad you made it there safely. The reason I am calling is, first, of course, to say hello. But, I have a second and more serious reason as well." And, he launched right into it. "I think that you need to be very careful. Grandpa and I both feel that Joana and Matt are in this together, and are after that copper sheet for what it says. I think that you should wait for me to get there and not go outside at all."

Nicole had figured that Joana was probably up to no good but was unaware of a connection to Matt. Be that as it may, she took a breath and let it out slowly. "Okay. I will be careful but I can't just hide out at Ingvill's house. Besides, if they are trailing me, and Joana knows Ingvill has the sheet, then she is in danger too. Look, stay by your phone. I am going to talk to Ingvill about all of this and call you back when we have a better idea about what is on the sheet, and what we need to do about it."

Before Jason could say anything, Nicole was gone. He stared at the phone and waited, impatiently.

Nicole went to the kitchen just as Ingvill finished pouring two cups of tea. Ingvill smiled and handed Nicole a cup.

They sat at the table and Nicole started. "Ingvill, we need to talk."

Twenty-one

Plans and More Plans

Hugin arrived at the hotel where Matt was registered but he couldn't find any hotel information on Nicole. He was not a detective or a con artist or a spy so he had no idea how to find someone and, once found, how to follow them. He was beginning to think that he was in way over his head. Well, his grandfather trusted him and gave him full confidence, so he would have to figure this out somehow.

XXXXX

Matt watched Ingvill's house. He wanted to go straight inside, grab the copper sheet, and run. However, that seemed too dangerous. One, there were two people inside and one of them might get a chance to call for help or knock him on the head or both. Two, there were too many neighbors out walking, doing yard work and going or coming in their vehicles. He would wait to see if only one came out.

Kevin watched Matt watching Ingvill's house. He had to figure out a way to get Matt out of the way and out of the picture.

XXXXX

"Ingvill, I have to tell you something about this copper sheet and this situation." She paused to gather her thoughts.

Ingvill jumped in. "Look, Nicky, I have already guessed that this is not just a simple search for a treasure by some interested archaeologists. As a result, I am guessing that there is a dangerous element here, especially after meeting Pamela, I mean Joana. She comes off as a sweet person, and seems sincere about her request. But, I felt that there was something about her that went deeper."

"Yes, yes." Interrupted Nicole. "We, that is Jason, Dr. McGuire and myself, have determined that she may be working with one of the dig volunteers to steal this copper sheet and secure for themselves whatever this map leads to."

"What might be their motivation? Just the possible wealth they might find? Or is there something more?"

Nicole took a deep breath and said, "Yes, there is more. I'll be as brief as I can because they are searching for me and the copper sheet right now." Ingvill quickly glanced at her door, saw that it was unlocked, and went over to lock it. She sat down with Nicole.

"There were two bodies inside the mound. The burial box contained the body of a Viking warrior who was captured by the Indians but then accepted into the tribe. He married, had children, became a great warrior, and eventually a revered chief of the tribe. There was also a body under the burial box that was more-or-less tossed there. We are pretty sure that it contained the body of the only member of the tribe who refused to acknowledge the Viking as anything but someone to kill in battle. When the Viking became chief, he was advised to get rid of the trouble maker, but he did not."

Nicole continued telling Ingvill about both men passing down their legends – the Viking's escape, the treasure's location, and the trouble maker's hatred of the Viking and all his descendants. She also told her about Jason being one of the descendants of the Viking and that they suspect that maybe Joana or Matt or both could be descended from the trouble maker.

Ingvill was totally fascinated with Nicole's story. She knew many other stories like it since the ancient archives of the Norse people were full of them. When Nicole finished they both sat for a moment then Ingvill started. "Okay, all of that is good to know. Here is what I suggest. I have translated the copper sheet so I'll give you the translation and you can call Jason to tell him to go to Iceland where you'll meet him."

"Once you have done that, we will discretely pack necessary items in boxes and put them in my car. Someone may be watching, so we will make it look like we are taking some items back to the university, which is exactly where we will go. Once there, we will go into the faculty garage where I will take one of the university vans. We will take the stuff from the car, and put it in the van then you and I will dress like male employees and leave in the van."

Ingvill looked over at Nicole and saw a huge smile on her face. "What are you smiling about?"

"Ingvill! You are so clever and secret 'agent-ish'! I love this side of you. Go on!"

Ingvill chuckled. "Yes, well, desperate times call for secret 'agent-ish' action! Once we are loaded up, we will drive north to a spot where my elderly uncle used to operate his fishing boats. He has since passed but I still know many of the guys who used to work for him. One of them was in desperate need at one point and my uncle helped him. Since then, he has since been a very good friend to me and my family. He will do me a favor and take you to Iceland secretly."

"What about you? Where will you go? How will you be safe?" Nicole came over to Ingvill and sat next to her. She grabbed her hand and held it tightly.

"Nicky, don't worry. I will be fine. There is an old hunting cabin well north in the dense forests that I will go to until you contact me to tell me it is safe to return."

"Ingvill, I can't ask you to do all this. You have a career, an important job, friends, family, what will you tell them?"

"It will be fine. Another colleague can take over my next set of classes, and I will call the school in some random place and tell them that I need to take care of some family issues. Also, I have never taken a vacation in the 4 years I have been with them so this will be good for me."

"I just hate the idea of all of this falling onto you so suddenly. I am so sorry. I wish I hadn't come." She leaned into Ingvill and hugged her.

Ingvill hugged her back briefly then gently pushed Nicole's arms down. She held Nicole's hands, looked into her eyes and smiled. "Don't say that. I have missed my little American sister and should have used some of that vacation time a long time ago to visit you. Instead, I worked and worked. When you decided to come here, I was overjoyed and would not have wanted this trip be anything else but what it has been – you and I having fun together while making your mom mad at us for the trouble we sometimes caused."

Nicole remembered those days and smiled. "Okay, what's next, my Norwegian big sister."

Ingvill grinned. "First let me get the copper sheet and my translation. We'll go over it then you can call Jason. And, while you do that, I will start packing."

XXXXX

Kevin had no idea what was going on inside the house. It would be night in a few hours and he worried about losing track of Matt if he snuck out of his car or if he just drove off. He decided to take action now rather than wait for something potentially bad to happen.

Invill's house was located a block and a half from a large wooded area, and Matt was parked almost at the corner of the street that bordered the woods. Kevin was on a residential street, so he backed away from where he could see Matt's car, and parked across from the wooded area where there were no homes. He lifted the hood of his car and walked to where Matt was located.

As he walked to Matt's car, he opened his jacket, pulled out one side of his shirt, and started looking left and right with frantic motions. He walked slightly passed Matt but then quickly turned back like he had just noticed him sitting there.

He moved to the driver's side window, bent down, peered in, and tapped on the glass. Matt ignored him at first but then as the tapping became more frantic, he rolled down his window. "Yea?" he asked curtly.

"Oh good. You speak English. I need help. My car broke down and I need to get to a job interview in an hour. I don't even know if I will find the place. This is a really great opportunity for me. You have to help me. Please help out a fellow Yank. Come on. I'll show you. It's just around the corner. Please."

Matt mumbled a no then turned away. He started to roll up the window. Kevin grabbed the door handle and opened the door. Matt looked like he was going to attack Kevin but held back since he didn't want to cause a commotion. Instead, he grabbed the inside handle and said, "Hey. What is wrong with you? I said no. Now go away."

Kevin held onto the door and leaned in so that he was only a foot away from Matt's face. "Look. I understand that you do not want to be bothered, but I am desperate to get to that interview. All I am asking is that you come with me, and take a look to see if you can help me. If not, then I'll try someone else. Come on, man. Don't be an ass!" He put on a 'stare-down' face and looked into Matt's eyes.

Matt harrumphed, said nothing, but he did get out of his car. He figured that he might as well go with the guy, look at the car, and tell him he couldn't help. Then, he could get back to his business. "Let's go and make it quick."

"Sure. Sure. I understand. You are probably waiting for your date to get ready. That's cool. The women here are really hot. Maybe if I get this job and move here I can meet one or two or maybe more. Huh? Huh?" He smiled lasciviously at Matt who never looked at him. Kevin wanted to keep him off balance so he continued his ramblings. "And, maybe if you live here, we can double date or just you and I can go have some beers together. I owe you one anyway for helping me. As a matter of fact, I'll buy all the beer for the night."

At this point they were about ten meters from Kevin's car. He started again. "Okay. Here is my rental. I don't know what happened. It was fine and then it just stopped dead in the road here. I had to push it out of the way to here. I checked under the hood but don't know much about cars, especially these foreign jobs. Here look. Can you see anything wrong?" They both bent down and leaned on the grill to peek at the engine.

Matt was thinking at this point that he would look around then declare that he had no idea what was wrong, and walk away from this knucklehead American. As he was about to say that he had no idea what was wrong, his head went forward hard onto the top of the radiator once, then again, and then again. He neither saw nor felt anything after the third plunge into the top of the radiator.

Kevin quickly eased Matt to the ground, closed the hood, and grabbed a bag that was sitting on the passenger seat. Next, he glanced around and saw no one, so he hoisted Matt up from under his armpits, and dragged him across the road into the trees. He continued to drag him about a hundred meters into the trees, found a clump of bushes about twenty meters in circumference, and thought, 'This will do'.

He laid Matt on the ground and started rooting in his bag. He pulled out zip ties, rope and duct tape. He secured Matt's hands behind his back, and then his feet with multiple zip ties. Next, he tied the rope around him under his armpits, dragged him into the bushes, and tied him to the lone tree growing in the middle of them. He checked his pulse and breathing then wrapped a long strip of duct tape over his mouth and around his head twice.

He backed out the same way he came in, and began brushing away the drag marks and foot prints. When he reached the edge of the tree line he checked to make sure no one was around then moved quickly to his car and drove around the corner to watch Ingvill's house.

As he pulled closer to the house, he sighed. The car was gone. He contacted the 'watcher'

The 'watcher' told him that she will keep an eye on Matt. She also told him that Joana was now in Oslo and that Jason has flown to Iceland.

Twenty-two

To Iceland

Once Joana realized that Ingvill was no longer in Copenhagen, she broke into her office that night. She searched everywhere including the safe but found no copper sheet. She had used another set of skills she acquired from one of the guys at a bar she had met. He had been in prison for five years after breaking into several businesses, and robbing them. She met him right after he was released so he was happy to share his knowledge with her since she had shared her bed with him.

Joana found no evidence that Ingvill was coming back to this office or where exactly she had gone. So, since she had said that she was heading back to Oslo after she finished with her class in Copenhagen, Joana planned to do the same.

The following morning, she bought a train ticket, and arrived in Oslo late that afternoon. She checked into the Comfort Hotel conveniently connected to the train station. When she got into her room, she tossed her small bag on the bed, and opened her laptop on the small table next to the bed. She signed into the hotel's free WiFi, and began a search for Dr. Bergstrom and Oslo University where she taught.

Finding the school was easy. She converted the language to English, and located Dr. Bergstrom in the faculty list. She did a search on the internet for any additional information about her, especially an address. She had tried her phone number but it was not in service anymore. It had probably been a temporary phone plan while in Denmark.

Her search turned up articles and research papers she had written as well as awards she had received but there was no mention of a home address. She decided she would go to the university tomorrow to see if she could find her or any information about her. She finally decided to head down to the restaurant to get something to eat and to work on a plan of action.

Kevin knew Joana was at the same hotel because the 'watcher' sent him a text as soon as she saw that Joana had checked in. He had planned to leave tomorrow for Iceland since he figured that Nicole would go there to meet up with Jason. But now, he decided to wait a day and follow Joana around to try to determine what she might seem to know.

Kevin saw Joana enter the restaurant and watched as she moved to a table by the window that over looked the plaza in front of the train station. The teenagers seemed to enjoy hanging out there, and were now gathered in groups around the perimeter of the plaza. Most of them smoked which seemed strange for a country that focused so much on health and fitness. But, then again, *when do we ever understand the minds of teenagers.*

XXXXX

Nicole and Ingvill had been driving for about two hours, and were now fairly certain they had not been followed. They saw a roadside rest area so Ingvill pulled in, parked, and they changed out of their university employee disguises. Ingvill climbed into the back of the van, and hid them in one of the boxes she had used to stuff cloths and personal items. She didn't want either of them to tote a suitcase around since that would not go along with their 'sneaking away' plan.

After that was done, Ingvill rooted in another box then stepped out of the van with a large sheet of opaque white plastic, a role of tape, and a large pair of scissors. Nicole gave her a questioning look. Ingvill smiled and motioned for her to follow.

Ingvill stopped at the passenger door and pointed. That's when Nicole realized what she intended to do. Emblazoned on the door in six centimeter sized letters was the university's name and phone number.

Ingvill smiled. "Watch." She cut the plastic sheet in two and gave one half to Nicole. She took the other half and rolled off a long strip of the wide packing tape then handed the roll to Nicole. Ingvill stuck the end of the strip of tape in her teeth and proceeded to hold the plastic sheet against the door until it covered all of the university's logo and information. She then carefully applied half of the strip of tape to the top of the plastic and the other half to the door. She finished taping all sides of the plastic in the same way. She did the same thing to the driver's side door.

Once done, she turned to Nicole. "Ready to go?" They jumped into the van.

After a couple of hours of chatting about old times, Ingvill asked, "Have I ever told you the story behind my name?"

"No. I don't think so. At least, I don't remember."

"Well, my father named me after an ancient Norse god named Yngvi. However, since the people from Scandinavia entered northern Europe and the British Isles it has had other spellings. In old German it is Inguin and in old English it is Ingwine."

"In Norse mythology, Yngvi was the progenitor of the Yngling lineage, a legendary dynasty of Swedish kings from which the Norwegian kings are also descended. My father didn't elaborate as to why he thought that was a good name for his daughter but I liked it, so I never really cared. Many other given names also come from Yngvi. However, the Ing way of spelling the name survived into modern times so names like Ingmar, Ingvar and Ingrid are all names you can find commonly in Norway and Sweden."

"Cool. That is such a great story." Nicole was quiet for a few minutes. "I have no idea why mother and father chose my name. I never really knew my grandparents or other relatives but maybe I am named after one of them." She was quiet again then, "Actually, over the past fifteen years, I have felt closest to the McGuires and Jason. Well, and my mother too, of course."

Three hours later, they were getting close to where Nicole would be shipping out to Iceland so Ingvill briefed her on what will happen. "When we get to the port, I will park near a house, go in, and you will wait here. Don't worry. You will be safe here." She gave Nicole a reassuring smile.

"I'll probably be inside the house for several minutes while I explain to Lars what I need from him. He is the one I mentioned before about being indebted to my family. Okay?" Nicole nodded.

They pulled in front of a small but pretty cottage, and Ingvill went to the door, knocked, and was let inside by a woman. Nicole waited in the van and looked around the small village.

There were probably a couple dozen of the pretty cottages, some larger and some smaller but all well maintained. There were very few cars but she saw a half dozen pickup trucks and a couple of vans. Maybe they all shared the vehicles for trips to town to sell their catch or pick up supplies. The port was a bit farther away but she could still make out several good size fishing boats anchored there, and they were bobbing up and down in the moonlight. It was actually a very pretty scene, and would have made either a great photo or painting. She also thought it would be a fantastic film location.

As she continued to scan the area, Ingvill and a large man, she assumed it was Lars, came out of the house and toward the van. As they approached, Ingvill waved Nicole out.

Ingvill stepped up to Nicole and Lars stood to her side. She began talking to Lars in Norwegian and occasionally glanced at Nicole. He would nod, and scrunch his eyes together, and tighten his lips every-so-often.

Finally, she turned to Nicole and said in English, "This is Lars and he will be taking you to Iceland. I assume Jason will fly into Keflavik then make his way into Reykjavik to find a place to stay. Lars will take you as close as he can to the harbor at Reykjavik. Either way, he will escort you into town, and help you to find an acceptable hotel."

Nicole nodded. "I should pay him something for all of the trouble he is going through."

Ingvill shook her head. "It is not necessary. He is happy to help me do this for you since you are my dearest friend. He would refuse any payment offers anyway, and would actually be offended if you did offer."

"Well. Okay. Thanks." She smiled at Lars who smiled back. At this, Nicole went to the van and grabbed her box of belongings. Lars gently took it from her, and they moved down to one of the boats docked in the harbor. Lars immediately got aboard, and disappeared with the box into the hold of the vessel.

Nicole turned to Ingvill. She had tears in her eyes. Ingvill immediately grabbed her and pulled her in tight. They stayed that way as they listened to Lars giving orders to the men on his boat. He must have already called them and told them they had a sailing to undertake.

The two finally separated and smiled. Ingvill spoke first. "I am so happy you came. I know it was because of a difficult problem you and Jason were working on, but it has made me very happy. It also showed me just how much I love and miss you and your family. I hope after all of this is over, we can change that and spend more time together."

"Oh Ingvill. You don't know how happy this has been for me, and I promise that I will always make time for you if you can get away from your work."

They hugged again and stared at each other a moment. Then, Nicole sighed, turned and walked to the boat. Lars was waiting for her, and gently took her hand to help her aboard.

Nicole stayed where she was, and watched the distance between she and Ingvill enlarge. She waved along with Ingvill until they were no longer within sight of each other.

As Nicole stared back at the small village, she swore to herself that she would keep that promise, and make sure that she and Ingvill spent time together each year whether in Norway or Ohio.

She finally turned and headed to Lars who pointed to a spot in the small bridge where she could watch their progress. It would be a long ride, so she would likely be staying in a room somewhere below. She figured Lars would show her where when he had the time.

Twenty-three

All the Rest

Jason was beside himself with worry. He was staying at the Guesthouse Lena just off of the pond. He sat in his room and worried because he could not reach Nicole nor could he get through to Ingvill. He finally called his grandfather and asked if he had heard anything, but he hadn't. He resolved to wait several more days before reporting Nicole missing.

XXXXX

Matt had been awake for several hours. He could see but, because of the tape, he could not make any sound that could be heard beyond a few inches of his head. He also could not move more than side to side by rolling onto his shoulders. His mind raced to try to figure out a way out of this mess. One thing he was sure of, if and when he did get out of this, he would kill that bastard who put him here. The guy should have killed him, even so, Matt was glad he hadn't. But, first things first, *How the hell am I going to get free?*

Matt could hear and he eventually heard noises that sounded like someone or something was moving through the area, and he hoped it was a person and not an animal. He decided to make as much noise as possible to attract the attention of the people, but scare off any animals. He started thrashing around as much as possible. He rolled. He twisted. He kicked his legs and stomped his feet. He stopped every few seconds to listen, and hoped the 'people sound' came closer and did not go farther away.

Suddenly, Matt saw a bright light intermittently through the bushes. He started wildly thrashing around creating as much noise as possible. He finally paused, not because he wanted to listen some more, but because he was exhausted.

He still saw the light going back and forth but seemingly closer. Suddenly, the bushes where he had last seen the light burst open, and a shotgun barrel was pointed at his head. He wet his pants at that point and shut his eyes. Then he heard talking. He didn't understand any of it but it was clearly human. He opened his eyes to see two men in dark clothes peering in at him and discussing something.

Finally, one of them reached in with his hand and grabbed Matt's shirt at the shoulder. The next thing he saw was a huge knife start coming at his head. If he hadn't already wet himself, he would have done it now. *They are going to cut my head off!* He closed his eyes.

The next thing he felt was a lot of tugging and pulling, and then he was moving. They were dragging him out of the bushes. They had apparently cut the rope that held him to the tree, and one of the guys was now pulling the tape from around his mouth while the other proceeded to cut the zip ties. The guy pulling the tape off, finished first, and moved a few feet away continuously pointing his shotgun at Matt. Once the other guy finished with the zip ties he pulled way next to his buddy, and also pointed his gun at Matt.

Matt worked his mouth and arms and legs trying to get the stiffness out of them. One of the men had pulled out a cell phone and was now talking rapidly to someone on the other end. They both continued to hold their guns on Matt as they talked. When the guy finished his call, he said something to his friend, and then turned back to Matt. He spoke rapidly then stopped and stared.

Matt figured he was trying to ask him what had happened so he tried responding in English. "Some guy ambushed me from behind and put me here." Both men looked at him with confused expressions. Matt sat up then started to try to stand but the men began talking rapidly and pointing their guns at him. He got the hint so he sat back down and waited.

About a minute later he heard a siren. *Crap. They had called the police*. He should have figured they would. I mean, this probably looked suspicious. Matt sat silently.

A moment later he heard more rustling in the woods in the opposite direction from where the men had come. After a few minutes, two uniformed police officers appeared with their flashlights and guns pointed at Matt.

The two officers looked at the two gunmen and nodded. Apparently, they knew each other. They all started talking and pointing at Matt. After a few minutes of this, the two gunmen wandered off with a wave, and one of the officers helped Matt to his feet. He appeared to ask Matt something but Matt only shrugged. The officer nodded and led Matt to their vehicle, and motioned him into the back seat. Matt sighed and complied.

XXXXX

Hugin sat in his room and worked his fingers across his keyboard. He still found no record of Nicole's whereabouts and Matt was still checked into the same hotel. He decided to go back to his search program and tell it to sort his data for anyone who flew from the same two cities to Copenhagen, Oslo or Reykjavik on or near the same day as Matt and Nicole.

A few seconds later he had a list of a dozen names that had traveled within two days before or after Matt and Nicole. He applied the same logic and had it identify any who had an association with the dig and only one name appeared, Jason Swenson, who had flown to Reykjavik. He next took those eleven other names and asked for ages, gender and pictures. Three were children under eighteen so he discarded them along with their parents. That left four people, but two were over sixty so he discarded them. He now had two more people, Joana Wells and Kevin Rivers.

He searched on hotel reservations for both of them. They were both staying at the Comfort Hotel. Matt stayed not far away at the Clarion and Nicole had no reservation anywhere. Jason had gone to Iceland so he remained in the picture since one or more of these folks, if involved, would also go there. He now had five names.

He did several searches on social media sites to find any pictures, and found pictures of Jason and Nicole but not the others. He did a search on various academic sites for current and former students. He got a hit on Matt. He tried several searches on different media, including police and FBI databases, but found nothing on Kevin or Joana. He tried the airlines again to get a passport photo but had no luck.

He finally decided to wait near Matt's hotel to see if he arrived with any of the others.

XXXXX

Lars had shown Nicole on a map where they had left from and where they were going. They had started from a small harbor near the town of Tananger and were heading to Reykjavik. He wrote the number of days it would take on a pad of paper and Nicole gasped. He had written '7'. Seven days! She had to contact Jason but, unfortunately, she had no signal. She pointed to her phone and shrugged at Lars. He led her to the bridge, and showed her how to use the ships radio. She thanked him, but she couldn't call Jason on that so she sat down to think.

About that time, one of the men came in and said something to Lars who went outside. After a few minutes, Lars came back in and picked up the radio. He began talking rapidly to someone on the other end then hung up. He immediately went out again and started talking to his men. Nicole figured that something was wrong or some important issue had to be dealt with.

Five minutes later, Lars came in trailed by one of the young men in his crew. The young man immediately removed his cap, and looked shyly away from Nicole. Lars said something to the man, and the man turned to Nicole.

"Umm, I speak little English. I Sven. Lars say something me and I say you, okay?" Nicole nodded. He turned to Lars and waited while Lars spoke then stopped. "Lars say bad storm coming. Must turn, go back." He turned to Lars again. "He say go to Stanvanger. You fly plane Reykjavik."

He motioned her to the map table and pointed to where they were, then to Stanvanger, then to Reykjavik. He turned to Nicole and smiled.

She said, "Okay".

He turned to Lars and waited while Lars spoke some more. At one point he looked worried but Lars just smiled. When Lars finished, the man still faced him but then Lars gently turned him to Nicole.

The guy shifted his feet a little. He looked at Lars again then back at Nicole. She was really wondering now what this new set of instructions were about. Sven started, "Umm, Lars say I go with you to help you go fly." He paused and looked down then back at Nicole. "Umm, okay?"

Nicole smiled and said, "Yes, okay."

He smiled. "Yes, okay." Then he turned and quickly left the bridge.

Lars got to work plotting their course to Stanvanger.

XXXXX

Joana was seriously mad and ready to kill someone, anyone. She didn't know where any of them were, and she had lost Nicole. She hadn't seen Matt and who knew what Jason was up to. She had to think.

XXXXX

Kevin sat in his first class seat on his way to Iceland. He still had no information on Nicole but he knew Jason was there and, if he was there, then Nicole would not be too far behind. He reminded the 'watcher' to let him know as soon as Nicole re-appears.

He also asked the 'watcher' to continue to keep an eye on both Joana and Matt. He mentioned to her that Matt might be unseen for a while but might reappear on a police scan or blotter.

Finally, he asked the 'watcher' to book him a hotel reservation not far from Jason.

XXXXX

Matt was released after making a statement which corroborated what the two hunters had said about how they found him. The police asked for a description of the guy who did this to him, and Matt gave him a description of one of his former college friends. He did not want them interfering with his plan for the guy.

They asked where he was staying and for how long. He told them his hotel, and that he'd be here a week but that could change if his business needed him elsewhere. He also gave them his phone number. It was a burner phone, and he was planning to toss it his first chance. They let him go.

He headed back to his hotel planning to check out the following morning. He decided to head for Iceland. Nicole had to have gone there. After all, she had the map by now, and knew that the treasure was there.

He got back to his hotel just after 7 am and was exhausted. He showered and lay down to get some sleep.

XXXXX

Lars piloted the boat into the Stavanger harbor and the men quickly got it tied down. Lars walked Nicole and Sven off the boat then gave Sven a few more instructions. Sven nodded vigorously.

Lars turned to Nicole and smiled. He said in very broken English, "Sorey. Sven good boy. He takes car you." He smiled and gave her a hug, and Nicole hugged him back. He turned and went back onboard. He waved as she walked away with Sven.

Sven smiled. "I take ai … um, arpot… um".

Before he continued, Nicole smiled and said. "You will take me to the airport. Yes?"

"Yes, yes." He tried again slowly. "I take you to airport." He smiled triumphantly.

Nicole smiled, and they headed away. He insisted on carrying the small backpack, which Ingvill had given her, containing her stuff.

When they were away from the harbor area, Sven waved a taxi over to them and they got in. He told the driver where to go, and they were off.

On the ride to the airport, they were silent for the first fifteen minutes. Then, Sven asked her, "You go home now?"

"No. I am going to meet someone. He is a friend of mine."

"Oh. Meet boyfriend." He looked disappointed.

"No, not a boyfriend, just a good friend."

"Okay, understand." He looked a little more relieved. Then he asked, "I am your friend too?"

"Yes, of course. You have been a very good friend."

"Yes, very good." He puffed up a little at that.

About that time, they pulled up to airport check-in and the departure gates. As they got out he asked the driver to wait. He walked her inside and pointed to the SAS ticket counter. "I wait. Make sure, okay."

Nicole smiled. "I must make a phone call first."

He nodded.

She walked to a quiet corner, and turned her phone back on. She had turned it off while on the boat to save the battery since it was impossible for her to get a signal. She entered her mother's phone number.

"Hey mom." Pause. "Yes, I am okay." Pause. "Yes, I will be careful. Listen mom I need to get going. I need to ask you to do two things for me. Please move $5000 from my savings account to my checking account. And, second, please call Dr. McGuire and tell him I am okay, and I am on my way to Iceland to see Jason." Pause. "Mom, I am sorry I don't have time now. Dr. McGuire can fill you in. Thanks. Love you." She let her mom say love you too before hanging up on her.

She next called Jason. When the call was answered, the first thing she heard was, "Oh my god, I am so happy to hear from you. I have been worried sick. Where are you? What happened? Who ..."

"Jason, stop. I am fine. I don't have a lot of time before my flight. I am flying to Reykjavik and will be there in about five hours. Can you meet me?"

"Yes, yes. What ..."

"Jason. I really have to get going. We can talk when I get there. I have to go now. Bye." She didn't wait for Jason to start rambling again.

She went to the ticket counter and purchased a seat on the next flight to Reykjavik. It would land at Keflavik airport, which is a short bus ride into the city.

She came back to Sven. "Well, I have my ticket." She showed it to him. "Thank you so much for all of your help." At that, she gave him a big hug, and a quick kiss on the cheek.

He was so surprised by the hug and kiss he could only stammer out, "Yes, okay, bye." He smiled and waved as she went to security then to her gate. As she disappeared, he turned with a smile and headed to the taxi.

Twenty-four

Planning the Hunt

Hugin knew he had to decide what to do. *Should I head to Iceland where I know Jason is or stay here to try to locate the other four? I think Matt is probably still here. Should I hope that he will lead me to the other three people?* He was no closer to identifying his American relations which told him that he was going to have to approach one of the five in order to find out. But, which one.

Well, he knew where Matt was located so that seemed the logical place to start. He was staying at the Comfort Hotel as well so he wandered the short distance to a café across from the Clarion and waited while reading the London Times.

After three hours he wondered if he should leave and wait at the hotel to see if he might get a hit somehow on Joana or Kevin. He had no idea how since he did not know what they looked like but it seemed better than sitting here and doing nothing.

Just as he was about to leave, Matt came out of his hotel and headed to the Comfort Hotel. Maybe he was going there to meet either Joana or Kevin. Hugin quickly paid and followed Matt.

Matt went into the attached restaurant and headed up the stairs to the second level where they served the free breakfast for the hotel guests. Breakfast was over and the area was now open for lunch. He sat near a railing that gave a good view down towards the entrance. Hugin went up there as well, and sat against the window that overlooked the plaza but still gave him a good view of Matt.

They both eventually ordered lunch. The meals were served, and Matt ate, and sat sipping a Heineken. They both ate slowly, and it seemed to Hugin that Matt was waiting for someone. Hugin wondered if it might be Joana. He had never seen her so he hoped this would give him the opportunity.

XXXXX

Joana had spent the past thirty-six hours searching for anything on the location of Jason or Nicole or Bergstrom. She found out that Jason was still in Iceland, thus Nicole will probably go there too. She found nothing on Bergstrom. She decided that her only option was to head to Iceland to try to find Jason and Nicole. It was now early afternoon, and she was hungry, so she decided to head to the restaurant.

Before heading to the restaurant, she booked a flight to Reykjavik departing at 10 am tomorrow morning. That would give her plenty of time today to decide where to stay, and to do one more set of searches for Nicole. She gave up on Bergstrom.

She entered the restaurant and sat in the back at the window above Strandgata street. She reviewed the menu.

Matt had watched her enter and sit in the back where he had no view. His food was half finished so he stuffed a few more bites into his mouth, and used the rest of the Heineken to wash it down. He dropped enough kroners on the table to cover the bill, and went downstairs.

He guessed she might know more about where Jason and Nicole were, and what they were doing than he did. He still wasn't sure exactly why she was here but he was willing to try this approach to find out.

He acted like he had just walked in and was surprised to see Joana as he walked towards her table. He approached her and said, "Wow, what a small world. Imagine my surprise when I saw you sitting in the same restaurant I was entering." He waited and smiled.

Joana had seen him coming but quickly pretended to be studying the menu. She decided to act like it was a surprise, and that she was wondering the same thing about seeing him. "Oh my goodness. Matt, right? I remember you from the dig site." And from the motel, and from his bed. But, she set those memories aside.

"May I sit with you?"

"Sure, please sit. I am so sorry to keep you standing. I guess I was just so surprised to look up and see you standing there. So, what brings you here to Oslo?"

"Well, sadly, I had to leave the dig because my brother went back on drugs again. As his older brother, I felt compelled to take care of him since our parents are gone now. Tragically, he died before I got to see him. So, I stayed, and helped with the funeral and burial. After all that, I was exhausted, and decided to take a vacation. Oslo came to mind, so here I am. How about you? What brings you to this lovely city?"

"First I am so sorry about your brother." She knew full well that he didn't have a brother, at least one that he cared about. "I guess I wanted a little vacation after the busy summer I had so, like you, I came here for a break. I had always heard how nice the people were and how beautiful the city is."

Hugin did the same as Matt, quickly paid, went downstairs, and pretended to have just arrived. He walked to an empty table a couple of tables away, sat, checked the menu, and picked up his newspaper. He hoped that he could overhear what they were discussing. The fact that Matt seemed to know the girl made Hugin believe that this must be Joana.

Matt and Joana exchanged small talk at first then moved on to what they had seen and planned to see in Oslo. Matt also started to wonder if he really wanted to involve Joana. He decided to wait and decide later. He started to talk about leaving to do some sightseeing.

Joana wondered. *Do I want his help or not? Maybe I do. Maybe he knows something that I don't.* "Hey, Matt." He sat back down, and looked at her while waiting for her to say something. "I'd like to talk to you about something. Do you have some time? Is there someplace quiet we can go?"

He looked at her for a few seconds then decided to see how this played out. "Sure. I think I saw a big park a short walk from here. The weather's nice so maybe we can find a quiet place there to chat."

"Great. Let's pay and head out."

After they passed Hugin, he waited a few moments then quickly dropped enough kroner on the table and followed. He stayed behind them and tried to blend into the crowd of tourists roaming the area. They crossed in front of the hotel then turned right onto Karl Johans Gate Street. Most of it was pedestrian only so the crowds thinned a little since there was more room for the window shoppers to move out of the way of the strollers.

They chatted and pointed along the street, and to Hugin, they appeared to be doing it to look like they fit in with the tourists – they were just a young couple out enjoying a little vacation to Oslo.

As they passed Rozenkrantz Gate St. they moved into the park and headed along one of the many footpaths. After about fifty meters they moved off of the footpath, and sat on one of the many benches around the small pond that is used as a skating rink in the winter.

Hugin chose one on the opposite side of the pond with a good view of Matt and Joana.

After they sat, Joana scanned the area, and once she was comfortable that they had some privacy, she turned to Matt. "I know where the map is."

Matt was stunned into silence. *How did she know about the map? Why does she have any interest in all in this?*

Joana could tell that he was confused so she continued. "I overheard McGuire, Jason, and Nicole talking about the copper sheet at lunch one day. McGuire said that it could be a map to some kind of treasure. The day after you left early, I saw Jason talking quietly to McGuire by one of the containers. At one point he took out an object wrapped in a cloth, and opened it enough to show McGuire what it was. Right before I looked away, I saw a flash of yellow, probably a reflection from the sun."

"He put it away quickly, and they both started scanning the area for anyone nearby. That's why I quickly looked away, and continued serving sandwiches."

"Then, over the next few days Nicole left, then not long after, Jason was gone." She paused and looked around again. "I grew up poor and have always lived hand-to-mouth. I never did anything bad but I always thought, 'Why can't I have stuff like others!' Anyway, I decided to follow them but lost Nicole. I'm pretty good with computers and learned simple hacking techniques from a friend, so I searched airline reservations, and found out that Jason went to Iceland, and Nicole came here to Oslo."

She waited but he didn't say anything. She sighed, "I propose that we join forces. Maybe the two of us can work better than each of us working alone."

Matt was thinking the whole time she was talking, that Jason must be the one that robbed him of the map. He also thought about what he wanted to do to the jerk. He figured that Nicole may have gotten the map from Jason and came to Bergstrom to get a translation. He was already planning to head to Iceland but maybe Joana and he would be better in this than only himself.

He also knew there was some other guy out there but he had no idea what he was up to. He finally decided that he would agree to join with Joana. She seemed pretty tough so maybe she could help.

"Okay, Joana. Let's join forces. They are in Iceland and I have already booked a flight there for tomorrow morning. Can you leave tomorrow?"

"Absolutely. Thanks Matt. I know we will succeed in this. What flight are you on? I'll get a seat on the same flight." He told her then they walked back to their respective hotels.

Hugin watched them go. He had thought about approaching Matt, not Joana, thinking that he was the one that might be an American relative. But now, he decided to wait and follow him.

He went back to his hotel room, searched, and found the flight Matt was on, and booked a seat on the same flight. He also searched on Joana, and found that she was now on the same flight as well. *Interesting indeed.* He wondered.

The 'watcher' contacted Kevin and told him that Nicole was on her way to Iceland, and passed on the flight details. She also told him that Matt and Joana were on their way as well.

Kevin thought *Well, this should be interesting with all four of them back together for the first time since the dig.*

Twenty-five

Iceland

Kevin sat at a table in the arrivals hall of Keflavik Airport drinking a small coffee. He watched the arrivals board, and noted that the plane carrying Matt and Joana had landed. After about thirty minutes he saw both of them exiting the baggage claim area together. They walked side-by-side and chatted as they moved outside to the taxi queue.

He was surprised to see Matt and Joana together at first. But, after thinking about the odd match up, he reasoned that it was probably a good idea. They both had similar agendas, and probably figured that together they would be more successful than separately trying to achieve their goal. He wondered who had approached whom.

He let them pass out into the sunlight and continued slowly sipping his coffee. His attention was now diverted to Jason, who had emerged from a shop nearby, and was now pacing back and forth just outside of the secure area. Kevin watched him look at his watch then up at the arrivals board then pace a few feet then look at his watch. He kept repeating these basic actions while he waited for Nicole to arrive, which would be in about twenty minutes. After deplaning, and passing through immigration and customs control, she would then have to wait for her bag, if she had any. It could be another hour before she walked through the doors into the hall.

He called the 'watcher' and asked her to let him know as soon as she gets the information on where the four of them are staying. He also asked her to book him into the same accommodations as Jason and Nicole. With Matt and Joana close by, he wanted to keep a close watch on them. The 'watcher' told him that Jason and Nicole were staying at the Centerhotel Plaza, and that their rooms were near to his room.

XXXXX

Hugin waited in the same area as Kevin but still had no idea what he looked like or what his involvement might be in this, which wasn't any better than his knowledge of the other four people. He had no idea if one or any of them were descendants of Ingvarr or Aki or even had an interest in the hunt for the treasure. He pulled out his laptop and started searching for any new information on the five people he felt might be involved in all of this.

He didn't find anything new on Jason and Nicole other than that they were staying at the Centerhotel Plaza. Matt and Joana didn't appear to have a reservation yet but Kevin was also at the Centerhotel Plaza. Hugin made a reservation there.

Hugin knew he had to do something soon. He had to approach one of these people to find out what was going on. They all seemed to be connected in some way since they had come from the same area of America to this place at around the same time. Jason and Nicole seemed to be working together and now Matt and Joana seemed to be as well. It could not be just a coincidence. Was Kevin a loner or was he also working with someone that hadn't appeared on the scene yet? He knew what the other four looked like but not Kevin.

He watched Jason pacing and glancing at the board.

XXXXX

Kevin looked up at the arrivals board and saw that Nicole's plane had landed, as did Jason because he now stopped pacing and focused like a laser beam on the door leading out of the baggage claim area. But, he still kept looking at his watch and the board.

Kevin tossed his unfinished coffee into the trash and went to stand against the wall on the opposite side of the hall from Jason. His eyes moved from Jason to the door.

XXXXX

Hugin noticed the movement of Kevin to the wall. He also noticed that the man's eyes were mostly on Jason but also on the arrivals door. Hugin wondered. *Could he be Kevin? If not, then why was he so interested in Jason, and apparently, Nicole?*

Hugin decided that this 'possible' Kevin needed more attention, and he planned to give it to him.

Suddenly, the door to baggage claim opened and a group of passengers exited. The flow continued for several minutes then Nicole appeared.

Hugin knew that Jason would move to her right away but he wasn't watching Jason. He wanted to see what 'possible' Kevin did.

As he watched him, the man stopped leaning against the wall, stood, and watched both Jason and Nicole as they moved to each other, hugged then kissed. The man also kept quickly scanning the other people as though he was searching for something or someone.

Hugin figured that this had to be the elusive Kevin. There was no other explanation for this behavior other than that he knew the two people but they did not seem to know him. He had come from the same location as they did so this wasn't likely to be a coincidence. But, what exactly was his role in this? He was behaving more like he was worried about them. But what could he be worried about. The only threat that Hugin knew about was that someone descended from Megedagik could be involved in this. As a matter of fact, as Hugin watched and waited for him to approach the couple, he never did. In fact he seemed to try to recede into the crowd of people but not so much that he could not keep an eye on them. To top it off, when Jason and Nicole exited the hall, he followed but kept well behind.

Hugin needed to think about this development. He was glad that he decided to stay in the same hotel as Kevin and Jason and Nicole. He would now have the opportunity to watch all of them even more.

XXXXX

Jason and Nicole stood in the taxi queue. "I'm so happy you are finally here. I was so worried about you, especially when I lost access to you yesterday."

"I'm sorry about that, Jason. I'll tell you all about my time in Oslo when we are rested and alone. Have you seen Matt or Joana?"

"No, but I haven't exactly been looking for them around Reykjavik. Do you know when they may have arrived?" Jason answered.

"I don't know anything about Matt because the last time I saw him was at the dig site. He might still be there for all I know. But, I have seen Joana and she is likely here now. I will tell you more about that later."

"By the way, we are both staying at the Centerhotel, which is located pretty much in the center of Reykjavik. We have two rooms next to each other. It is a nice hotel and I like the location. There are plenty of places to eat so maybe once we get settled, we can wander over to one of them. I happen to like the Hard Rock Café which is only a few blocks away. We can get a booth, and talk about the translation and Oslo."

"Sounds great. But, don't keep me out too late. I am very tired and need to get my beauty rest."

Jason shook his head and said, "No, no. As always, I will be the perfect gentleman." At that, he leaned over and gave her a nice big kiss, and Nicole didn't mind at all.

Jason and Nicole arrived at the Centerhotel Plaza and checked in. They took the elevator to their floor and walked down the hall to their rooms.

"Let's meet downstairs at around 5:00 pm. Does that sound good?"

Nicole yawned and said, "That is perfect. I really need to rest."

Jason kissed her and they both went into their rooms.

XXXXX

Matt and Joana had two rooms at the Hotel Hilda located about a half a kilometer from the city center. The taxi let them off, checked in, and agreed to rest for a few hours then meet later in the afternoon for dinner and to discuss a plan.

XXXXX

Kevin watched Jason and Nicole head up to their rooms before moving from the bar to the reception desk to check into his room. He went to his room and checked with the 'watcher'. She had nothing new to report so he lay on the bed with his eyes open staring at the ceiling and wondered what he was going to do about Matt and Joana.

All along he had hoped that they would just go away but that was obviously not going to happen now. He didn't want to hurt either of them but he would not fail in protecting Jason and Nicole no matter what the cost.

XXXXX

Hugin watched Kevin check in while he read a magazine seated in one of the lobby's chairs. He really wasn't reading it, not because he was busy watching Kevin, but because it was in Norwegian.

Once Kevin went to his room, Hugin left for his room. When he entered it, he tossed his bag on the bed then sat and opened his laptop. He wanted to try to do some searches to see if he could get a better identity on the people he was tracking. After half an hour, he still hadn't made any progress so he set the laptop aside.

He began to realize that his best gambit in this was to make contact with Kevin. He seemed to be the least likely threat to Jason and

Nicole, and actually seemed to really be concerned about the young couple. Hugin had finally decided that most of the danger was coming from Matt and Joana.

And, if all of that is true, then he really had to talk to Kevin and explain his own role in all of this. There was certainly risk involved by revealing himself to Kevin especially if Kevin wasn't someone Hugin could trust. But, he felt it was a risk he had to take.

Now he had to figure out the best way to make contact with him.

Twenty-six

Team Building

Jason and Nicole made their way down to the lobby and out to the small park across the street. There were kids playing with a soccer ball, and a few tourists pointing and shooting selfies with their cameras. They dodged the picture takers as best as they could then made their way onto Austurstraeti street. As they walked along, Jason reached over and took hold of Nicole's hand.

They passed bars and restaurants and shops. At Laekjargata Street they turned right and entered the Hard Rock Café. The inside was fairly typical of most of the Hard Rock restaurants. There were various guitars, albums, and framed clothing items hanging on the walls, most of them signed by the musician or group who donated them. There was a large rectangular bar just as you entered with stools all around it and small stand up tables lining the walls behind the bar.

They moved to the bar and the bartender introduced himself as, Gunnar. "What can I get for you two?"

"What lager beer would you recommend?" Jason asked.

"I would suggest the Egils Premium Lager. It is brewed by Egill Skallagrímsson Brewery, an Icelandic brewer. Would you like a sample?"

Jason looked at Nicole and she shrugged. Jason turned back to Gunnar and said, "Sure."

Gunnar brought them two small glasses of the Egils. They tried it and Jason looked at Nicole. She nodded. So Jason said, "We'll take two glasses, please." When he brought them their glasses, Jason paid, and they moved to one of the low tables near the back, away from the speakers.

They toasted each other with the beer. Before they had a chance to start talking, a waitress came over. "Hello. I am Christina. I see that you have a beer so would you like a food menu?"

Nicole said, "Sure. Thanks."

Christina went a few steps away and pulled two menus from a tray on a small serving table. She handed one to each of them and said, "I'll come back after a little bit to take your orders."

They thanked her then quickly scanned the menu to pick something so that they'd be ready when she returned. Jason looked at Nicole when she finished making her choice and asked, "So, what happened in Oslo?"

Nicole smiled, sighed, and started. "Well. It was pretty weird." She then related her adventure, her visit with Ingvill at her home, the trip to the university, the disguise, the van, the escape, the boat ride, the return to Stavanger, and the plane ride. Half way through the tale, Christina came back and they ordered the same thing – cheeseburger and fries. When their food arrived, even though they were both starving, they took their time and talked in between bites.

Nicole eventually finished her tale, and Jason shook his head and rolled his eyes. "Wow. What an adventure. We are really going to have to keep an eye out for Joana."

After several minutes and a few more bites of her burger, Nicole asked, "Did you get to compare our DNA results?"

"I did, and on the surface we seem to have come from two different areas of the world. But, as you know, that just means whoever our ancestors are, they eventually migrated to America." Nicole nodded and ate a fry. He took a bite of his burger and a sip of beer. "Next, I decided to look at our second analysis which looked for common ancestry. Did you have a chance to review it?"

"No. Things started happening with this stuff, plus I had to contact the school to tell them I was skipping a semester, plus talk to my mom, and well, it just got too busy to look at it. What did you find?"

"It seems to me that we might have at least one common ancestor." Jason smiled when she looked at him quickly and almost chocked on the swig of beer she had just taken.

"I'm not sure of this, so we'll need an expert to clarify what I am seeing. Anyway, as I said, it is only a hunch. But even if we do, it is so far back that it doesn't make any difference now. I mean it's not like we are siblings or cousins or anything that close."

"I suppose you are right. I took an introductory class on DNA a couple of years ago, and only touched on this kind of stuff briefly. But, yes, from what I remember, when you go back past three or four generations, there is no real issue with any relationships in the present." Suddenly, she blushed and looked at her plate.

"Are you okay? Are you feeling okay?" Jason started to get up.

"I am fine. I'm okay. Please sit." She took a drink of beer. Once she swallowed, she continued. "It just struck me that talking about not affecting a relationship in the present seemed to imply that, well, that, you and I were going to be a, you know, couple." She smiled at Jason.

He stared at her for a few seconds. "Oh, yea. I see." He looked at Nicole and asked, "I wouldn't mind that. Would you?"

Nicole acted like she was giving the idea serious thought but she abruptly smiled and said, "Hell no. I would definitely not mind."

They smiled at each other then looked away and continued eating.

XXXXX

Hugin was sitting in the lobby when Kevin came down from his room. Kevin couldn't really call either Jason or Nicole and ask where they are since they knew nothing of his existence and purpose. However, he could make some pretty good guesses after tracking them for so long. Plus, he could always contact the 'watcher'.

At that, he pulled out his phone and called her, but she had no new information for him.

He glanced around the lobby then figured he would head to the Hilda to watch Matt and Joana to make sure they stayed away from them.

He was about to exit when Hugin came up to him. "Excuse me sir, but may I have a moment of your time?"

Kevin smiled and said, "Not right now. I really need to be going. I am supposed to meet a friend in a few minutes." He turned to head for the door.

Hugin softly said. "Is your meeting with Jason and Nicole?"

Kevin turned into Hugin and stared at him. "What are you talking about?"

Hugin was now convinced that Kevin was someone who was very concerned about their safety and, if appearances could be trusted, he was very effective at it. "Please, please. I am no danger to either of them, you may rest assured of that. I would really like to talk with you because I too am concerned for their safety."

Kevin continued to stare at Hugin even after he had finished. He motioned Hugin to the bar, and they sat at a table well away from the bartender. Before they could begin, she came over and asked what they might like. Kevin ordered a Doppelbock and Hugin ordered the same.

They sat eyeing each other until she came back with the beers. After she moved back to the bar, Hugin started. "Mr. Rivers, and before you become more concerned, yes, I searched my database to learn who the five of you were. The other four being, as you know, Jason, Nicole, Matt and Joana."

"However, please let me begin at the beginning. You see, I am descended from Ingvarr's grandfather, Aki.

XXXXX

Joana waited in the lobby of the hotel for Matt. It was almost 6:00 pm and they had agreed to meet at 5:00. Joana thought, *Maybe this was a mistake teaming with Matt. He really doesn't know anything that I don't already know. Besides he is such an asshole.*

Just then Matt walked out of the elevator toward her. He hadn't slept long, mainly because he wasn't that tired, but also because he had a nagging thought that Joana was somehow familiar. Unfortunately, he hadn't been able to bring up a clear memory of her from someplace in his past.

Joana stood and pasted a false smile on her face. He didn't even try to smile back. He walked to her and stood. She asked, "What?"

"Where have we met before? I know that I somehow know you. Tell me why that is!"

"I have no idea what you are talking about. You know me from the dig. Come on, let's eat and figure out how we are going to find Nicole and get the map."

"No. I want to be able to trust someone I am working with and I do not trust you. You and I have met and you know it, so you better tell me right now!" He was getting a little loud and several people in the lobby looked over at them. Hopefully, they thought that it was some kind of lovers' quarrel.

"Matt, keep your voice down. Let's go outside and talk about whatever this is." Joana headed for the door without waiting for a response. As she walked to the door, she decided that she couldn't work with this idiot. He hadn't been any real help so far, and she didn't see that status changing anytime soon.

Matt stood for a bit then followed her outside. When he stepped onto the sidewalk he didn't see Joana at first then saw her leaning against the wall of the hotel. She was wedged into a small corner of the hotel where the drain pipe descended from the roof gutter to the street. Her arms were folded across her chest, and she was glaring at him.

He stepped up to her. "You had better tell me the truth or we are through. As a matter of fact, if you continue to pursue your search for Nicole and Jason, I will stop you, and I will hurt you bad."

Joana sighed. "Okay. Follow me to a less visible area, and I will tell you." At that she moved off toward the harbor. While Matt was still in his room, she had come to the lobby and asked for a map of Reykjavik. She had originally thought that they could use it to navigate around the city in search of Nicole and Jason. Now, she would make use of it for a different purpose.

She had noticed that the harbor was only about five blocks from the hotel. It also appeared to be a working harbor and not a residential one. At this time of day, work would be stopped or at least at a minimum. But, even more importantly, it looked like one area was not yet developed. She headed in its direction.

Matt hadn't followed at first but then decided he wanted to hear what she had to say. Even though he couldn't remember exactly how he knew her, simply the thought of their lives crossing sometime in the past, and him not remembering it, bothered him. He stayed a step behind as she lead the way.

After a few blocks she turned left, went another hundred meters, then turned right onto a small roadway that passed between two almost empty parking areas. After another hundred meters she turned off the roadway and into a grassy area with several abandoned buildings around it. She stopped and turned to face him.

"Now, what is it you are accusing me of, Matt?"

He stopped a few feet from her and looked around. They were completely alone, and about ten meters from the harbor. "I am just saying that I know that we have met before and you know it too. I want you to tell me how we met, and don't lie because I'll know it."

Joana smiled at him. He is such an idiot. She really wanted to tell him about how many times she had hated being with him when they were having sex. She wanted to tell him how she got him drunk and toyed with his sexual desires in order to get him to talk about his quest for the treasure. She also wanted to tell him how she beat the crap out of him and stole the copper sheet.

So, she did. As she related the hatred of the sex with him, she saw his face get redder and redder. She noticed his hands clenching and unclenching. Then she told him how she got him drunk and played with him in order to get him to talk about the treasure.

"And, then I followed you to the dig site to see if any clues turned up there. You didn't even recognize me. How do you even get dressed in the morning? How do you remember which foot your shoes go on?" She was spitting the insults at him, and he backed away a little with each one.

"And, you little prick, I stole the copper sheet from you. I beat you up and I wish I had just killed you but, I didn't, and now I have to deal with you again. If you ever touch me again, I promise, I will kill you." At that, she turned and started to walk away.

He was stunned at first and just stood still. But, his fury took over as he thought about her laughing at him, and playing him for a fool, and stealing the copper sheet. He charged after her, grabbed her by the shoulders, turned her around, and slammed her against the building. As he raised his fist and looked at her face, he hesitated ever so slightly, because she was smiling.

The next series of actions happened so fast he had no time to react. Joana jammed her knee into his crotch which caused him to let go of her shoulders. Now that her arms were free, she grabbed him by the hair with her left hand and punched him twice in the throat. As he continued his fall to the ground, she rammed her knee into his face then dropped her elbow along with her entire weight onto the back of his neck.

As he lay face down on the ground, she stomped several times on the back of his neck then kicked him in the side of his face. Her anger was so elevated she continued to kick him in the face and his side. Each kick was a count of the many times her father had raped her, and for each of the men he had sold her to so they could do the same thing.

Panting hard and bent over now, she finally stopped. After several minutes, she caught her breath, and gained control over her rage. She straightened and looked down at the mess that was Matt Williams. She felt nothing, and it seemed that her anger was temporarily sated.

She turned and walked away. She didn't care if he was alive or dead. She would finish this hunt on her own, alone, just like she had been her whole life.

Twenty-seven

Watching

Jason knocked softly on Nicole's door. After a few moments it opened and Nicole smiled him into her room.

The first thing Jason noticed was the sweet smell of her fresh shower and what appeared to be the scent of lavender on her. Her hair was pulled back into a ponytail, and she wore a long sleeve cotton sweater with a pair of jeans. Her feet were bare, and he noticed the pick toenails.

"Hey, Jason. You are punctual as always. I cleared some space at the small table and moved it closer to the bed. I'll sit on the edge of the bed and you can sit on the chair. I also remembered to bring a small world Atlas. It probably doesn't have enough detail but it will give us something to start with. We can always buy a better map at one of the shops along Austurstraeti."

Jason nodded. "Okay. Let's have a look."

Nicole leaned back and grabbed a small folder that could also hold a small laptop. She unzipped it and removed a large clasp envelope. She opened the clasp and carefully reached into the envelope and gently removed a folded sheet of paper. A she unfolded the paper, she began. "Ingvill wrote out an exact translation of both sides of the copper sheet. She then rewrote the translation into English and combined the two sides into its proper order. She also included the copper sheet if we think we might want a second opinion."

"Now, all of that would have been wonderful, but she also added a map. She did the best that she could to try to mark the directions in the translation onto the map. The map isn't to scale and shows only the route with the current names of the places in the translation that she could find on a modern map. She apologized for not doing a better job, but she had to move quickly because she knew Joana would be coming soon."

Jason peered at what she had. "Okay, let's take a look."

As she opened the map then laid the translation next to it, Jason found that he was looking at it upside down. He looked up at Nicole just as she had realized the problem. She scooted a little to the side and said, "Come over and sit next to me on the bed." She patted the spot she had just vacated.

He moved to the other side of the table and sat next to Nicole. Since it wasn't a huge map, they had to sit right next to each other in order for both of them to get a good view of it.

Nicole pointed at the English translation. "Ingvill told me that she did the best she could but some of the locations listed on the copper sheet no longer exist today. She tried to compare some of the oldest maps she had with a current map in order to find a location that might be comparable to the original location. She explained that in some cases she could only say with twenty-five percent probability that she was correct."

"The locations that she was at least ninety percent sure of are underlined. Those are Mosfellsbaer and Lake Hvalvatn which are basically the starting point and the half-way point. She is only about fifty percent sure of Skjaldbreizzur Mountain. But, if that is in fact the last point, then she is sure that the directions to get to the cave are correct."

"The main problem with the directions to the cave is that over the past 1000 years erosion and earthquake activity could have made some changes to the terrain on the side of the mountain." Nicole paused and watched Jason look intently at the map. "So, what do you think?"

Jason didn't hesitate. "This is wonderful. I wish she were still here so that I could thank her personally. But, I understand why she had to get away and hide for a while. Anyway, I bought a pretty good map of Iceland one afternoon while I was waiting for your call." At that, he pulled it out of his back pocket. "If we assume that the start point and the lake are correct then we can drive up to Skjaldbreioarhraun and start our search there. It is located just past the lake on the way to the mountain."

"It's about 100 kilometers so it shouldn't take us more than two or three hours to get there. If we feel the need, we can go backwards toward the lake in order to assure ourselves that we are on the right track before proceeding to the mountain. Or, we could just head straight for the mountain and take our chances that it is the right end point. It is probably at least a three to four hour hike to get to the south base of the mountain by the look of the map here. By the time we get there we will not have much daylight left, so I think we should plan to spend the night there. If we do stay the night, then we will need a tent, sleeping bags, flashlight and other camping gear, as well as food and water. How does all of that sound?"

"It sounds good to me. Let's go shopping!" Nicole grabbed Jason's hand.

XXXXX

Kevin believed him. He hadn't known about Ingvarr's extended family in England but he did know some of the story regarding how he left his homeland and family, traveled to America, fought a battle with the tribe and was the only survivor. All of that was tribal legend. The stuff about a battle and three ships and a treasure in Iceland was all new to him. Hugin seemed sincere so, well, he decided to believe him.

"Okay, Hugin, so what is the reason you are continuing to try to make the connection with your American family?"

"When my grandfather told me the family history, I was fascinated by it. I was also saddened that our connection with that line of the family had been broken. It certainly isn't about the treasure, if it still exists. My family has become quite wealthy and we have no need for additional money. But, as I said, I do feel that the families should become acquainted again."

Hugin paused and before Kevin could interrupt, he continued, "And, it would be fascinating to learn what artifacts might be included in this so called treasure pile. Who knows, maybe there will be items that can give us links to some past generations. Those would be exciting finds. But, I am worried about the other people in our assembly. I am not at all sure that Joana and Matt have good intentions in this."

"Well, you are right to be concerned. Joana is descended from a line of family that goes back to when Ingvarr first arrived in America." At this, Kevin told Hugin about the Megadagik family vow of revenge and about Kevin's family vow to protect all in Ingvarr's family.

"Yes, I see now why you are so concerned for Jason and Nicole's safety. I understand Joana's interest in this but who is Matt and why is he a part of all this?"

"I truly do not have a clue as to who Matt is and why he is here and, to be truthful, at this point, I don't care. My only concern is that he seems to be interested in Jason and Nicole which makes him of interest to me. But, now, I must push all of this family history aside and focus on helping Jason and Nicole, which means I need to get moving."

Hugin smiled. "Yes, the American need to get to the point and to take action. I am enjoying this quest very much. What do we do next?"

"Ah, Hugin, you should not be involved in this. Both Joana and Matt are dangerous and determined people, which is a very bad combination. It usually means that they will do anything to achieve their goal, and that could mean extreme physical harm. I think you should wait here until this is over."

"Please let me help. We are talking about my family too you know. As a matter of fact, Kevin, we are all family and descended from the line of Ragnvadr, the king of our tribe in Norway over 1000 years ago. I deserve to be a part of this as much as you do."

Kevin sighed. He knew Hugin was right. They were family and he deserved to be there as much as Kevin did. "Okay, but please let me take the lead in this. I have lots of experience in the realm of protection."

"Of course, of course. I will defer to you in this matter but I would like to be of help in any way possible."

"Okay, good. One thing that you will be helpful with is watching or following Matt. He has seen me but not you so he won't be suspicious of you. But, for now, let's go see what Jason and Nicole are up to."

XXXXX

Joana walked the short distance back to her hotel. She changed and showered then packed her bag and checked out. If she needed to stay in Reykjavik longer she would use another hotel. Right now she wanted to see what Jason and Nicole were doing.

Twenty-eight

Preparations

Jason and Nicole finalized their plans for the next day's journey to the mountain. As Jason left for his room, he asked Nicole, "What time should we meet to head out?"

"I'll be ready in about forty minutes."

"Okay, I'll make a reservation for a rental car for, what do you think, four days?"

Nicole thought a moment. "How about a week since we really don't know what it is going to take to get to that cave. Besides, most companies give you a break if you rent for an entire week."

"Good idea. See you in a half hour."

Once Jason was in his room, he changed quickly then called the front desk to have a car brought around tomorrow morning at 6 am. When that call was finished, he called his grandfather.

"Hello. This is Mrs. McGuire." Jason was using a burner phone so she had no idea who was calling.

"Hey grandma. This is Jason. Is grandpa okay?" There was desperation in his voice to hear a 'Yes' response from her.

"Oh yes. He is fine. He's just resting since he worked late last night on the dig report. How are you and Nicole doing?"

"We're fine. We are going to do a bit of exploring tomorrow."

"Well, you two be careful. That Megadagik bunch are mean bastards. And, yes, James told me the family history right after Erik told him."

Jason was taken aback by the fact that she knew the history and that she used a word he had never heard her say in his life. "Yes, we will be careful. We think we have identified two possible people who might be a descendant of his. One is the food truck girl, Joana and the other is one of the volunteers, Matt. Grandpa knows both so if one or both shows up any time in the future, he should stay clear of them."

"I'll tell him."

"Oh. Grandma. Before I forget, would you please move $5000 from my savings account to my checking account?"

"Sure, honey. Again, please be careful and take care of Nicole."

"I will. Okay, I must meet Nicole in a few minutes, so I need to get going. I'll call again in a few days or so. Bye. I love you."

"Bye, honey. I love you too."

Jason put the phone in his backpack and headed to Nicole's room.

They went to the front desk and Jason asked, "Can you please recommend a good camping equipment store for us?"

"Yes. The Iceland Camping Equipment Rental shop gets wonderful reviews. I have used it myself and would not go anywhere else. They have everything you need and the staff is very helpful."

"Is the equipment in good condition?"

"Absolutely. The person who helped me reviewed the equipment with me to make sure it was in good condition before I walked out of the store. And, you rent it, which is great if you are a visitor here and just need the equipment for your visit, and the prices are very reasonable."

"Great. How do we get there?"

"Here, I'll show you on the map. It is located here on Hverfisgata and it is about two kilometers from here." At that, he traced his finger on the map from the hotel to the store.

"Thanks." He and Nicole walked out the door and made their way to Iceland Camping Rentals.

XXXXX

Kevin was watching Jason and Nicole stroll down to the lobby and move to the front desk. After several minutes of discussion and map pointing, they turned and headed out the door. Kevin followed.

At the same time, Hugin watched the front of entrance of Joana and Matt's hotel. He saw Joana enter but there was no sign of Matt. Hugin figured he had stayed in his room. An hour later, Joana came out with her bag and headed in the direction of Jason and Nicole's hotel. He followed her there.

Kevin, Jason and Nicole had already left by the time Joana and Hugin reached the entrance. Joana entered and Hugin followed. He saw her go to the front desk. After several minutes of discussion and pointing at a map, Joana quickly moved out of the hotel. It was all he could do to keep up with her. She moved down Austerstaeti then cut over to Hverfisgata.

About five minutes later, Hugin looked past Joana and he could see the back of Kevin's head up ahead. His mind went crazy. *Was she after Kevin? No, he said that Matt knew him but not Joana. Or, was it the other way around? I should call Kevin. No, Kevin said no phone calls because that might alert the person being followed. What should I do? I'll distract her.*

He walked quickly and came up next to Joana. "Excuse me. Can you show me where the Maritime Museum is located? I fear that I am lost", he asked politely.

Joana slowed a little but did not look at him. "No."

"But miss, I could really use your help." He reached for her arm.

It happened so fast. She had a tight grip on his arm, and he was hustled out of the crowd then into an alley. Joana flattened him face first into the wall then did a quick look around. She saw no one. Her anger came quickly back again. She hit him twice in the right kidney, and as he doubled over she hit him in the back of the head. He went down in a heap and stayed still.

Joana stood and stared at him. *Why did I do that? What is wrong with me? Every little thing is getting me angrier and angrier.* She shook it off, exited the alley, and walked quickly to catch up with Jason and Nicole. She saw them in the distance just as they entered the store.

Kevin sat in Emilie's coffee shop across from the equipment store sipping a cup of delicious coffee. Joana suddenly appeared and he became instantly alert. As he watched her, she continued past the store and out of his view.

At that moment his phone quietly buzzed him. He figured it was the 'watcher' with an update on someone and he answered it without looking at the screen. "Go ahead."

"It's me." Said Hugin.

"What? Why are you calling? What's wrong?"

"Joana," he had to pause while his head cleared. "Joana suddenly attacked me."

"Are you okay? Why'd she do it? Never mind, where are you?"

"I'm sitting in an alley off of Hverfisgate. I'll be okay. Stay with Jason and Nicole because I think Joana has gone off her senses. I don't think she even knows why she attacked me. She didn't even ask who I was or what I was doing there."

"Are you sure you are okay? I am actually on Hverfisgata at a coffee shop across from a camping rental store where Jason and Nicole are. I could easily come to you."

"Yes. I am okay. Stay on Jason and Nicole. I'll clear my head and come to you." He ended the call.

Kevin was actually getting scared. Not for himself but for the two he had vowed to protect. He did not want this to be the third failure for them in the past century. He shook his head. *It is not going to happen. I need to get focused on Jason and Nicole. Stay sharp.*

Hugin stood on shaky legs and leaned on the wall until they settled. He finally stood away from the wall and took a few steps. He walked slowly out to the street, and headed to Kevin. It had only been a few minutes since the call so Hugin hoped he was still there.

Joana went about twenty meters past the store and entered the Skuggi Hotel where there was a bar and restaurant with large windows that looked out onto the street. She bought a cup of tea and sat at a table where she could look back at the front of the store.

A she took the first sip of her tea and set the cup down, her heart started racing. *I need to get a grip on myself. I can't keep beating people up. Matt deserved it but that other guy didn't. He was just asking for directions. I shouldn't do stuff like that because sooner or later it is going to attract unwanted attention to me.*

She started breathing deeply and willing herself to get calm. It seemed to work. Her heart rate slowed, and her mind relaxed.

XXXXX

Jason and Nicole spent over an hour wandering through the store looking at the different items to rent and discussing whether or not they really needed it. After all, the more they took with them, the heavier their packs would be and the slower they would be able to travel.

In addition, if the treasure existed, then what? Would they try to get it out at that time or come back to Reykjavik to seek help? They decided first things first – find it, then decide what to do.

Once they decided on what they needed, they sought out an employee to help them with the rental procedure. They found a young woman straightening some tent rentals and asked for her help. She smiled and asked them what they needed.

They moved with her to show her what they wanted. As they moved through the store, they pointed to each item. She occasionally said okay or muttered a few uh huh's. When they finished, she asked, "Now, tell me what it is you plan to do."

They told her about driving to the lake and hiking to the mountain but nothing about the treasure. She asked if they planned to hike up the mountain. They said yes but not to the peak. She asked them about their hiking experience and what they felt was their fitness level.

She nodded at all of their responses then proceeded to walk them around the store and tell them what they actually needed to take. About half of what they thought they needed was not on the young woman's list and what she substituted was lighter and less costly than what they had thought they should have.

When they finished wandering the store, the girl stopped and asked, "What do you think?"

Jason looked at Nicole and they both said in unison, "We'll take what you said to take."

"Good let's gather it up and do the paperwork." When that was finished, she said, "I will put it in a locker for you and you can come by when you are ready to go. Here is your key and you do not need to ask for any assistance unless, of course, you require it."

As they walked out, Nicole turned to Jason, "Now that is customer service. I love it." Jason nodded and smiled.

Twenty-nine

A Long Trek

Kevin watched Jason and Nicole leave the store and head back in the direction of the hotel. He finished his tea and headed out to the street just as Joana walked by, obviously following the couple. He shook his head, took a deep breath and followed.

Hugin watched Jason and Nicole go by him on the opposite side of the street. A short distance behind them was Joana. Hugin turned quickly and stared into a shop window. He prayed that Joana had not seen him. He really did not want to get another beating from that woman.

When he was sure that she was well ahead, Hugin turned and crossed the street to follow. He suddenly felt a hand on his shoulder and begin to turn him around. He thought. *Please don't let it be Joana.* He closed his eyes.

"What are you doing? Hugin, open your damn eyes."

Hugin opened them and saw Kevin. He did a most un-British thing. He hugged Kevin. "Thank goodness it is you. I was afraid that it was Joana again."

Kevin smiled. "Well, we may yet have another encounter with her since she is following Jason and Nicole again."

"Yes. I saw her go by right after Jason and Nicole went past."

"Anyway, we can't worry about what she will or will not do. Since the two of them were in a camping store, we must assume that they are going camping or, at the very least, hiking. Thus, I need to get some gear as well."

"As do I."

"No, Hugin, you do not. We have no idea where they may be going and how long of a trek it might be. I can't have you along slowing me or, worse, getting injured."

"No. No, I must go. I am as concerned about them as you are. I have a right …"

"NO!" Kevin paused and took a breath. "Hugin, I know you care about them, but I really can't have you along on this effort. I would rather you stay here and heal, number one, and, two, do your computer magic and try to find out more about Matt and what his interest might be. He is still out there somewhere and we do not know where or what he might be up to."

Hugin saw the logic in this and knew Kevin was right. He finally sighed and said, "You are right. I would not be a very good companion out in a wilderness area. But, I do know how to make magic on the computer with my fingers." He held up his hands and wiggled his fingers for Kevin.

Kevin smiled and nodded. "Good. We'll follow Joana and Jason and Nicole. Once I see that they are safely in their rooms or some public place then I will leave you to watch Joana and make sure she doesn't try anything with them. I will come back here and rent some gear then meet you back at the hotel."

XXXXX

Matt opened his eyes but quickly closed them. After a few moments, he slowly opened them again. Nothing had changed. He still saw only blackness. As he stared into the distance, his eyes slowly began to come to life and he began to make out small lights very far away. Next, his mind came to life. They were not lights, they were stars. He was staring up into the night sky. But why and where was he.

He suddenly remembered and started to rise. But, he just as quickly lay back down. *Oh, that hurt. It hurt a lot.* He took a breath and closed his eyes again. He needed to remember what had happened.

He took inventory. *My head really hurts, my side hurts, my … oh hell. I hurt all over.* Then he remembered why he hurt all over. It was that bitch Joana. He now remembered her in his bed and his room as he must have blabbed about his plan to get rich. She must have followed him to the dig site. Then he remembered that she had told him that she had beaten him up and stolen the copper sheet. Okay, he was now going to kill her and the guy who beat him and left him in the woods.

But, first things first. He had to get up. He turned onto his stomach and pushed himself up into a four-point position. Next, on his hands and knees he walked to a wall a short distance away, and plopped over onto his butt and leaned his back against the wall. *Oh, that really hurt.*

He painfully pulled out his phone and glanced at the time. It was almost midnight. He had been there for hours. *Wow, this really is a deserted area. Now what do I do?*

XXXXX

Hugin was getting tired.

After Kevin had returned with his outdoor gear, they both went to their rooms then met a short time later to go to dinner. Kevin had asked if he had found anything on Matt yet and he told him that he had not.

Kevin asked him to keep trying then asked if he could search on Joana to see what she might be up to. He had smiled at Kevin as though he were a three year old child who had just asked if his father could drive a car like his friend Billy's dad.

Kevin got the hint and simply asked what he had found. Unfortunately, all he had found was that she had checked out of her hotel but that Matt had not. Kevin had mumbled something then proceeded to finish his dinner.

After dinner, Kevin suggested that Hugin go to his room to search some more while he watched for Joana. Hugin searched all evening and found nothing on Joana. Who knows, maybe she left, but that was extremely unlikely.

Hugin finally closed his laptop, turned out the lights and fought to get to sleep.

XXXXX

Joana paced across the small room for the thousandth time, or maybe it was double that, she had no idea.

After following Jason and Nicole to their hotel she had wandered around the area until she found a small cheap room located above a bar. Her room was spartan – no phone, no TV, no chair. All she had was a lumpy twin bed and a small table. She also had to share the bathroom with both male and female renters. But, it was cheap, it was near their hotel, and it was only going to be for one night.

She reasoned that Jason and Nicole were in that camping gear rental place because they were going out to a remote area. And, she reasoned, they were leaving tomorrow. She had found a small military surplus store down a back street, and bought a pair of boots, a heavy jacket, and a knife for gutting big game.

She knew she had to get some sleep but she was agitated. She still couldn't shake the feelings that had overwhelmed her when she beat Matt and hurt that poor man in the alley. She felt such hate in both cases. She could understand feeling that way toward Matt. He was easy to hate, but not the man on the street.

Well, tomorrow she would get up early, watch their hotel, and follow them as soon as they left.

Thirty

On the Move

Hugin and Kevin sat in the hotel restaurant, each with a cup of coffee. They had eaten a light breakfast of jam and toast. While waiting to see when Jason and Nicole might leave, Hugin glanced out to the street. He turned quickly back and Kevin asked, "What's wrong?"

"Joana is across the street watching the hotel. I don't want her to see me."

"Go up to your room. I can watch for Jason and Nicole and keep Joana away from them. You can start searching for Matt. I am really worried about what he was been doing the past two days."

Hugin reluctantly nodded and headed out of the restaurant. He kept to the side of the room and walked with his head away from the exit and the windows. He reached the elevator just as it arrived. When the door opened, Jason and Nicole stepped out with their bags and moved to the reception desk.

Hugin quickly entered the elevator and pressed the button for his floor.

Kevin watched them at the reception desk. They were obviously checking out but they were also discussing something else. The receptionist waved the concierge over and he nodded, went to his desk, went back to Jason, and handed him a set of keys and a folder.

Kevin felt foolish. They had rented a car. This really complicated the situation. He had to think quickly. He needed a car or motorbike in order to follow them.

He waited until they walked out the door and, once they were out and driving away in the car, he walked to the concierge. "Excuse me. Where might I rent a motorbike near here?"

The concierge told him that there was a rental office two blocks away and pointed in the direction to go. Kevin walked out the door and saw that Joana was gone. He ran the two blocks, went in the store, chose a bike, and impatiently waited for the paperwork to be completed and the keys handed over.

He thanked them, hopped onto his Honda Rockstar Dirt Bike and took off for the hotel. He figured that Jason and Nicole needed to go to the camping gear place to get their stuff so he hoped that he had time to catch them. But, he needed to get his stuff from his room then call Hugin.

XXXXX

Joana was shocked when she saw them climb into the rental car. Shocked at herself for not realizing they would probably do that and to prepare for it. Well, it was too late now to chastise herself, she had to move. She quickly moved down the street searching for a rental place. She finally saw a guy pull in front of a building about 200 meters away then head inside.

She moved quickly toward the building. When she reached it, she turned to the door the guy had entered. It looked like an apartment building so she entered. There were three doors around the small lobby with a set of stairs heading up. She also saw a small storage closet along the side of the stairway. She moved to it and waited.

About five minutes later the guy came bounding down the stairs. As he reached the bottom, Joana bent over and started to moan loud enough for him to hear. He stopped and turned toward the storage closet where he saw Joana bent over. He took his helmet off, stepped up to her and spoke. She assumed he was asking if she was okay.

She quickly punched upward and caught him under his chin as he bent toward her with his hand outstretched. She followed that with another punch to the side of his head. He went down. She reared back her foot, and was about to deliver a crushing kick to his head when she stopped. She was panting and staring at the guy with hatred.

She quickly opened the storage closet door and dragged the guy in. She searched his pockets, found the motorbike key, picked up his helmet, and closed the door. Hopefully, he will be out long enough for her to be well away.

She put the helmet on then exited the building. She climbed on the bike, started it and headed to the camping gear store. She reached it just as they were bringing out their stuff with the help of one of the store clerks. Once it was all sowed away, they drove off.

Joana followed but had to keep increasing the distance between them as they got farther away from the city, and the traffic became sparse.

XXXXX

Kevin grabbed his stuff from his room and banged on Hugin's door. He finally opened it and Kevin started talking right away. "They rented a car so I rented a motorbike and will follow. Watch Matt and Joana." He turned to go but Hugin ran to him.

"Here. It is a satellite phone. My company makes them for government use and certain private organizations. I had one sent to me by express when I realized the other day that the hidden items will probably be located in some remote area."

Kevin smiled as he looked at the phone. "Thanks. Great idea, Mr. Smart Guy!"

Hugin nodded and stared at Kevin's back as he ran down the stairs, not bothering with the elevator.

Kevin drove to the camping store but their car was not there. Maybe they parked elsewhere. He parked and went inside. He looked around but didn't see them.

He approached one of the store employees. "Excuse me. I am looking for my friends, a young guy and gal age twenty-five. They left a small backpack in their room so the clerk gave it to me since they had already checked out. The clerk knew we were all here together so he hoped I'd be able to get it to them. They told me about how nice the people were here when they rented their camping gear so I am hoping that you can help me to find them."

"I didn't help them but I remember them. They looked very happy together. I think I know who did help them so let me find her." He wandered off.

A short time later, a girl came up to him and asked, "Are you the friend looking for Jason and Nicole?"

"Yes. Yes. They left a backpack and I'd like to get it to them. They told me they were going camping today for a few days but not where they were going since I was heading out to do some fishing on a charter boat."

"Well, they did not tell me exactly where they were going but, based on their description of the kind of hiking they were going to do, I think I can give you a general area. Follow me."

She led Kevin to a wall map of Iceland to the store area where they sold hiking boots. "Okay, I am sure that they are heading inland toward one of the mountains in the area. They mentioned nothing about going on any water, either rivers or lakes. The fact that they rented a car tells me that they will drive to some location and begin from there." Wow, Kevin thought. *She'd make a great search and rescue volunteer.*

"Based on how long they said they would be gone and the nearby road network, I would search for them in this area." She pointed to an area called Skjaldbreioarhraun.

He made no attempt to pronounce the name.

"If you have a vehicle then I would suggest leaving here on Highway 1 then east on 36 then north on a gravel highway. I would guess they might leave their vehicle somewhere in this area and head out on their hike. They also mentioned a mountain so I would guess they mean this one and she pointed at it." It was Skjaldbreizzur.

She reached into a drawer, pulled out one of the maps, turned, smiled, and handed the map to Kevin.

"Thank you so much for your help. You would make a great member of a search and rescue team, by the way."

She smiled. "Thank you for the compliment. I actually am a member of an elite team that is assigned to the most difficult search and rescue events."

"Of course." He smiled again and headed out the door.

XXXXX

Matt had finally made it back to his room at around 2:00 am. He didn't bother to change or shower. He simply collapsed onto the bed and fell asleep. It was now almost noon and he crawled painfully out of bed, showered, changed and went to a nearby clinic. It was located in a tourist part of town so he hoped they spoke some English and didn't ask a lot of questions.

He found one and moved to the small reception desk. "Do you speak English?" He asked.

"Yes. Not well, but good. What do you need?"

"I was hiking and fell down a small ravine." He pointed to the bruises on his face. "I also injured my side and ribs. Can I see someone for some help?"

"Of course. Please write this up." And, she handed him a small form written in both Icelandic and English. He wrote a fictitious name and address in the states. He gave his real phone number since it was a burner phone which he'd toss away one of these days. He handed it to her.

"Please go there and I will call you." She pointed to a seating area.

After about ten minutes a woman appeared and called his fake name. He followed her to an exam room. She asked a few questions and he lied. She treated his injuries and gave him a few pain pills and a prescription for a few more. She also gave him a small tube of antiseptic ointment and some extra bandages.

Matt thanked her and walked out of the clinic. *Now what?* He thought.

He knew it would be fruitless to try to follow them, so he decided to hang around Reykjavik to see which one of them showed up.

Thirty-one

The Hunt

As Jason drove past the Reykjavik city limits, he turned to Nicole. "Are you okay? You've been pretty quiet since we left the store."

"I'm fine. I was just thinking about all this family history and DNA stuff. It is a lot to take in. I mean, finding out we are related because we have a common ancestor from 1000 years ago is heavy stuff. I know it makes no difference today in terms of, well, you know." She smiled.

"Anyway, I was also thinking about this supposed treasure trove we are looking for. We don't even know if it really exists or, in the very least, if it did exist it may not be there anymore. And, is this whole pursuit worth what has been happening? I don't mean that this treasure may not really be worth anything even if we find it. I mean, is it worth the danger that has been created because of Joana and Matt? I feel so bad that Ingvill has had to go into hiding because of all this."

"Hey. Nicole. Ingvill is in hiding because of Joana, not you. You, rather all of us, were merely pursuing something of scientific interest when Joana and Matt decided to intervene."

"Yes, well, regardless of whose fault it is, I still feel badly for her." She leaned back in her seat and closed her eyes. After a few minutes she opened her eyes and looked out her window at the passing countryside. They were following the course of a river located just to her right.

"We just passed Mosfellsbaer and are now on Highway 36. We probably have 2 hours to go before we get to the area where we can pull over and begin our hike."

"Uh huh. Jason, if we find this treasure, what do you think will actually be in it? I mean, what could be so valuable that it brings out people like Joana and Matt who seem intent on hurting anyone in the way of this, so called, wealth?"

"I don't know why those two are after it or even how they know about it. But, the treasure could be worth a great deal monetarily and scientifically. The age, style and origin of the items would be worth a great deal scientifically. Some or all of it could shed new light on Scandinavian and Viking history."

"And, of course, there would most likely be a monetary value in many of the items that are made from precious metals or gems. There would also be a monetary value based on what one or more collectors might pay to have some of it in their collection." He looked thoughtful for a few moments.

"I recently read a report out of Denmark that a thirteen year old boy and an amateur archaeologist uncovered a unique trove of items from the tenth century which is thought to have belonged to the legendary Danish King, Harry Bluetooth. He is famous for being the founder of the Danish empire, and creating one flag, and bringing Christianity to the country. And, yes, his name is linked to today's Bluetooth technology."

"The subsequent excavation by archaeologists from the state of Mecklenburg-Western Pomerania uncovered more than 600 coins, pieces of silver, jewelry, neck rings, brooches, pearls and a Thor's hammer. A number of the silver coins bore images of a Christian cross. There would obviously be value in the silver and the jewelry to those who simply wanted the metal and gems they contain."

"But, for many of us, the true value is in what can be learned about that time period from the items themselves and what they have inscribed on them or what can be inferred from them based on the dates and styles. The obvious question for us, and you asked it, is will we find any treasure and what will be its value scientifically?"

"I guess we'll have the answers to those questions by this time tomorrow." Nicole turned to look out of the window at the passing landscape of short grasses, small streams, and pretty cottages. It was so idyllic.

XXXXX

Hugin wandered down to the hotel restaurant in mid-afternoon to get something to eat. He hadn't eaten since the day before and was starving. He ordered their fish sandwich and a beer. He also picked up one of the English language newspapers that were stacked at the front desk. As he took a break from his paper to take a sip of beer, he glanced out the window toward the street.

He was about to turn back to his paper when he thought he recognized Matt. Matt had never seen him but Hugin knew what he looked like. Matt was slowly walking to the front of the hotel. Hugin quickly picked up the paper and began pretending to read. As he watched Matt approach the door he noticed that he had a limp. He also saw that Matt's face had several bruises and small lacerations.

Just as Matt seemed about to enter, Hugin's meal arrived. And, just as suddenly, Matt turned away and continued his slow walk up the street into the tourist area with its shops, bars and restaurants. Hugin relaxed and leaned back in his chair. It was obvious that Matt's absence the past day or so must have had something to do with the injuries he now had. Based on what Joana had done to him, he wondered if she had also given Matt a thrashing.

He had to call Kevin.

XXXXX

Matt changed his mind. He had checked at his hotel to see If Joana was still staying there even though he knew the answer to his own question. She was gone. He had hobbled out onto the street, found a coffee shop where he sat, and drank less than half of his coffee. His mind was churning through the events leading to this moment and his options for what to do next. He was going to give up his quest for whatever treasure existed, but was not going to let Joana or Mr. Unknown Guy get away with beating him.

He angrily rose since sitting around was no solution. He left his unfinished coffee and started walking toward Jason and Nicole's hotel. As he stood, he immediately decided that moving was a must. It accomplished two things – it kept his mind working and focused, as well as unstiffening his body. Man he was sore.

When he arrived at their hotel, his intention was to enter and wait for them to wander into the lobby, but he rejected that idea. They knew him and probably suspected him being involved in this mess. Even if he tried to hide his presence in the restaurant, there was always the chance that he'd slip into view by accident.

No. His best option was to find someplace crowded with tourists nearby then wait there to see if they came back. He reasoned that they would eventually show themselves, and if they didn't, well, then he would come up with a new plan. He really had no other options at the moment.

XXXXX

It was early afternoon and the temperatures were getting warm. Joana had watched as Jason had stopped once at a gas station about a half hour ago but it only appeared that they needed to use the restroom. They were inside a short time and each had a coffee when they came out. They climbed in the car and headed back on the road.

Joana had used this time to take her jacket off and walk the stiffness out of her legs. She hadn't been on a cycle in about five years, and even then she was mostly a passenger sitting behind the guy she was staying with at the time. He did let her ride by herself several times which she enjoyed.

The little group was now heading north.

XXXXX

Kevin was well behind Joana. He had pulled off the road and hid behind a small grove of trees and bushes when they all stopped. He wanted to take action against Joana as soon as he could before she had a chance to confront Jason and Nicole. He needed to pick the right place and time.

The convoy had started to move onto the road so Kevin moved to his bike to get ready to follow Joana once she is on the move. As they moved back out onto the highway, Kevin followed. He liked this route. There were very few vehicles on the road and almost no development on either side of the road. This might be a good stretch of highway to waylay Joana.

After about an hour, the road changed from a surfaced to a gravel road. They were now passing through a shallow valley between several small hills. As Kevin looked ahead, he could see that Joana was staying well behind Jason and would actually lose sight of Jason when heading around the curves that were becoming more frequent on this stretch of the road.

Kevin could hear Joana's bike over the noise of his own bike. The Honda ran very smoothly and produced very little engine noise. Maybe he could use this difference to sneak up behind Joana and take her down. But, he knew it was a one-time shot. If he missed, then Joana would know that someone new was in the hunt. Worse, if he failed in this then Joana might accelerate her plan to take action against Jason and Nicole even before they found the treasure. He could not, would not, let that happen. Kevin backed away a little and watched the road ahead, looking for a sharp curve.

They were now following a small stream with small trees and a variety of bushes on both sides of the road. The car was kicking up a good bit of dust and dirt now, and Joana appeared to be pulling back even more in order to not become blinded by it. Kevin started accelerating, and slowly closed the gap between he and Joana.

As they entered a short length of straight road, Kevin noticed that the car was already around the next turn which looked to be a kilometer ahead of him. He made his move.

Kevin increased his speed and closed the distance with Joana rapidly. He actually decided to pass her for a brief second then drop quickly back and put her down. He figured she might be on alert once she heard him coming up on her but might relax a bit if he simply went by. She might figure that he was somebody out enjoying a fast bike ride in the countryside.

Kevin came up on her rear wheel, moved even with her, and noticed she took a quick glance at him. With his helmet on and visor down, she wouldn't be able to see his face. He hesitated slightly but then gunned past her. Kevin actually owned a Honda back home and loved to take it out on the back roads near his home in Kentucky, thus this was all familiar playtime for him. He and a couple of buddies used to ride together and do simple tricks with their bikes. His next move was going to be one of those tricks.

Kevin suddenly braked and did a 180 degree turn to face Joana. She reacted by turning to her left. He gunned his bike, and headed straight for the side of her bike intent on forcing her off of the road into the ravine with the stream.

He had her in his sights when she suddenly turned more to her right. He was now looking at her rear wheel which was spinning wildly in the gravel. And, unfortunately for Kevin, all of the gravel under the rear wheel of her bike was flying directly into his bike, body, and worse, his face. His vision was now gone.

Kevin tried to keep focused on the direction he had intended to go but now he had no idea if Joana was still there. And as it turned out, she was not. He only encountered empty air and, once the rocks stopped hitting his visor and he had vision, he did not like what he saw. No, not one bit. He was heading into midair and down into the ravine where

Joana was supposed to go. He hit hard with the bike, then flew off into the stream, hitting his head on a boulder conveniently located where his head wanted to land. He blacked out.

XXXXX

Joana looked back, and saw the other rider and bike fly into the ravine. She stopped and drove cautiously back to where he went over. She parked her bike, moved slowly to the edge of the ravine and peered down. The bike was trapped in a tight bramble of thick bushes with its wheels still slowly spinning. The biker was lying on his side in the stream.

She really wanted to go down and beat the guy to a pulp. She felt her anger rising higher than when she beat Matt. Her fists clenched and unclenched. Her breathing was rapid and her vision blurred. She forced herself to calm, taking deep breaths and closing her eyes. She finally felt her body relax and briefly thought about climbing down just to check the face of the driver. No, she needed to get going. Besides, he may not be completely out-of-it. But, who the hell was he and why was he after her? She figured it was a he because he was built more like a guy – tall and muscular. It didn't really matter what sex he was, she hated him for interfering.

She had to get going. She had no idea where Jason and Nicole were heading so she needed to keep them in her sights. She quickly climbed onto her bike and headed back onto the road in the direction Jason and Nicole had been heading.

Thirty-two

On a Hike

Jason stopped, and pulled out the map the camping gear store employee had given him. He opened it and they both looked it over. He found the lake and mountain and suggested they start their hike here. He pointed at it and showed Nicole. "This spot should be about another thirty minutes away. What do you think?"

Nicole liked that Jason always included her in the decision making process for everything they did together. He even called her sometimes when they were in different schools and asked her advice. "I agree. We just passed this bend in the river so we must be right here."

"Okay. Here we go." He pulled back onto the highway and began kicking up dust again.

Joana had just rolled up on her dusty machine. If she had been two minutes earlier, they would have seen her. She slowed and hung well back.

"Nicole. I forget to tell you that grandfather told me the name of the Viking who started this whole adventure rolling over 1000 years ago. His name was Yngvarr and he was the son of the Norse king who stayed to fight the invading force of the rival king. Grandfather told me that he was named after an ancient Norse god named Yngvi. Isn't that cool?" He glanced at Nicole and saw that she was staring at him and smiling. "What?"

Nicole shook her head smiling. "Well, Ingvill told me that her father named her after the same god. She explained that over time the spelling changed depending on where the Vikings were living at the time. In old English it became 'I-N-G' instead of 'Y-N-G'. It's pretty cool that we had the same story but from two different sources."

Just then, Jason started to pull off to the side of the road. "I think this is where we start making our way to the mountain and, hopefully, the treasure."

They climbed out of the car, and moved to the back to retrieve their backpacks and camping gear. They sorted through everything in their backpacks and decided to leave some of their extra clothes in the trunk. They repacked everything in the larger, and more comfortable hiking packs that they rented at the store.

Nicole put the two padded ground covers in her pack and Jason took the two small tents. They each took their own sleeping bags then crammed the remaining gear in whatever pack could handle it. Two items that they were definitely not going to leave behind were the small shovel and pick. Jason took the shovel and Nicole took the pick. They each also had a fully equipped Swiss Army knife just in case they needed one or more of the tools contained in it.

Once all was stowed in the car and the packs were on their backs, Jason asked, "Ready to go?"

"As I'll ever be. Let's go."

"Nicole, do you think we should backtrack to the lake to make sure we are in the right place?"

Nicole paused a moment looking one way then the other. "You know, I think we should just head to the mountain. If we hike for an hour or so and we still don't see the mountain off in the distance, then we can turn back and check. But, I really don't think we will need to do that. I have a good feeling about Ingvill's translation and the map we have been following."

"I agree." They both turned and headed to the mountain.

XXXXX

Joana watched Jason and Nicole sort their stuff then head off to the east. She was hidden behind a low bluff with several bushes to block her from view. She had rounded the last bend, slowed, and watched as the car's dust slowly started to settle back to the ground with no more spewing into the air. They had stopped so she immediately pulled off the road to the left and hid.

She waited until the two were well away from their car and almost out of sight before she made her way to the bike, and slowly drove the short distance to the car. She debated hiding her bike in case they came back before she caught up to them.

No. This is it. Either they would not be coming out or she would not. So, it didn't matter if the two vehicles were located together.

She parked behind the car and proceeded to fill her backpack with the few items she had stuck inside the carry bag on the back of the bike. Once she had everything, she headed east after Jason and Nicole.

XXXXX

Hugin grabbed his phone once Matt was well away and called Kevin. He didn't pick up. Hugin tried again and got the same result. *Was he dead? Did he turn his phone off? He would do that if he was close enough for someone to hear it.* Hugin decided to try again in a half hour then keep trying until, well, he didn't know.

XXXXX

Matt strolled around town all afternoon. *This sucks!*

He finally decided to eat. He had seen the Hard Rock Café on his wanderings, so he went there. He walked in and moved to a table against the wall next to the bar. Christina came over, introduced herself and asked, "What can I get you to drink?"

"I'll take whatever the cheapest light beer is that you have at the bar."

"Okay. Would you like a menu?"

"Sure." She retrieved one, handed it to him and moved to the bar to get his beer.

When she got to the bar and Gunnar brought Matt's beer, he said, "Man. It looks like that guy ran into a wall or someone who didn't like him very much."

"Yea. I noticed that too, but I'm not going to ask since he seems pretty edgy."

She brought his beer, and he ordered a cheeseburger and fries. Once she was gone, he mulled over his options, which were not many.

XXXXX

Kevin was rudely awakened when his face suddenly slipped into the water and he started to drown. His head jerked up, and he shook the cobwebs out, along with the water that had collected in his mouth, nose and helmet.

He sat up, pulled off his helmet, and tossed it onto the dry ground. At that point he noticed his bike amongst a mess of bushes and shrubs. He slowly rose, made his way to dry ground, and sat on a rock.

After a few moments the fog cleared from his head enough, and he began to remember what had happened. He couldn't decide if Joana made a dumb move or it was just luck or she knew what she was doing. He finally decided it didn't matter. He had to get moving.

He stood and picked up his helmet. It was damp but, other than a few scratches, seemed to be in good condition. He walked to his bike, set the helmet aside, and began tugging and pulling the bike from its bramble trap. It finally came lose and, other than some dents and scratches, it appeared to be in good running condition. He strapped his helmet onto the handle bars and began trudging up the shallow ravine.

After what seemed like several hours, but was only about twenty minutes. He finally made it to the top. He propped the bike onto its stand, and took a couple of slow breaths. He had to get going as soon as possible. Joana was on the hunt.

He put his helmet on, climbed onto the bike and started it. He was a little surprised when it started on the first try. Honda makes great bikes, he decided.

He pulled onto the gravel road and headed to Joana, Jason and Nicole.

After about four kilometers he saw their car and, unfortunately, Joana's bike was parked behind it. Ignoring any noise he might make he sped to the car, parked next to Joana's bike, and quickly grabbed his backpack. He didn't have much but he hoped he wouldn't need anything more. The most important items were the hunting knife and handgun he bought from a guy who knew a guy.

He saw the footprints and headed in their direction but only took three steps when his phone rang. He continued moving while he answered.

He saw that it was Hugin. "Yes." Pause. "No, I'm okay." Pause. "Okay. Keep track of him the best you can but do not, I repeat, do not approach him." Pause. "Yes. I have the sat phone. Listen, I need to get going. Joana has a head start on me and she is after Jason and Nicole." Pause. "Yes. I'll call.

Kevin's phone rang again. He wasn't going to answer but then he saw that it was the 'watcher'. He answered, "Yes?" Pause. "I figured they might drop off. Don't worry. I am following them now. I'll call later." He shut down his phone since, as the 'watcher' pointed out, reception was spotty at best out here.

Thirty-three

The Mountain

Matt finished his second beer and ordered another. He had finished his meal over an hour ago and spent the time since then thinking about his dilemma.

I could go back to Ohio. No. Not an option. I am mad and want to exact punishment on Joana and the unknown guy. Then, I want payment and will take all of whatever treasure there is. But, I have no idea where they went or what they are doing. I probably have enough money left to stay for a month, if I have to. The room is paid for and I have a return ticket so all I need is spending money, and the money I might need to get the treasure out.

He was staring at one of the waitresses when he decided to finish this beer and head back to his hotel. He was walking along Austurstraeti Street thinking about his options, when he suddenly pulled to a stop. *I need a weapon!* He quickly looked around to see if anyone heard him but no one seemed to be paying him any attention. Then he realized that he had only thought it and not said it. He needed to get some sleep.

He decided to make the gun his first priority tomorrow.

XXXXX

Hugin checked on the location of the Hotel Hilda where Matt was staying, and walked there to check the area. As he walked along the street near the hotel, he noticed that the area looked very residential. The buildings looked like large homes partitioned into apartments or flats for rent or lease. The only way he would be able to watch the comings and goings of Matt would be to rent a room directly across from his hotel.

Well, if that is what he had to do then that is what he would do. He noted the addresses of the three properties located directly across from the hotel and went back to his room. He pulled out his laptop and checked for rentals in the three addresses he had noted. He found one with a street view on the second floor of the building just to the left of the front of Matt's hotel. He submitted a request to rent it for two weeks. He set the laptop aside, called room service, and ordered the fish special from the menu. As he finished ordering, his laptop 'pinged' him. He opened it, checked his emails, and found a message from the apartment manager that confirmed his rental.

Tomorrow, he would check out of the hotel and move to his rental. He called his office and had them express deliver overnight to his hotel one of the company's high end surveillance cameras. He planned to set it up in his new room and tape Matt's comings and goings. He would also link it to his computer so he could watch Matt whenever and wherever he wanted.

About that time, his door chime rang and he retrieved his fish dinner from the delivery man. He had also ordered a bottle of wine. He poured himself a glass right away and toasted himself. He felt good about his plan.

XXXXX

Jason and Nicole sat on a couple of large boulders next to their small camp site. They had arrived at the Skjaldbraizzur Mountain an hour ago and quickly made their camp near the boulders. They offered some protection against the wind if it blew from the west, which was the tendency in this part of Iceland. It was just into the fall season so it would get pretty cold in the evening.

However, this time of year was a good time for them to climb around on the mountain since most of the winter snow was gone.

"Jason. I am a little worried about any kind of treasure we might find in the cave. I mean, we started out crossing grassy tundra with streams and small patches of brush. But, we then moved on to a very rocky expanse the rest of the way here. This mountain has all the appearance of an extinct volcano. That, of course, means that there were likely numerous small or even large quakes over the past 1000 years. Whatever treasure they hid might be strewn over a large area and may be unrecognizable."

"I agree. I am also worried about all of the hiking trails we came across. They indicate that there have been a large number of people wandering all over the area and the mountain. If the treasure had become exposed then it could already be looted of anything of value."

"Well, so what do you think? Do we continue up the mountain or call the whole thing off?"

Jason stared at Nicole with an incredulous look. She smiled back at him. He finally broke into a smile too and said, "You were kidding, right?"

"Oh yea. And, the look on your face was priceless." She knuckled his shoulder. "Come on. We have gone through way too much to stop now, especially since we are, supposedly, a mere 1000 meters away from it. I would have gone up on my own if you had decided to quit."

"I figured that you would." Jason looked over his shoulder at the mountain then turned back to Nicole. "Okay. We should probably eat something then get some sleep since it will probably be a long day tomorrow with lots of slow going over rocks and loose stones."

They grabbed their packs and each pulled out several energy bars and a bottle of water. They quietly consumed their 'dinner' then put all of their trash into a trash bag they had brought along.

"Well, I guess we should get into our sleeping bags." Nicole glanced at her tent and turned back to Jason.

He was looking at her. "Oh yes. We should do that. We need to get some sleep."

"Right. You said that before." Nicole observed.

"Oh yea, I did. Well, um, I guess I'll see you in the morning." Jason turned and looked at his tent.

"Jason."

He turned and saw Nicole standing close. He started to say something but she quickly put her arms around his neck and pulled his mouth to hers. She kissed him hard and he returned it. She was so warm.

Nicole rubbed her hands down the small of his back and began kneading the muscles of his butt. She felt him press into her and sensed his urging. She slowly pulled away, and looked at him, saying nothing.

"Nicole, I really don't want to let you go."

"And, I don't want you to let me go. I have loved you for so long and have thought about what, well, what the moment might feel like, but ..."

"I have thought about it too. You know, we could probably both easily fit into one tent, especially if we share a sleeping bag. It would be warm and really ..."

Nicole knew what he was driving at and she had wanted to go there as well. But, this was not the right time. She had no idea what that statement meant but she did know how she felt.

"Jason. Let's keep this moment as it is. Okay?"

He nodded, smiled, and kissed her again. He gently held her face in his hands. "Good night. See you in the morning."

Jason watched Nicole crawl into her tent. He smiled and mumbled, "Yea. Tomorrow." He went into his tent.

XXXXX

Joana watched the touching scene and scowled. She was going to make them both pay for what their ancestor did to her family. If their ancestor hadn't humiliated hers then her life might have been so much better. Her ancestors had all harbored hatred and evil in their hearts for centuries. As a result, their hearts had become stone, and that is the only inheritance passed on to her father making him the evil bastard he had become. And, he had passed it on to her.

She was going to stop this menace from going any farther by getting rid of the descendants of the perpetrators of it – Jason and Nicole. If she could wipe them out, she could set aside her hatred and live a normal life.

As she looked at the now empty scene she started to shake. At first, she thought it was the cold making her shiver. But, then she felt the warm tears streaming down her cheeks. They wouldn't stop. They started coming faster and bigger. The shaking increased because the sadness and hatred in her were fighting each other. She couldn't stop any of it, not the hatred or the sadness.

She finally moved from her hiding place and walked on violently shaking legs to a spot well away from view. She sat and leaned back against the side of a small boulder. She willed the tears and shaking to stop. Neither listened and they seemed to get madder. She took off her jacket and had no trouble ignoring the cold blast. She felt nothing except the war going on inside her. She dropped her head into her jacket and let the sobs come.

She hated them. She hated her father. She hated her ancestors. Most of all, she hated herself. *Why doesn't this all stop? Why have I never, ever been happy? I don't have even one small happy memory in my whole miserable life.* The sobs and tears increased.

A long time later, she woke to find her face still stuffed into her jacket. She lifted her head and looked around. She was still alone. Something she was very accustomed to. She had stopped crying and shaking. She was exhausted. She leaned back and closed her eyes.

XXXXX

Kevin was lying in his blanket in a small patch of bushes. He could see the edge of the rock area and the mountain well into the distance. He had eaten a couple of energy bars and drank one of his water bottles. He hadn't had time to get a sleeping bag and tent so he had only the thick blanket he 'borrowed' from the hotel. He expected that it would be a busy day tomorrow so he had stopped here rather than try to gain more ground on Joana in the dark. He lay back and closed his eyes.

Thirty-four

Skjaldbreizzur

Hugin sat in his room early the following morning packed and waiting for the concierge to call about his package. He was excited to get started with this new plan he had devised. He was finding that he liked this kind of stuff – hunting for clues about things or people, watching various people or activities, and he especially liked working with Kevin. Kevin was such a professional and, he felt, a really good guy.

The phone rang and Hugin was told that he had an express package waiting for him at reception. He grabbed his small bag and headed down to the lobby. Once there he went to reception and received the package. He also told the person helping him that he had a change in plans and would be checking out as well. She nodded and proceeded to print his receipt and thank him for staying with them. He stuffed the package into his bag and headed out of the door.

He headed to his new accommodation across form the Hilda Hotel. As he made the long walk to the apartment, he continued to mull over his thoughts about enjoying this kind of work and Kevin's professionalism.

After a couple of blocks he stopped mid step. Several people had to quickly side-step around him and he apologized to each. He was finally able to move to the side and was, fortunately, now standing outside a coffee shop. He entered, ordered tea and found a table to continue his 'mind-meandering'. His tea was delivered and he thanked the server.

His mind quieted for a few minutes then it tossed out an idea. *What if Kevin and I start a Private Detective business? I certainly have the computer skills and resources to do much of the online investigative work, and he is excellent in field work. I also have the finances to get us up and running, and keep us in business long into the future. I will have to propose this to him once all of this is over.*

He finished his tea and continued to the apartment. When he arrived, he checked the box inside the front door and found an envelope addressed to him. Inside, he found the key to his room, and all the information he needed for getting mail, where things were, and various contact names and numbers.

He entered his room and immediately pulled the package from his bag. After opening it, he started setting up the camera on the small tripod he bought the day before, and checked that it worked as he expected. He also checked the feed to his laptop and saw that he had a clear view of the entire front of the hotel.

The camera also had an infrared sensor attached. Hugin linked this to his laptop and verified that he had several signatures in the hotel. He did not know where Matt's room was located so he would have to wait to see him enter then track him to the location of his room.

Now the boring part begins. Sitting, watching and waiting.

XXXXX

Jason crawled out of his tent and looked toward Nicole's tent.

"Morning, sleepy head."

Jason turned and saw Nicole sitting with her back lodged against a rock. She was smiling and held a water bottle up in a toast to him.

"Good morning. What time is it?"

"It's time to get up and get started."

He grumbled, wiggled the rest of the way out, stood, and stretched. "Yes sir, general. What are your orders?"

She ignored his remark. "Would you like some orange juice? I brought some orange mix that you can mix with your water. It actually tastes pretty good."

"Sure." She tossed him one of the packets.

After he had his drink, he sat next to Nicole, who started. "Okay, the mountain is just over 1000 meters and the map says we need to go up 300 meters according to Ingvill's estimate. She had to translate the steps mentioned in the original instructions into an existing form of measurement. She used anatomical data from bodies, bones and footprints to come up with the number. It sounds good to me and I trust her judgment."

Jason nodded. "I agree. It says that we should move up the south side and look for a ledge to the right of the path." He stood and walked a short way to their right facing the base of the mountain. "This is the south side and there already appears to be a trail leading up. We might as well use this one since trails are normally there because they have been forged over many years by previous people." He looked over at Nicole for a comment.

"Sounds good to me. Let's get our stuff and head up."

They began digging into their packs and putting aside the items they felt they'd need once they arrived at the cave. They set aside more water, some energy bars, the shovel, the pick and a small spade. They emptied Jason's pack and put the items into it. They paused a moment and scanned the area.

"Well, do you think we have everything?" Jason asked Nicole.

"I think so. Besides, if we get up there and decide we forgot something, it isn't that far to come back here and get it." She paused a moment then turned to Jason. "Should we worry about Joana or Matt getting here before we have a chance to pack up and leave?"

"I am guessing that one or both of them are on their way here right now. They may even be close enough to see us." Nicole quickly looked toward the way they came. Jason saw her look out across the rocky plane. "Nicole. Let's just do this and worry about them later. Remember, we decided to go forward no matter what. Besides, we can see pretty far in the direction we came and will likely be able to see even farther the higher up we go. I am guessing we might see them before they get here which will give us some time to get away."

"Okay. But, I am carrying this." She pulled out her Swiss Army knife. "It's not much but it's something."

Jason pulled his out of his pocket and waved it around. "I agree."

They both put their knives away and Jason asked. "Ready?" Nicole nodded and they headed up the trail.

XXXXX

Kevin woke before the sun broke over the horizon. He couldn't start too early because the terrain was fairly treacherous, especially over the rocky plane leading to the mountain. As he carefully made his way over the tundra then the rocks, he hoped he wouldn't be too late to stop Joana from harming Jason or Nicole.

He often wondered how so many generations of descendants could hang on to a revenge vow. Why hadn't someone along the way simply decided to end it and devote their time and energy to, well, anything else – maybe a family business, a career in something they enjoyed, sports, something! He didn't know the answer, so he shook his head and got moving.

XXXXX

Hugin had been watching the hotel for the past two hours. It was now 9:00 am. The infrared showed at least a dozen people moving around. He guessed that half of those were probably various hotel staff. He had already replayed the video the camera took over night and had seen Matt go in late which probably means that he is still in there.

He sat back drinking the large coffee he made with the room's coffee maker and coffee selections. He also munched the muffin he had bought yesterday. He knew that this was going to be the boring part of his job but he didn't mind. He used the time to make notes about changes to the various products his company sold as well as possible new products.

He turned back to the laptop and watched for a few minutes. His mind wandered to the topic of his family's past. He knew that his ancestor, Aki, had come to York right before the great Norse migration. At that time all of the English kings were in the south of the country, so the migration went off with only small pockets of resistance from some of the ancient Saxon lords in the northern areas.

However, the Normans invaded the south in 1066 CE and everything changed. William the Conqueror became king and started a campaign to secure power throughout the country. The north rebelled and the conqueror's army brutally suppressed it, slaughtering men, women and children all over the area, especially in York.

Surely, many of his ancestors were caught up in the slaughter but there was no way to know who or how many. However, it is certain that at least one survived because the legend and vow made it to the present day. The traitor's actions were carried out during the reign of Charles II. He was brought to power when Cromwell was finally ousted. He had also been brutal to the people of the north. Maybe that is why the traitor decided to give up the relic and the vow.

Well, he was continuing the family vow now and hoped that they were successful.

His eye suddenly caught someone exiting the front door. He watched through the lens and saw that it was Matt. He scrambled to get his shoes on and make his way out of the house. When he reached the street, there was no sign of Matt. He decided to head toward the town center, figuring that would be the most likely direction he would take.

He chastised himself for not being ready to leave at a moment's notice. That would not happen again.

XXXXX

Matt headed for the harbor area where Joana had given him the beat-down. He guessed that it would be the perfect area to find someone who might know where he could get a gun.

The harbor area would be busy this time of day since work was just getting started on loading and unloading ships, as well as various maintenance tasks. He had a pocket full of kroners in order to 'help' the process along. His main problem was that he didn't speak any Icelandic. But, he did remember some Norwegian from all the years he had spent there as a kid and as a college student.

He wandered to the port and looked for men working or walking alone. He had wet his head wounds to make them look recent and painful. He also exaggerated his limping. The first four men he approached ignored him when he made his request. One of them looked almost ready to cooperate but then he was called away by someone from one of the buildings. But, Matt was not deterred, and kept at it for another hour.

He was thinking of quitting, but kept walking toward another man standing next to a large crane then someone behind him said something to him. It sounded like the word 'help' to Matt. He stopped and turned to the man who crowded close to him. He said something, which to Matt, sounded like 'need help, I can help'.

Matt replied in broken Norwegian, which he hoped the man would understand. "Yes. I need gun because." And he pointed at his head and lifted his shirt to show the bruises there.

The man stared at both sets of wounds but still looked skeptical. So, Matt added, "Man do my son," He held his hand down near his waist to indicate the boy was small. "Very bad thing." At this he looked around and then pointed to his crotch and his invisible son. He looked very sternly at the man.

The man seemed to get the idea. He nodded then wrote an address and an amount of Kroners on a piece of paper. He also listed a time. He handed it to Matt and said, "You come." He pointed to the address then the time. Matt nodded and the man quickly moved off.

Matt looked at the address but didn't recognize it. He would have to look it up on a map. The time that the man had written was noon. Matt walked back to his room, and proceeded to look at one of the maps he had, which had a more detailed view of the city and its streets. He found the street and estimated by the number that it was probably a corner location. It was in the Hlidar area.

It was about a mile from his hotel so he planned to walk about half way there and have an early lunch. He would then leave the restaurant, and arrive at the location sometime between 11:30 and noon.

Hugin had watched Matt return, and made sure he also watched for the infrared signature so that he could learn which room he was in. The room ended up being on the top floor in the front corner of the building. He would have to watch that area carefully to make sure he didn't screw up his surveillance again.

Thirty-five

Climbing a Mountain

Joana had been awake and watching Jason and Nicole since before they had roused themselves up and about. She had slept fitfully, waking up several times in a cold sweat. Her dreams were horrible. They all reflected her beatings, her rapes, and her life on the streets. They each ended with her being nearly dead and then she'd wake up, but it would start again as soon as she fell asleep.

She was still trusting that this revenge effort would finally change her life. All she wanted to do was to end this quickly, get whatever was of value from the treasure, and go back to the states. She planned to go to Wyoming and find some cheap cabin or house she could buy. She would live there by herself for the rest of her life. She hated people, especially men, and wanted nothing more to do with anyone ever again once this was finished.

She watched Jason and Nicole pack one of their backpacks and begin heading up the mountain. Once they had gone about 100 meters Joana moved away from her hiding place but not toward their camp. She stayed low to the ground and worked her way well out, and to the far left of their location. She knew that as long as they were in view then she would be too.

She finally made her way to the base of the mountain where she could no longer see the two of them. She crawled on her hands and knees the remaining fifty meters to their camp and hid behind a large boulder. She took a quick glance up to where she had last seen them and saw now that they were no longer in view. She slid her knife out of her pack and waited for one or both of them to return.

While she waited for them, she occasionally glanced back toward the vehicles. She had no idea who the crazy motorcycle rider was but he surely wasn't someone to be taken lightly. He definitely seemed intent on taking her out when he came at her on his bike. Dumb luck saved her when she tried to twist away and he flew off into the creek.

She didn't want to be surprised by him again.

XXXXX

Kevin was not heading directly to the mountain. He had found a perch near a large boulder earlier and had used his high-powered scope to watch what was happening ahead of him. It took him a good while to finally notice the two small shapes slowly moving up the mountain.

He didn't see Joana but he knew she was not far behind them. He also figured that she would be watching to the rear of her position in case the motorcycle nut was still after her.

Well, she was right. He was still after her

He was now well to the right of the trail that Jason and Nicole were using to hike up the mountain and approaching the base of the mountain. He couldn't see Jason and Nicole but he wasn't watching them. He was watching for Joana. He couldn't see her yet but he was sure she would be close to the trail.

He moved along the base of the mountain, stopping for a minute or so before moving another five meters and stopping. He suddenly saw movement about thirty meters ahead. He swept the scene slowly and saw the camping stuff they had rented, but didn't see the movement again.

Then he did. He caught Joana peeking over a large boulder up toward the trail. He didn't follow her line of sight. He stayed on her until she ducked down again.

He had to decide whether to take her out now or wait until she made her move. Logic told him to take her out now. He had his gun so it would be easy. However, his gut and his instincts told him to wait.

He listened to his gut, at least for now.

XXXXX

Matt left his hotel at 10:00 am to go eat some lunch before his meeting.

Hugin was diligent this time, and had seen him leave his room, and move down to the front of the hotel. He was ready, and at his front door when Matt turned and headed toward the town center. He followed at a safe distance.

Matt finally reached Austurstraeti Street then walked a short way to the Apotek café. He entered and settled down at a table.

Hugin waited and wandered around looking in shops at the various items for sale. He kept the front door of the restaurant in view. After about thirty minutes he wandered into the Apotek and sat at a table behind and to the right of Matt's. He placed an order with the waitress and pulled out his ever present newspaper.

Finally, at 11:20 am, Hugin noticed Matt getting ready to leave. He had already paid his bill and, it seemed, he was merely sipping his coffee to bide his time. Hugin had already paid too, so after Matt had left and turned to the right, he quickly gathered up his paper and left.

He followed Matt to a residential area that looked fairly old. It may have been built in the 50s by the looks of it. He had to stay well behind to avoid being spotted. Matt suddenly stopped at one of the homes on the corner, walked up to the door, and knocked. After a short time, a man opened the door and invited him inside.

Hugin kept walking past the house and decided to go around the opposite block. He moved to the street, crossed and headed away from the house. He soon lost sight of it, moved down the next street, turned at the next corner heading back to the house that Matt had entered. When he was about halfway to the corner he saw the door of the house open and Matt exit.

Matt crossed the street and started walking back the way he had come. Hugin quickly adjusted his location and fell in behind Matt two blocks away.

Matt never stopped. He went directly back to his hotel and up to his room. Hugin did the same.

Hugin entered his room, and quickly went over to his laptop to watch the infrared output. He saw Matt walk from the front of his room to an exterior wall. He reached up and made a motion that looked like closing the curtains. He then moved to the center of the room and sat on his bed. Next, he reached over and grabbed something.

It must have been a package because his hands moved around it and pulled and tugged at what appeared to be wrappings. Matt finally set the wrapping material aside and stood. He had something in his hand, and he began holding his arm straight in front of him and moved his arm side to side and up and down. He moved whatever was in his right hand to his left hand, and that is when Hugin saw what it was.

When the object was taken by his left hand, Hugin got a brief heat signature of what looked like a handle. Then he realized that Matt had bought a gun.

Hugin quickly took out his phone and called a number that no one in his family had. When it was answered, Hugin began.

"Hello, Winston. How are you today?"

"I am very well, Hugin. To what do I owe this honor? I haven't heard from you in several months, not since we went out to the Orkneys to hunt."

"Yes. I have been quite remiss and I do most humbly apologize. However, grandfather has put me on a special project for the family, and it has kept me very busy these past couple of months."

"Oh, no need to apologize. When Lord Wilkinson asks, we all hitch up our pants and get to it, eh."

"Yes, well, I have a rather discreet and delicate favor to ask of you Win. I am currently located in Reykjavik as part of this special project, and I need an item that I trust you'll be able to provide, rather quickly, I might add."

Winston didn't respond right away. He was probably staring off into space wondering what he had gotten himself into now.

"I see. What is it that you require?"

"I need a gun. Small and inconspicuous would be best."

Hugin waited while he let Winston mull this over.

"Is this an illegal adventure?"

"No. Not at all. It is just that this aspect of the project has encountered some rather ignominious persons involved. I would never use the weapon unless and only if I or a colleague is threatened with immediate harm."

He waited again while Winston digested that.

"Very well, Hugin. I will get on this, and will notify you by secure email when and how your package will arrive."

"Brilliant, Win. Thank you so very much, and I owe you for this gesture of true friendship."

"Well you could let me win in our next snooker tournament."

"Well, that is a bit much to ask, but I will do it."

They ended the call and Hugin went back to watching Matt. This project had taken a very serious turn.

Thirty-six

Treasure

"What do you think? Have we reached 300 meters yet?"

Jason tried again to check his phone. The battery was definitely dead. Nicole had reported hers dead earlier in the day as they began their hike up the mountain. "My phone is still dead." He looked down the trail and then up. "Three hundred meters is slightly less than one third of the height of the mountain. I would suggest that we are close but not quite there. I think we should start looking for the ledge to the right."

"That sounds good. Besides we don't know how accurate the 300 meter distance is. Even Ingvill admitted that she had to translate the clue written in the old Viking language and she wasn't positive about her estimate."

Jason turned and continued up. He began scanning left and right just in case this trail was too far to the right of the actual trail. Nicole did the same.

They walked for another forty minutes. Jason walked around to the left of a large rock outcropping and then moved back to the right to continue up.

"Jason." Nicole shouted from in front of the outcropping.

Jason turned but couldn't see Nicole so he backtracked down to her. "What is it?"

Nicole waved him to her. When he was in front of her and looking at her with his eyebrows up, she reached up and put her hands on his shoulders. He may have thought, or hoped, she was going to pull him in for a kiss, but that is not what she did. She turned him around to face the rock he had just walked around.

He looked up the mountain past the rock, and was about to turn and ask Nicole what she was looking at when his eyes settled again onto the rock outcropping. He smiled and turned to Nicole who was already smiling.

"This is it. This is the rock ledge."

She smiled and said, "Yup. Shall we turn right?"

He grabbed Nicole and gave her a big hug and she returned it. They pulled apart and started to the right. "Okay, Invill's translation says to go twenty meters and look for three large rocks that are set in a triangle about two meters to a side. The entrance to the cave is in the center of the triangle."

Jason moved to the right. There was no trail here, so they were blazing one of their own. Every few steps a rock or the ground would give way and roll out from under them. The good thing was that they were not on top of a steep drop-off. Still, they did not want to fall or twist an ankle or both.

Suddenly, they stopped, looked at each other, and smiled. This had to be the place. There in front of them were three large rocks. They weren't set in a triangle since the rock which might have been the top of the triangle was now lying next to the rock anchoring the lower right of the triangle. They both studied the scene.

Finally, Jason suggested, "I really think this is it but let's go another five meters just to see if we find another set of rocks that might also be what we are looking for." They moved another seven meters then stopped. They both shook their heads and decided to head back to the first spot.

As they checked that scene again, Nicole offered, "My guess is that the rock that was at the top of the triangle was not in its natural position. I think the Vikings moved it there so that it more clearly marked this spot. Over time, the various quakes and weathering simply dislodged it, and it rolled to this spot. But, there is no doubt in my mind that this is the entrance to the cave." She looked at Jason for agreement.

She received it when he said, "Shall we have some fun and play in the dirt?"

Nicole shook her head and smiled. "You're such a goof. Get to work or I'll send you back to our camp to think about what you did."

Jason grabbed the shovel and Nicole pulled the pick from the backpack. They also put on work gloves they had bought a few days before at the hardware store where they bought the pick and shovel.

Nicole started dislodging rocks and compacted gravel, and Jason shoveled it off to the side. After five or ten minutes they were both glad they had thought to get the gloves. Their hands were already sore but would have been a lot worse with no gloves.

XXXXX

Matt paced his room while holding the gun in his right hand. Occasionally, he shifted the gun to his left. He couldn't sit. Now that he had the gun, he wanted to take action against Joana, the unknown guy and anyone else who kept him from his treasure.

He had begun to theorize that the treasure was in fact his. It had been stolen by those who were fairly defeated by the new king. The treasure should have stayed with the new king and his warriors. His ancestor was one of those warriors and, since no one from the king's men were around now, he was the rightful owner.

And, he would have it!

The problem was how would he get it? He had no idea where it was or where Joana, Jason and Nicole have gone. He had to think. He needed a plan.

XXXXX

"Did Ingvill say anything about how deep we needed to go before reaching the cave entrance? We've already removed about a meter of rocks and gravel from the mountainside."

"No. The directions stopped here, but having said that, I can't imagine the cave entrance being too far back into the side of the mountain. My guess is that we will find it ..." She didn't finish because Jason put his hand up to her.

"Listen." He took his shovel and struck hard into the gravel. It only penetrated about half the distance of the blade when it stopped and there was a muffled 'ding'. He looked at Nicole. "Did you hear it?"

"Oh yea. Come on let's get this cleared away." She began digging feverously with the pick while Jason shoveled the debris away as fast as it piled up.

Ten minutes later they were looking at a wall of medium to large stones. They were neatly placed so that the gaps between them were minimal. Jason took the pick from Nicole and started with the top most stones. He pulled one away then quickly stood back in case the whole thing tumbled down. It didn't. He went after the one that had been next to the first and it came away easily. Nicole rolled them off to the side and clear of the cave entrance.

After fifteen more minutes of work, they were looking at a cave opening. It wasn't large but it would accommodate one of them easily. Nicole grabbed a flashlight and started to crawl through the opening. Once her feet were clear of the entrance, Jason grabbed the other flashlight and followed her in.

As Jason's torso cleared the entrance he stopped because he was blocked by Nicole's butt. She had stopped and was now up on her hands and knees shining her flashlight around the cavern. Jason slowly wedged by her and got to his hands and knees as well. He began moving his flashlight around the cavern as well. His eyes went wide.

He remembered when he had entered the mound with his grandfather on the first day. They had done the same thing. They had shined their light around at the many objects around the chamber and marveled at the sight of it.

This view beat that by leaps and bounds. The place was packed tight with rough wooden crates and leather bags. Some of them had broken open and strewn their contents on whatever surface was below it. Sometimes it was a crate and sometimes it was the cave floor. And, there wasn't much floor. Jason and Nicole were literally in as far as they could go because of the crates blocking them.

Jason looked at Nicole and she looked back at him. They had no words for how they felt. Jason finally asked, "How far back does this cavern go?"

"I have no idea and the instructions said nothing about it. However, if you look at the sloping of the ceiling and how far it might be before it gets down close to the floor level, it seems to me that it is at least three or four meters deep."

"We are going to need trucks and people to clear this out. We also need to hire a lawyer to represent us to the Iceland government if we want to excavate this and remove the objects. I think we should reseal the entrance and get back to Reykjavik so that we can call my grandfather to ask if he knows anyone who can help us."

Jason backed out and Nicole followed. Once out, Nicole suggested, "Jason. Let's take a representative sample of the objects in order to show the importance of the find."

"Great idea. You go back down and grab your backpack. We'll use it to carry the items back to the car. I'll select a bunch of items from the cave, bring them out then I'll reseal the entrance."

"Okay. I should be back in a little less than an hour." Nicole turned and headed back to the trail and down the mountain.

Jason crawled back in and began selecting objects that he thought would fairly represent the overall importance of the find. As he carefully checked through the crates and bags and loose items his mind raced. *Wow, grandfather would love to see this. I am seeing gold coins, silver coins, beautiful ceramic pieces, gold and silver jewelry, and military items – swords encrusted with various gems, knives with the same decorations, and armbands.*

He created a group of about twenty objects and carefully arranged them in a relatively flat area near the cave entrance. He then started placing the stones at the entrance, and piling the dirt and gravel over them.

Thirty-seven

Confrontation

Kevin watched Joana watching the trail up the mountain. They had been in this position for the past ninety minutes. He didn't know about Joana but he was getting stiff from the lack of movement. He still wondered why his gut was telling him to wait before doing anything. He was endangering Jason and Nicole by not taking her down now.

Suddenly, Joana seemed to tense up and Kevin saw why. Nicole was coming down the trail. He pulled his gun from his pocket, checked that the safety was off, and that there was a round in the chamber. He saw Joana move around to the side of the boulder that made it unlikely Nicole would see her.

Nicole moved quickly to their small makeshift camp and began removing items from her backpack. Once she seemed satisfied that the pack was empty she grabbed a small brush, several items of clothing, then inserted them into the pack.

She stood and turned toward the trail. Her back was now to Joana.

Joana quickly rose and grabbed Nicole from behind. She had her left arm around Nicole's waist and her right arm around her neck. She also had a knife in her right hand that was wedged up under Nicole's chin and threatening her throat.

Just as quickly Kevin rose and aimed his gun at Joana. "Joana, let her go or I'll shot."

If Joana was surprised, she didn't show it. She looked over at Kevin and said, "No. You won't. You might hit her and I am guessing that you do not want to do that."

She was correct up to a point. Kevin knew several ways to shot someone while they are holding onto a hostage. Unfortunately, most of those required wounding the person they are holding. For example, he could hit Joana by shooting Nicole in the fleshy part of her side which would allow the bullet to continue through and hit Joana behind her. The one way that was not available was to hit Joana as she poked her head around Nicole, but Joana was so small she didn't present much of a target even when she did.

Joana seemed to recognize his dilemma and smiled. "So. What now? Do we stand here looking at each other? Do we have a chat? Do I just slit her throat and then try to duck your aim? Do you just go ahead and shoot her in order to hit me?"

"You know, Joana, I have been here almost as long as you have. I could have taken you down any time before now. But, I chose not to do that. I have been doing this job my entire life and I have learned to trust my gut instincts and they told me to wait. To wait and see what you would do once you could kill either Jason or Nicole or both."

Joana stopped smiling. Her mind raced. *What am I going to do? If I cut Nicole's throat, he will shoot me for sure. The longer we stay like this, the more likely it is that Jason will show up. Then, I will be facing three people.* She couldn't decide.

Nicole seemed to sense Joana's hesitation. She even began to feel Joana's arm start to shake very slightly. Nicole reflected back on all of the martial arts training she had taken. *Was I taught a move to counter something like this? I can't remember, but maybe if I simply grabbed her arm, it will throw her off balance and that guy can take her out.*

Joana felt her confusion rising along with her anger. *Why does this always happen? I am thwarted at every turn when trying to help myself. I should just kill her and duck behind the boulder and try to get that guy. Yes, I will kill her.*

She tried moving her knife hand into her throat but it started to shake. Tears sprung to her eyes. *I can do it. I am a killer. This is my destiny.* The shaking became more pronounced.

Kevin could see it from his position. She was hesitating but she also still had the knife at Nicole's throat. He was going to have to act soon or ....

Nicole felt the shaking increase. She decided to make her move. She quickly reached up and grabbed Joana's arm and started pulling it away from her throat but Joana was strong.

Joana screamed "No. It is mine. Mine. Mine." She could hear the desperation in he own screams.

Nicole gave one mighty pull on her arm and it moved away a few inches and then a few more. She kicked back and stomped on Joana's instep. She dropped down and pushed away from her.

Kevin fired.

Joana dropped the knife and fell forward to her knees. She screamed once then she sobbed uncontrollably.

Kevin rushed forward before either Nicole or Joana could move toward the other. He put himself in front of Nicole and told her, "Please. Move back. I'll check her."

Nicole moved back and sat on the nearest rock.

Kevin moved to Joana, picked up her knife and tossed it well behind him. He put his gun away and very slowly and carefully bent to Joana.

Joana felt his touch and reacted. She screamed and started to punch him. Instead of pushing her away, he pulled her into himself. He held her and kept talking softly to her. "Let me help you. Let me help you. You have been shot. I need to get you some help. Please, Joana. I want to help you. Please let me help you." He felt her relax.

Kevin slowly let her step back but she immediately collapsed back into his arms. He looked down at his coat and saw that it was covered with blood.

He gently laid Joana on her back, pulled open her coat, and ripped her shirt open. He had hit her in the left side, just below her breast. He gently rolled her up and put his hand on her back where he found an exit wound. He also saw the bullet hole in the back of her coat. Good. It didn't hit something hard or stay in her. It went straight through.

But, she was losing blood. He shouted to Nicole. "Hand me some clothes. Anything. T-shirts, underwear, anything. I need to stop the bleeding. Nicole grabbed the backpack she had just filled, and pulled out a couple of t-shirts, some underwear and socks. She had intended to use these to wrap the objects in order to protect them from damage.

As she tossed them to the man, he immediately picked them up, and begin trying to pack the wound. "Do you have any duct tape or any kind of tape or glue?"

"No. We didn't bring any with us."

"Okay. Come here. Put pressure on the wound and try to stop the bleeding. I need to make a phone call." He pulled out his sat-phone and called Hugin.

"Hugin. Shut up. I know you have connections and resources. We need help here. Joana has been shot and she needs medical attention right away. Shut up, would you. Use the GPS coordinates you see for my phone and get here fast." He disconnected without waiting for Hugin to respond.

Kevin took over for Nicole and she sat back against the boulder. "Who are you? What is going on here?"

Before he could say anything, Jason came scrambling down the trail yelling, "What's going on? I heard a shot. Who is that?"

Nicole rose and moved to waylay Jason from the scene. When he reached her, he immediately hugged her tight. Without letting go, he asked, "Are you okay? What happened?"

Nicole pushed away and held his eyes. "I am fine. Joana has been shot. She had a knife to my throat. This man saved me. He has called someone and asked for help to get here immediately. That is all I know. Come on sit. Calm down. I am fine."

Kevin was frantic with worry that Hugin wouldn't get here in time.

Thirty-eight

Help

Hugin sprang into action. He contacted his company's representative in Reykjavik. When he answered, Hugin immediately started talking. "Dag, sorry to be so abrupt, but I have an emergency request. Do you have a helicopter at your disposal?"

"Yes, Mr. Wilkinson. What do you need?"

"A friend of mine has been hiking out in the area near Skjaldbreizzur and there has been an injury. How many passengers can it handle?"

"It can accommodate four people comfortably and five if there is no additional baggage."

"Great. I am located at an apartment near the Hilda Hotel. Where can I meet it in order to get taken to the site?"

"There is a port located near your location. I will have the helicopter land there and wait. I will send a car to pick you up and take you to it. What is your address?"

Hugin gave it to him. "How long before the car gets here?"

"No more than ten minutes."

"How long is the flight?"

"Based on the location you gave me, it should be no more than thirty minutes. The problem will be finding a suitable landing spot. It is very rough ground out there."

"Okay. I have a sat-phone and can keep in touch with my friend and he will guide us to a landing location."

"Great. The car is already on its way to you."

"Thank you so much my friend. I will tell you all about it when we have a chance to meet. Goodbye."

He knew that he would not be able to tell Dag the whole story, actually not much at all, but he would cross that bridge when he had to. He gathered up his phone and his laptop and moved downstairs to wait for the car. He'd call Kevin from the car.

XXXXX

Kevin felt that Joana was stabilizing but he still worried that she had already lost a lot of blood. He kept checking her blood pressure, and although it was a little weak, it was steady and had not dropped since he first checked. He just hoped that Hugin would come through and help would arrive soon.

He glanced over at Jason and Nicole and saw that they were watching him. "Would one of you care to take over putting pressure on the wound?"

Jason stood and came over. He held his hand above Kevin's and, as Kevin moved his hand away, Jason dropped his hand over the wound.

Kevin stood and shook some feeling back into his hand. Nicole had come over too and sat next to Joana. She gently took Joana's right hand and held it, lightly stroking the back of it.

Kevin watched the two of them gently care for the woman who had planned to kill them. He smiled at them and took a breath.

"You …" Just then his sat-phone rang. He held up a hand and answered. He listened, then said thanks and turned off the call.

"That was a friend of mine telling me that help would be here in about thirty to forty minutes." He paused and started again. "I suppose you'd like to know who I am and what I am doing here. So, here goes. My name is Kevin and I am here because of our ancestors." He proceeded to tell them about how Alsoomsa had made her brother vow to protect Yngvarr and all of his descendants and that he was currently their assigned protector.

He told them that Joana is descended from Megadagik and was intent on killing both of them to get at the treasure. He told them that Matt is an unknown but that he also seems intent on harming them and taking the treasure. Finally, he told them about Hugin and how he is descended from the grandfather, Aki, and that he has been helping him protect them.

"So, you see, all of us, you two, me and Hugin are all related."

"Wow. That is quite a story. I believe it, mind you, but it is still a remarkable tale." Jason turned to Nicole to hear what she was thinking.

All she said was, "Great. I can contact Ingvill and tell her that she is safe now."

"Actually, you need to wait. Matt knows about Ingvill. He followed you and Ingvill to her house because he knew that Joana gave her the copper sheet to get it translated. He also knew that you knew her and that she was now sharing the translation with you."

"How do you know that?"

"I was following Matt because he was following you. Joana had lost track of you so I decided to follow Matt since he was the more immediate threat. I caught up with him as he was watching Ingvill's house after you and she arrived there. I decided to waylay him then left him tied up in the nearby wooded area."

Nicole asked, "Why did you try so hard to save Joana? She seemed ready to kill us all, yet you were desperate to keep her alive."

Kevin smiled. "Good question." He thought a moment. "Gut feeling is the only reason I can think of. I think Joana is a very troubled soul. I suspect that she was abused as a child and that it left severe marks on her feelings and emotions."

He took over for Jason and put his hand over the wound. He looked at Joana's face then back at Nicole. "I have spent the past fifteen years of my life doing this and a big part of it is reading people in order to learn what they might do or not do. I have to do that in order to be ready to act and protect. At first, I read Joana as an angry descendant and a psychotic. I watched her carefully because I didn't want to fail in protecting you."

"By the way, there is also another protector that has been helping me. She is also a relative of ours. Her official name is the 'watcher'. She is a computer wizard and tracts people. She helps me to know where any one person is and what they are doing. She uses hotel reservations, airline tickets, traffic cameras, social media, and probably a bunch of tools that I know nothing about. When I was following Matt, she was tracking Joana along with you and Jason."

"Anyway, as I followed and watched Joana I kept getting a more and more confused feeling about her. Don't ask me why, it just happened. My approach to her changed from wary to caring about what had happened to her. Of course, when she grabbed you and held the knife to your throat, I was ready to take her down in order to protect you. But, once that was done, I wasn't going to let her die, so, well, I did this." He pointed to the bandages. Just then they all heard the helicopter approaching.

"Nicole. Please take over. I need to guide the helicopter to a landing spot."

Nicole stepped in and applied pressure while Jason followed Kevin to a clearing that was free of the large stones and boulders. They stood to the side and watched as the helicopter landed.

Once down, Hugin jumped out, bent over, and ran to Kevin. He shook his hand then turned to Jason. "Hello. I am Hugin. I hope Kevin has filled you in on me and my involvement here."

"He has. Come. Let's get moving. We need to get Joana to a hospital."

They all moved quickly away while the pilot kept the helicopter ready to depart. Once they were at the camp site, Jason and Kevin began to fashion a liter to use to carry Joana to the helicopter. They used one of the sleeping bags and several of the tent poles. Once completed, Jason and Kevin gently lifted Joana onto it while Nicole continued to apply pressure to her wound.

It was a good thing she was small because they were barely able to wedge her onto the floor between the forward seats and the back seats. Jason held Kevin's arm and shouted over the noise. "Nicole and I will wait here. There is no room for us. We'll be fine."

Kevin nodded and climbed in the back with Joana. Hugin sat in front next to the pilot. Jason and Nicole stepped well back and the pilot lifted the craft into the air and turned back toward Reykjavik. Hugin put on the headset and motioned for Kevin to do the same.

Once they were both on the radio, Hugin said, "I have contacted the Landspitali University Hospital and told them that we would be arrived with an emergency patient. I told them that there had been an accident when a gun accidentally went off." He glanced over his seat back at Kevin, who nodded.

XXXXX

Jason and Nicole made their way back to the camp. They each sat on one of the small rocks littered around the area. Jason started. "Wow. That was a lot to take in. I actually believe Kevin's explanation of his role and of Hugin's relationship to us, but it is still bizarre to think that this whole revenge thing has continued for a 1000 years. It is also amazing that we have met two more of our family's descendants."

"I know. And to think, Kevin and his ancestors have been protecting our families for those 1000 years."

They were both quiet for a few minutes just looking around the area.

Nicole finally asked, "Well, what now?" She looked at the mess that their camp had become.

"I think that we should pack up and head for the car. We only have the one sleeping bag and tent, so even if we did decide to share, there just isn't enough room. I say we pack up what we can in my backpack and put the items from the cave in your backpack."

"I agree. How about, I will start packing up our stuff in your pack and you can take mine up and pack the cave items. Take whatever is left here that you think will help to protect whatever items you took out of the cave."

They both stood and started moving. Jason grabbed some shirts and the sleeping bag, stuffed them into his pack and headed up the trail. He turned about two meters up the mountain and said, "Try to save some room for the shovel and pick."

"Okay." He headed up and she bent down to dismantle the remaining tent.

An hour later, they were heading across the rocky field to their rental car. They figured they'd arrive at the car just about the time the sun drops behind the hills to the west.

Their trek was purposeful and they said little to each other along the way. Just as it was getting almost too dark to see where they were stepping, they arrived at the road and their car. They loaded the packs into the trunk, got in, Jason pulled out onto the road, turned, and headed back to Reykjavik.

XXXXX

Matt finally grew tired of pacing during the day. He got drunk last night at the Hard Rock and woke up this morning with a headache and was now pacing again. He stopped in the middle of the room and made a decision. He would go to the hotel where Jason and Nicole were staying and watch for them. Maybe they would show and maybe they would not. Regardless, it was better than this. He'd watch for a couple of days then decide what to do from there.

XXXXX

When they arrived late yesterday afternoon, the hospital's emergency room staff met them and took Joana into triage.

Hugin told Kevin that he would handle the hospital's questions about their arrival and the circumstances around the injury. When Kevin looked at him with a worried face, Hugin smiled and winked.

"Hugin. Is Matt still here? I don't remember if you told me anything new about him."

"He is still here and he now has a gun."

"Hmm. Okay. Tell Nicole that she can call Ingvill, but tell her to make sure that Ingvill stays in Oslo." Hugin nodded.

As the staff took Joana away and Kevin followed, Hugin thanked the pilot and gave him a very generous tip. The pilot raised his eyebrows at the amount, but didn't try to give it back. He just smiled and waved as Hugin wandered into the hospital reception area.

He looked around and saw Dag sitting in one of the chairs reading a magazine from the rack. He walked over and sat down next to him. "Thank you so much for your help, Dag. Without your help, I fear my friend's life would be in grave danger. There will be a bonus included in your next payment."

"Thank you so much Mr. Wilkinson. Your generosity is humbling and I am grateful that I was able to help." He shifted in his seat then turned back to Hugin. "Then, it was an accident with a gun?"

"Yes. Poor dear. Mr. Swanson had it along with him since they were very far out into the Skjaldbreizzur area and he had his two female friends along. He felt the need to be fully equipped to protect them should something become a threat to them."

"Well, Miss Wells, who has no experience with weapons of any kind, found it in his backpack while searching for an energy bar. She pulled it out and held it up to look at it. When he saw her holding it, he told her, I fear too loudly, to put it down. His voice must have startled her and she dropped it and, as you might guess, it went off. It struck her in her right side but, fortunately, Mr. Rivers was nearby and immediately came to her aid."

"Mr. Rivers was in the American military. Infantry, I believe was his specialty. He has years of experience with weapons and treating wounds. Thank goodness, I might add. He went into action right away. He treated her wound, set about making a stretcher, and instructing the others on their duties. He was able to contact me because Jason and I are related and have been sharing family histories over the past few years."

He stopped and shook his head sadly. "I do hope Miss Wells is in no danger." He looked at Dag with the question he did not want to verbalize but asked with his look.

Dag nodded. "Oh, I think Miss Wells will be treated well by all who meet her. She is in very good hands and no one seems very interested in the circumstances surrounding this terrible accident anyway. After all, these things happen."

"Yes. Yes, they do, unfortunately."

"Well, I must run. Business calls me. It was lovely to see you, sir, and I hope to see you again soon."

"I too am glad to have gotten a chance to see you too, even though in not the best of circumstances. Perhaps, I can pop over in a few months for a nice dinner one evening."

"Til, then." Dag shook Hugin's hand and exited the hospital.

Hugin thought as he watched him leave, *I will, of course, pay for his dinner. Such a helpful man.*

Just then, Kevin came into the room. He moved to Hugin and motioned him outside. Once outside, he asked, "Is everything taken care of?"

"Yes. My colleague was most helpful and Joana will not be hampered with any additional treatments or paperwork."

Kevin reached for Hugin's hand with both of his and shook it. "Thanks. I really, really appreciate your help. I don't know what we would have done had you not been here in Reykjavik."

"Yes, well, thank you for your kind words, but this is what family does for each other. We help in whatever way we can." He paused then said, "Matt has a weapon in his room. I am really worried about him." He chose not to mention that he was about to get a weapon too.

Kevin frowned and looked down at his feet. "This is a very troubling turn, and I don't like it at all. He now bears even more careful watching. I'm afraid that you will need to do the watching, at least until I can get Joana back on her feet and on our side. If I can't get her to give up the revenge vow then I'll have to do something else."

He sighed. "Anyway, I am going to stay here with her. They said they would let me stay since she is an American and I am her only relative." He smiled. "I told them that I was her step-brother and that we were on vacation here."

Hugin smiled. "Yes. We must sometimes improvise in order to accomplish worthy goals. Don't worry. I will watch Matt and as well as Jason and Nicole. They should be getting back sometime this evening. Do you think I should stay at the apartment or move back to the hotel?"

"I think you should move back to the hotel so that you are closer to the two of them."

"I agree. I will move as soon as possible after I leave here. I'll also try to meet them as they come back to the hotel. Should I update them on all of these developments?"

Kevin mulled for a moment. "I think you should. They have been brought into this fully since seeing what happened out at the mountain, so they should know about Matt, the gun and me staying with Joana."

"Okay. Keep me informed of your progress with Joana and I will let you know when I can about Matt's actions." At that he walked to a taxi queue and got into the first one in line.

Kevin went up to Joana's room and quietly entered. She was awake and her eyes went wide when she saw him. He quickly moved to her side and began talking to her gently.

Thirty-nine

Decision Time

Jason and Nicole arrived back at the hotel just before midnight. They parked in an area that the hotel designated for its guests. They sorted through the two packs and put whatever clothes they had left into the pack with the items from the cave and left the camping stuff in the trunk. They'd return that stuff tomorrow and pay for the damages and missing items.

They headed into the hotel, went to reception, reserved two rooms, and went straight for the elevator.

Hugin was sitting in the hotel bar drinking tea when they came in. As they stood at the elevator, he walked over and quietly said, "Let's go to one of your rooms quietly."

They said nothing more at the elevator door and stayed quiet until they entered Jason's room. At that point, both Jason and Nicole started asking questions, most of them about Joana.

Hugin filled them in on the flight, the status of Joana, and what Kevin was doing. "Now, I must tell you about Matt. He is staying at a small hotel about a kilometer from here but he knows where we are staying so he will probably be watching for you. He doesn't know me yet so I can move about freely around him. The bad news is that he has acquired a gun."

Neither Jason nor Nicole looked surprised. Hugin figured that because of all that has happened in the past few days, the surprise emotion has probably been knocked out of them.

"I imagine that Kevin would be glad to hear that you two are okay. So, I will call him tomorrow."

Nicole said, "I want to see Joana. I want to tell her how sorry I am that all of this has happened."

"I want to see her too." Jason added.

"Well, I suppose that will be okay, but we'll need to check with the hospital. I think many hospitals limit the number of people who can go to a patient's room. However, we need not worry about that now. I am sure you are both tired and would like to get some sleep. I am staying here as well one floor below you. Here is my room number." He handed them a slip of paper with his room number and his phone number. "Call or come by anytime. Shall we plan to meet in the morning at the restaurant, say about 8?"

Nicole looked at Jason, he nodded, and told Hugin, "Sure. We'll meet you there."

As Hugin headed for the door, he turned and asked, "By the way did you find the cave?"

Jason smiled and nodded. "And, the treasure. As a matter of fact, we brought some with us to show to whoever we will eventually need to get approval from in order to set up an archaeological dig operation."

Hugin nodded, thought a moment then said, "I think I might be able to help with that. Please do not talk about this with anyone until we have a chance to talk again. Okay?"

"Sure." Jason looked at Nicole then back at Hugin. "We were actually hoping you'd say something like that."

Hugin nodded again and left.

Nicole turned to Jason, "Wow, these past twenty-four hours have been crazy. I mean, a knife at my throat, a treasure, two relatives we knew nothing about, Joana getting shot, what else can happen?"

"Now, you've done it. By saying that, you've now jinxed us to have something worse happen." Nicole looked crestfallen. Jason quickly added, "Sorry. I'm just kidding. That kind of thinking is dumb."

"Okay. Well, I think I'm going to go to my room. I am really tired."

"I'll walk over with you."

They headed out and stopped at Nicole's door. She opened it and turned back to Jason. Without hesitation, they both hugged and kissed. They slowly eased away from each other and Nicole entered her room. Jason stood a moment then went back to his room.

Hugin let himself into his room and immediately checked his computer for messages. He had one from Winston. It told Hugin to be at the port at 6:00 am and to look for a fishing vessel by the name 'Jasmine'. The captain will have a package for him. Hugin smiled. Jasmine was Winston's daughter's name.

XXXXX

Kevin held Joana and stroked her hair while quietly reassuring her that she was fine and everything was going to be okay. He finally felt the tension go out of her. He stood then sat on the bed next to her. He reached out and gently held her hand.

Joana stared at him for a long time. *Who is this guy? He shot me. Now he is comforting me. The only time a man has ever comforted me was when they wanted something from me, usually sex. Well, he'll get nothing from me, especially that.*

Kevin watched her as she stared at him. He noticed the hardness come back into her face, especially in her eyes.

"Joana, my name is Kevin and I have been told about your family's vow of revenge against Jason's family." He decided to keep this simple and not talk about Nicole's relationship to the family as well as his and Hugin's.

"My family has known Jason's for some years and I have sometimes traveled with Jason. I served in the Army's Special Services units so I have lots of skills. I met Nicole a year or so ago and I like her, she is a nice girl. In fact, I am pretty sure she and Jason like each other." He smiled a little shyly.

"Anyway, I decided to make this trip with Jason. But, then all these dangerous things started to happen to him and Nicole, and I became concerned. I followed them when they suddenly left on the camping trip. I was worried. When I saw you following them, I reacted too quickly and I am very sorry for that. I should have a approached you and tried to talk to you. Again, I am sorry."

"When I woke in the ravine, I became very worried and rushed to catch up to them, and that was when I saw you hiding. I was confused. I didn't know at the time if you were a friend trying to surprise them or someone who was lost or, well, someone wanting to harm them. So, I just stayed quiet and watched."

"When you suddenly grabbed Nicole, I was scared." He squeezed her hand. "You know what I mean? Here was someone I didn't know threatening my friend and I was scared." He looked down and mumbled. "Again. I am very, very sorry." He felt a very slight squeeze back from Joana.

"I mean, you were holding a knife at her throat. You were yelling. I always carry a gun – force of habit, I guess. I pulled it out but I didn't want to shoot you. I really didn't. Please believe me." This was the most truthful statement so far. He slowly reached his other hand over and lightly touched her cheek. "I really, really, really am so sorry."

"As soon as the gun went off, I ran to you. I held you and talked to you and told you over and over how sorry I was. Then, you fell to the ground and I saw the blood and I grabbed whatever I could to stop the bleeding. Then Nicole came over and helped me. She held your hand and put pressure on the wound so I could call for help."

He let go of her hand and put his hands on each side of her face. He leaned down and kissed her cheek. "Please believe me. I am truly sorry and will do everything I can to make sure you get better." At this point, he moved off the bed and plopped into the chair across the room and dropped his face into his hands just above his knees. He wasn't making any of this up. He felt horrible.

He knew that the revenge vow had driven her to this point in her life. She was too young to be mixed up in this. She should be dating and enjoying her friends. Then, he suddenly looked up. Had he heard something? Then, he heard his name spoken very softly.

"Kevin." Joana tried a little louder. Her throat was sore from lack of use and whatever else she had been given by the doctors and nurses.

"Kevin, please come here." He quickly came over and stood by her bed. She reached up and took his hand. She pulled on it until he sat on the bed again and she let it go.

"Kevin." Her voice was getting better. "Please lie next to me."

He was taken back at first but then he slipped his legs up and nuzzled up against her. Joana moved her arm up and around his neck. She laid her hand on his check. He moved his left hand up and across her chest just above the wound.

He had no idea how long he laid that way but when he woke, Joana was sleeping quietly. He glanced at her face. It looked so peaceful and serene. He put his head back down in the crook of her arm and closed his eyes.

He next woke up to Joana stroking his cheek. When he opened his eyes, she was staring at him and smiling. He smiled back. Joana asked him, "Help me to sit up."

He quickly got off of the bed and gently put his arm under her shoulders with his hand lodged in the armpit of her right arm. He used his other hand to push the pillows back up and against the headboard then he eased her back against it. "How is that? Do you feel okay? Here let me get you some water. It is just over there on the small table." He got her a cup of water, came back and handed it to her.

She took several sips and handed it back to him. He set it on the table next to the bed. "Are you hungry? Let me go get something for you." He turned.

"Kevin, please sit with me but not on the bed. Pull up the chair and sit facing me. I like looking at you." She smiled.

Kevin pulled the chair over and sat. He reached over and held her hand. She squeezed it as soon as he held hers.

She looked at him for a minute or so. "I am going to tell you about my life. I will not ask you about yours. I don't care. I have already guessed that you are more than 'just a friend' but truly," and she squeezed his hand again, "I do not care what you did before or why you were in Iceland or why you are hanging around with Jason and Nicole. I only care about you now, right now. I like you. I really like you. This person is the one I want to know." A tear rolled down her cheek. Kevin felt that he should leave it there.

She looked away then back at him. "As I said, I have surmised some things about you and this whole situation and part of it is that you already know about the revenge vow my idiotic ancestors started. My father told me about it because he had no male children, just me. When he told me, I only half listened. It sounded crazy to me but, I pretended to take it seriously."

"Now, I am going to tell you the rest of my story. Maybe hearing it, you'll understand a little better why I am at this point in my life." She told him about her childhood and the horrible way her father treated her. She told him about the rapes and the other men and her sixteenth birthday 'present'. She watched the expression on Kevin's face darken, especially in his eyes. She told him about running away and living on the streets and doing whatever she could, in order to survive. She told him about the stuff she learned – martial arts, computer hacking, picking locks – and how these all came at a price.

Kevin looked on in horror as she related her story. He tried to be an impassive listener but it was hard. He wanted to go back to that time and give her father a piece of his mind and, well, some, no a lot, of physical pain. As she continued he thought, *How did she even make it this far in her life? I can't, won't, let anything like this happen to her ever again. There was once a sweet kid in her but that life has been beaten into a small pebble deep inside of her. She will be that little girl again someday.*

She told him about meeting Matt and his story about the treasure and the Vikings. "I thought briefly that he might be a descendant of the old Viking but then he went on about what he was going to do with it and I realized he was just a greedy bastard out for some easy money."

"I followed him to the dig, and on the day he ran away. I stole the copper sheet from him and almost beat him to death. I found out about Dr. Ingvill and found her in Oslo. She must have guessed that I was up to no good," She smiled at Kevin and he grinned. "Anyway, she took off and met up with Nicole. Nicole ended up with the translation and we all ended up on the mountain. Then, of course, you showed up and I ended up here." Kevin looked aside.

Joana let go of his hand and reached over to stroke his cheek. She winced at the pain but she smiled at Kevin who had turned back at her touch. She looked at him for a second. "And, it has been the best twenty-four hours I have ever spent in my entire miserable life. And, Kevin, I have you to thank. So, thank you. Now lean up close so I can give you a kiss on the cheek."

Kevin quickly stood and leaned toward Joana. She winced but held his face in her hands and pulled his forehead to her mouth and kissed it, then she moved his face a little to the side and kissed his right cheek, then she moved it the other way and kissed his left cheek.

She sat back, let go and Kevin saw the tears roll down her cheeks. Kevin leaned in and kissed those away.

Kevin sat back on the chair and held her hand again. After a couple of minutes, he looked at her and asked, "Well, Joana, what do we do now?"

"I would like to get the hell out of here and go see Jason and Nicole. I need to tell them that I am sorry."

Kevin nodded. "I think we can manage that."

"I knew you were a man of action." She smiled as he stood and headed to the door.

Forty

The Visit

Kevin forgot that it was late evening when he told Joana that she could leave. He was reminded when he went to the reception desk in the hospital.

"May I help you?" The receptionist asked when he arrived.

"Yes. I am wondering if Miss Joana Wells can be released. She really wants to get back to her room to continue her recovery. She is actually feeling very good and believes she will be fine."

"I am sorry, sir. There are two issues here. It is past 10:00 pm so we would not be able to process a release until tomorrow morning. Also, our liability coverage instructs us that we must always keep anyone who has been admitted into the facility for care by a doctor, under watch for a minimum of twenty-four hours." She gave him a weak smile and said, "Sorry."

Kevin nodded and went back to Joana's room. He knocked lightly then entered. "Sorry. The rules say that you must stay here for a minimum of twenty-four hours. We arrived around 5:00 pm today, so we'll get you out as soon as we can tomorrow afternoon."

Joana nodded sadly then smiled. "Will you be able to stay with me tonight?"

"No. Sorry. They have been generous so far, letting me stay well past the visiting time. Besides, I need to see Hugin and talk to him about what we can do next to get you home." He immediately regretted saying that. Joana looked away. She had no home.

"I'm sorry. We'll figure something out. I also need to check on the status of Matt. He is still out there and I am worried about him."

Joana turned back to him, nodded, and looked away.

Kevin quickly went to her bed. He sat and laid his hand on her shoulder. He gently turned her to look at him. He was smiling. "Joana. I will not abandon you, ever. I am your friend and I think you know that you can trust anything I say." He held her stare.

She reached up and stroked his cheek. She smiled. "I do know that. I don't know why but I trust you, which is strange for me. In my entire life, I have never trusted a man to tell me the truth. In my experience, they always lie. I guess I am just nervous and scared about my future."

"Hey. Hey. You have me now. You have Jason and Nicole. You even have Hugin. We are your team now. We are your friends. You do not need to worry ever again about whether or not you have a friend to help you." He leaned over and kissed her on her forehead.

He slowly moved off the bed. "Get some sleep. We'll probably be busy tomorrow." He turned and left the room.

Joana gave a sigh and closed her eyes. *Yes, sleep would feel good.*

XXXXX

Kevin knocked on Hugin's door. Hugin opened it. "Please. Come in, Kevin."

Kevin followed Hugin to the small table and sat in the lone chair. Hugin asked, "Tea?"

"Beer?"

Hugin smiled and grabbed two beers from the small refrigerator. He handed one to Kevin and sat on the edge of his bed. He held his bottle out to Kevin, who tapped it with his.

After they both had a good swig, Kevin started. "How do you know Kevin has a gun?"

"I followed him the other day and he stopped at a house then went inside. He exited with it, and must have bought it from someone in there. I have not seen it, except for the infrared view that shows him waving and holding it. Obviously, I cannot see the gun itself. I can only form an opinion about it based on the circumstantial evidence of the meeting with someone, the package, and him waving it back and forth."

Kevin nodded. "There is no doubt in my mind that he has one. My concern now is how does he intend to use it? Maybe you should go back to the apartment and continue watching him."

"Okay. I'll go back there tomorrow morning, early. I didn't exactly check out. I also left my equipment in the room."

"Good. By the way, Joana is doing very well and I think she has truly given up the whole family revenge vow. She wanted to check out this evening because she is desperate to see Jason and Nicole in order to apologize. But, I checked, and she cannot check out until she has been there for twenty-four hours."

Hugin thought a moment then said, "I could try to talk to my contacts here and get her released early."

"No, that's okay. She will get better rest there than back here in a hotel room. I'll reserve a room for her adjoining mine. I want to keep an eye on her. I worry that she might crack at some point or, of course, that Matt will show up."

"Well, I can warn you if Matt leaves his room, and if he does, I will follow him and give you updates."

"Thanks, Hugin. You've done so much for us in this. You are a true friend."

"Nonsense. We are all family."

"Well, thanks anyway. By the way, I cannot share the details, but Joana has been through hell her whole life. It is a wonder that she has survived this long."

"Yes, I can only guess at her trials and tribulations, especially as a young girl. But, she seems to be very resourceful and strong, and I am glad that you were there to help her." Hugin then remembered. "Oh, Jason and Nicole want to see her as well. I was planning to take them over tomorrow. But, now that you are here and I must watch Matt, maybe you can take them to see her sometime tomorrow morning."

"Sure. Joana will be happy to see them. Okay. I had better go downstairs and secure rooms for Joana and me. You have my stuff right?"

"Yes. I brought it all here when I came back." He walked to his closet and grabbed Kevin's pack. "Here you go."

"Thanks. See you tomorrow, maybe."

"Yes. Maybe. I'll be busy watching Matt."

Kevin went to the lobby and booked two adjoining rooms. Once he had the keys, he went to his room, showered, and climbed into bed.

Forty-one

The Next Day

Hugin was up early. He packed a few items and headed to the apartment, which was actually on the way to the port. At 5:00 am he arrived at the apartment, dropped his bag on the bed, and immediately proceeded to turn on his surveillance equipment. Once it was up and running, he left for the port and the Jasmine.

He arrived at the port about ten minutes prior to the arrival of the Jasmine. As he waited, he thought again about his idea to start a security service with Kevin. He was excited about the idea but unsure what Kevin would think. He wondered if Joana might … He heard a boat horn.

Hugin turned and scanned the port. He saw her. The Jasmine was just now pulling into a berth about 100 meters away so he headed in that direction. As he arrived, so did the port authority representative, who boarded the Jasmine, and spent about fifteen minutes chatting with the captain and getting signatures on various documents, then he left.

The captain eventually came down to the dock and walked over to Hugin. Hugin noticed that he had a small backpack with him. He approached Hugin. "Mr. Wilkinson? I am Donald."

"Nice to meet you, Donald. Shall we sit? There is a small coffee shop a short distance away."

"Yes. That would be splendid."

Hugin led him around a corner and down another block to a small coffee shop set in the ground floor corner of a large apartment building. They entered, ordered coffee then sat in the back corner.

Hugin asked about the journey and the weather. Donald asked him about his time in Iceland and the weather. Their coffee arrived and they each took a sip.

As they were sipping the coffee and exchanging idle chatter, Donald nonchalantly opened the backpack and removed another one that was folded in half. He placed it on the seat next to his. After another few sips of coffee, they rose, shook hands, and exited, each grabbing a backpack. Donald headed back to the boat and Hugin headed to his apartment.

He arrived at 7:00 am and quickly checked the camera. The infrared still showed Matt in his bed. He moved to the table in the corner and opened the backpack. He pulled out a box that was wrapped like a birthday present. It even had a bright pink ribbon.

He removed the ribbon, and the paper, and opened the box. He pulled out a solid object nestled inside of what looked like a small, thin towel. He removed the towel and set the shiny 22 revolver on the table. He looked in the box and pulled out another heavy object wrapped in cloth. He removed the cloth and found a box of ammunition. There was also an envelope that contained all of the required paperwork, including a medical authorization and a sports club membership.

He had been raised around guns, and had often gone with his father, grandfather and cousins out to ranges for shooting practice. He had handled many types of weapons over the years, and was very familiar with the 22 revolver. He made sure the safety was on then loaded the gun.

XXXXX

Joana had had a fitful sleep for the first three hours. She kept having dreams of her father that caused her to wake startled. She would jerk awake then softly cry out with pain as her side reminded her that she had been shot. But, each dream became shorter and less about her father and more about her.

She didn't know how long it had been since the last nightmare but she felt well rested as she turned her head and saw Kevin sitting on the chair watching her. She smiled at him.

Kevin rose and came over to the side of her bed. "How are you feeling this morning, Miss Sleeping Beauty?"

She couldn't help it. She started to cry. She had never ever been called a beauty, let alone a character like Sleeping Beauty. She had seen the cartoon story once when she was a little girl.

"I'm sorry. I didn't mean to upset you." Kevin blathered.

"No. No. I am fine. I, it, oh, I'm just emotional. That's all."

"Okay. Did you sleep well?"

"Better than I have in a long time." She looked at the small clock on the little table and saw that it was only 7:00 am. "How did you get in here? Don't visiting hours start at 10:00 am?"

"They start at 9:00 am but the receptionist felt generous toward me, I guess."

"Yes. You seem to have that way with people, especially the young ladies."

"Okay. Okay. Flattery will get you anything. Now, I met with Hugin and he said that Jason and Nicole would like to see you too. Here is my question, do you want me to go pick them up later this morning or would you rather wait and meet with them when you are checked out of here?"

Joana thought a moment then, "I'll wait until we can get out of here. I'd like to eventually take a shower and change." She looked under the covers and saw that she was dressed in a hospital gown. She looked over at Kevin and sheepishly grinned.

He saw her look and knew exactly what she was thinking. "I assume you do not want to put on your bloody clothes. I also assume that your other clothes are somewhere out in the wilderness with your stolen bike." He saw her give him a look which he gave right back.

"Yea, I stole it. Maybe we can leave 'an anonymous tip' with the police about where it is? The few items of clothing there are worth nothing to me."

"Sure. We can do that. Would you like me to go shopping for you? I could also ask Nicole to come along. You know, just to have a woman's viewpoint on the items I pick out."

"Sure. By the way, when can I check out?"

"I'll ask when I go back downstairs. I'll also ask them to send you a clean hospital gown and some soap and shampoo."

"Thanks." Kevin smiled and turned to leave. She grabbed his hand and pulled him over for a hug.

He finally moved away and smiled. "See you soon. Any preferences for the clothes?" She shook her head no and he left.

XXXXX

Kevin arrived back at the hotel and entered the lobby. He looked into the restaurant and saw Jason and Nicole, so he went to their table, and they made room for him to sit.

Nicole said, "Wow, you were up early."

"I went to the hospital to check on Joana.   She's doing really well and wants to check out as soon as possible."

"When will they let her check out?" Nicole asked.

"I convinced them to let her out at 2:00 pm. It's earlier than they like but they agreed that she was responding well to her treatment so they said okay. By the way, Nicole, she asked if you and I wouldn't mind doing some shopping for her. She has nothing to wear except for her bloody clothes."

"Absolutely. I'd love to help find some cute outfits for her. When do you want to head out?"

"Give me an hour. I need to shower and change. I also need to check with Hugin on Matt's activities. Hugin moved back to his apartment so that he can watch him for us. But, even so, you guys need to be careful. He is out there and he is armed. I am very worried about him and you should be too. Do not, I repeat, do not simply go out without contacting me."

"Hugin and I are in direct communication so we should always know Matt's whereabouts. However, that is no guarantee. He slipped away on Hugin once before and he might do it again. And, I repeat, he is armed. The fact that he purchased an illegal weapon tells me that he is serious about inflicting grievous injury on someone. Understand?"

"Yes." Jason looked at Nicole as he said it. "We will always talk to you before going anywhere. Is there a way for us to call you or Hugin?"

"Sure." He gave them his and Hugin's cell numbers. "Okay. I'll come to your room, Nicole, when I'm ready to go shopping."

XXXXX

Matt finally rousted himself from bed at 11:00 am. He really needed to stop hitting the bars until they finally closed. He moved slowly to the bathroom and spent another half hour in there shaving, showering and other stuff. He came out and checked that the gun was still hidden well back in the small closet. He let housekeeping in twice to clean, and to change the sheets and towels, but he stayed in the room the whole time.

He finally headed out but not before hanging the "Do Not Disturb" sign on the door. It was close to 1:00 pm and his plan was to go to the hotel again to watch for any of them to return. He had been doing that for the past three days with no luck. It was getting close to the end of his funds, and he hoped he'd finally see them today or tomorrow.

XXXXX

Hugin watched Matt move to his door and step out. He grabbed his bag and headed down the stairs to the front door of the building. He watched Matt walk out and turn right toward the city center. When Matt was fifty meters away, he began to follow him.

As Hugin walked along the shaded street he pulled out his phone and called Kevin. When Kevin picked up, Hugin quickly told him that Matt was on the move. Kevin had just left Nicole after shopping for Joana's clothes, so he quickly turned back and went up to Jason's room.

Jason let him in and he saw that Nicole was there too. Kevin started. "Good. You are both here. Hugin reports that Matt is out and headed this way. Please stay here until I come back to your room. Can I borrow your rental?"

Jason handed him the keys and told him where to find it. "Good. I am going to take this stuff to Joana then check her out and come back here." He turned and headed out the door.

Forty-two

The Meeting

Once Kevin left, Jason looked over at Nicole. They had been reviewing the items he had brought out of the cave. They were trying to determine the value, provenance, and origin of each item. The coins and jewelry, especially those made of gold or silver, would be worth a good bit both to collectors and to those who would simply want to extract the gold and silver from them.

The ceramic objects, non-precious metal coins and jewelry, and other objects could have little value or a great deal depending on what they represented to a collector. Was the object from a royal household? Was it very old? Did it have a special relationship to an actual event? All of these questions would need a lot more time to determine.

Based on what they had brought out and what they estimated remained behind, they figured the total value could vary from a couple of hundred thousand dollars to five times that figure. Experts would need to be brought in to make that determination.

"Do you think Hugin will be able to help us get the permits and licenses to operate a dig at the cave?" Nicole had no idea what was involved.

"I really don't know but I do know that we would be lost if we tried to do it on our own."

Nicole was quiet then asked Jason, "What are you going to say when we meet Joana? I mean, what do you say to someone who took a vow to kill you?"

Jason smiled. "Well, I've never had to deal with a situation like this before so I guess I'll just 'wing it'"

"I think I will say something like, 'I am glad that she is okay and that I hope we can be friends'."

"Sounds good to me. The way Kevin talks about her, I think she is remorseful for her role in this and really wants to turn her life around. I mean, Kevin couldn't even tell us about it since it was so bad. I really feel badly for her and I really do not want to continue this revenge stuff."

"I guess we'll see what happens in an hour or so."

XXXXX

Hugin followed Matt to the hotel where Matt entered and sat at the bar. Hugin stood outside for about fifteen minutes. While waiting he texted Kevin to let him know where Matt was located. Once finished, he entered and went to the reception desk to ask for a newspaper. Once he had it, he went into the restaurant and sat on the opposite side from Matt. He ordered a tea and began reading the paper.

XXXXX

Kevin had just pulled up to the hospital when he received Hugin's text. He read it, thought about it then entered the hospital. He went to Joana's room, knocked lightly, and she called him in. He entered and saw her sitting on the edge of the bed swinging her feet back and forth. She smiled when he entered.

He walked to her bed and set the bag of clothes on it. She jumped down and came next to him in order to see what was in it. He could feel her body touching him along his arm and hip. He turned to the side so he could watch her root through the clothes.

She looked at the items for a minute or so then turned to face him. She smiled and hugged him. She had done it so quickly, she had pinned his arms to his sides so he couldn't return the gesture. She was warm and her hair smelled of lilacs. It was still a little wet. She felt and smelled good and he was relieved when she moved away.

"Did we do a good job?"

"Oh, my goodness. Everything is perfect. I love it. Thank you so much. She hugged him again but this time he had his arms free so he returned it.

She finally stepped back over to the clothes and began selecting her wardrobe for the day. She picked out a light blue blouse with short sleeves. She chose a pair of skinny jeans that had blue stitching along both legs and a tiny stitched design of a dragonfly on the back just below the belt line in the middle of her butt. She grabbed a bra and a pair of panties.

He moved to the chair to wait until she came out of the bathroom, except she did not go into the bathroom. She turned her back to him and pulled the panties up under the hospital gown. She put the bra on under the gown then took it off and set it aside. Still with her back to him, she put on the blouse then the jeans.

When she was finished, she turned to Kevin. "How do I look?"

She looked really, really pretty. "You are still as beautiful as you were when I saw you this morning."

She smiled and came over to him in the chair. "Really? You are not just saying it are you?"

"Do you remember that I told you I would be your friend for life? Well, I grew up in a home where you never lie to your friends and family. So, yes, you are really beautiful."

She leaned over and kissed him on the lips. It was quick and light. She turned and stared at herself in the mirror.

"When can we go see Jason and Nicole?"

"They told me they would give you an early release because you have healed so well. However, I am sure that they will have you sign some forms that say if anything goes wrong with the wound after you leave, you can't blame it on them and sue them.

She waved that off and said nothing.

"Why don't you get you stuff together then we'll head to the reception area and get you out of here."

Joana grabbed the bag he had brought and put the rest of her new clothes in it. She slipped on the cute sneakers Nicole had picked out, and looked over at the closet where her old clothes were folded and placed on a shelf. The hospital had cleaned them for her, and brought them in along with the clean gown Kevin had asked for. She stared at the items then moved to them, picked them up and dropped them in the trash.

She turned to Kevin and said. "A new life does not need old clothes." She walked by him into the hallway, and he followed.

XXXXX

As they drove to the hotel, Kevin filled Joana in on what had been happening over the past twenty-four hours. He told her that Matt had a gun and was now waiting in the bar in the hotel lobby. He said that he didn't think he was carrying the gun now but, even so, they needed to avoid him.

They pulled up to the back of the hotel, went in through the back door, and headed up the stairs to their rooms, one floor below Jason and Nicole. He handed her the key to her room and she entered. He moved to the adjoining door and opened her side. His side was already open.

"I hope you don't mind that we leave these open. I feel it is safer until we can figure out what to do about Matt."

Joana thought it was so cute that he cared so much about her privacy and security. She smiled. "I definitely do not mind. I feel much better knowing that you are close by."

Kevin nodded and turned to go into his room. *Did she have a twinkle in her eyes when she said that?* He shook his head and let her in just to show her around.

When she turned back to him, he asked "Would you like to go meet Jason and Nicole now? I know they are anxious to see you."

She heaved a big sigh and said, "Yes. I am ready."

They exited her room and headed for the stairs. They went up one floor and entered the hallway. Joana's heart was beating like crazy. Kevin stopped at a door and turned to her. She nodded. He knocked.

The door opened within seconds. Jason smiled. "Please come in."

Joana entered first followed by Kevin, and Jason closed the door behind them. Nicole immediately came over to Joana and took her into a tight hug. She whispered, "I am so glad you are okay. You are okay, right? I have been so worried about you. Do you like the clothes? I had to guess on the items."

Kevin finally suggested to Nicole, "You might want to give her a chance to answer one question before asking another."

Nicole let go. "Of course. Of course. Sorry, Joana. Please sit. We brought the extra chairs from my room so we could all sit together."

Joana took the seat that Nicole had indicated. Once Jason and Nicole were seated, Kevin turned to go. They all said at the same time, "No. Kevin. Stay."

He stopped and turned. Joana was especially imploring him to stay. "Okay." He sat in the only empty chair left.

Joana started. "First of all, I want to sincerely apologize for the past troubles I caused all of you, and, frankly, many others who are not here." They started to say something and she waved them off. "Please let me say my piece before I start crying and run away." They sat quietly. Joana looked at Kevin. "Did you tell them what I told you about my life?"

He shrugged then said, "Some. Not much."

She smiled at him. She knew that meant that he hadn't told them much at all. She turned to Jason and Nicole. "I know that you, Jason, are descended from Pajackok and that you, Nicole, are descended from Alsoomsa. I am, as you know, descended from Megadagik. The family vow of revenge and the story behind it was passed down to me as it was to you." They nodded slightly.

"When I heard it, I thought it was so stupid. I couldn't believe that, supposedly intelligent people somewhere along the way, didn't put a stop to it. Although, I found out recently that Hugin's family had done just that 400 years ago."

"Anyway, I cared nothing about the revenge thing but I did want the treasure. Here is why I wanted that treasure." She related her life story in the same way with all of the details she had related to Kevin. When she finished, Nicole was beside herself. She started crying at the first mention of the rapes beginning and she never stopped. Jason kept getting more and more angry. Kevin mostly turned away.

She ended it the same way she did with Kevin. "I told Kevin that what all three of you have done for me and shown me over the past twenty-four hours has completely changed my life. The caring and love and concern you have shown me is the first I have ever had in my entire life. I told Kevin that the best thing he did was to shoot me. Since then, these past hours have been the happiest time of my entire miserable life. So, thank you so much for getting me shot." She smiled.

Kevin and Jason smiled back but Nicole jumped of her chair, went to Joana's, knelt down in front of her and pulled her into a hug on the floor. She was crying and that got Joana started. Jason and Kevin watched the two woman quietly.

Joana finally calmed and whispered to Nicole, "Sorry, my wound is still a bit sore."

Nicole quickly pulled away and laughed. Joana did as well. They both sat back in their chairs.

Jason stood and walked to the middle of the room. The rest finally turned to watch him. He looked at Joana. "Joana, let us do what our ancestors did not do." At that he held out his hand.

Joana looked confused then she remembered. She stood and walked to Jason. She stood in front of him and reached for his hand. They slid past their hands and grasped each other's forearm just as would have been done those 1000 years ago if the offer had been taken seriously.

They held it for a minute then slowly let go and came to each other in a hug. Joana whispered, "Never again."

Jason whispered, "Never again."

They all sat back down and began talked about where to eat.

Forty-three

One More Vow

Matt had been good the night before and had gone back to his room shortly after having a late dinner. He was in bead and asleep by 11:00 pm.

He woke at 6:00 am feeling pretty good. He decided the night before that he had to make something happen. He couldn't believe that no one was back yet. He supposed they could have all simply left the country but he didn't think so. He quickly dressed and headed directly to the hotel.

He walked into the lobby and moved quickly to the front desk. He acted all anxious and nervous. When the receptionist approached him he immediately started talking.

"I am sorry but I am very worried. I was out last night with my friends and I am worried about whether they got back here okay. They had a good bit to drink but I finally got them to head back to their hotel. I am staying at a different hotel but I came here with them, told them to get some rest, and I'd see them today."

"As I headed off to my hotel, I turned around to see that they went inside. I saw them heading back to the bar. I caught them and insisted they go to their room but they brushed me off and continued on their way. I was frustrated so I went to my hotel."

"I called about twenty minutes ago and no one answered. Can you check to see that they are even registered here and did not check out and leave, please? They are Jason and Nicole, a young couple, very nice. Thanks."

"Just a moment. They are still checked in and I have seen them a couple of times over the past couple of days. Maybe they were still asleep when you called. I can try for you." She picked up the phone.

"No. No, that will not be necessary. I don't want to wake them. I'll just wait and try later this morning. Thanks. Bye." He walked out.

Now I know they are here. I am sure that they will show themselves sooner or later. He headed to the Restaurant Reykjavik about twenty meters from the front of the hotel. He ordered a coffee and sat by a window.

XXXXX

Hugin woke and went to the equipment to check on Matt. He looked three times through the lens and at the laptop with the infrared reading. Matt was not there. Hugin quickly dressed and started for the hotel. He stopped at the door, turned and retrieved his gun from the closet. He also grabbed his jacket. He put it on and stowed the gun in one of its large pockets. Satisfied, he left.

When he reached the Centerhotel, he walked into the lobby and took the elevator to Kevin's room. It was almost 7:30 so he figured Kevin would be awake. He knocked. Kevin opened the door and Hugin entered.

He saw that the adjoining door was open and he heard the shower running in Joana's room. He followed Kevin to the table and sat in one of the chairs. Kevin sat in the other and asked, "What's wrong?" He figured there was, otherwise Hugin would be busy watching Matt.

"Matt is out on his own. I got up shortly after 6:30 and, as usual, I checked my equipment. Matt is no longer in his room."

Kevin wished now that he had not had to turn his gun over to the police after they explained the 'accident' that happened to Joana.

"My guess is that he is probably watching the hotel. I think we need to move. Would you mind driving Jason's rental to the camping gear rental place and turning the stuff in for them. Since some of it was ruined, there will probably be a charge. Please pay it and I will reimburse you."

"No need. I'll get the key from Jason and do it now." Hugin left for Jason's room.

As the door closed, Kevin heard the shower turn off. After a few minutes, Joana peeked around the corner of the door. "Good morning." She had a towel wrapped around her torso and another one around her hair.

"Good morning. How are you this morning? How is your wound healing?"

"I am doing great and so is the hole in my side. The doctor did a great job with the stitching and it has already stopped seeping out stuff. I'll get dressed and be right back." She headed back into her room.

Kevin smiled the whole time she was looking in his room. But, as soon as she left, he frowned. *This is not good. I think we need to move. When Hugin gets back, he and I will head out to get my bike so I can return it. I can't report it stolen because that would entail another police report.*

Joana finally walked into his room and sat where Hugin had been sitting. "So, what is on our agenda today?"

"Well, unfortunately, I think we need to move somewhere else. Matt knows we are staying here so he will be watching. I don't want to risk one or two of us heading out and him following. I think he intends to hurt someone soon."

"He is tough, that's for sure. I have given him two good beatings and he just keeps coming back." Joana smiled.

"Yea. I beat him up too then tied him in the woods when he was getting too close to Ingvill and Nicole. Yet, here he is again, and with a gun. Hugin saw him buy it."

Joana shook her head. "Oh, that is very bad."

"Let me go get Jason and Nicole so we can discuss how to go about the move." He headed up to their rooms and they all came into Kevin's room fifteen minutes later.

Nicole and Joana hugged and Jason said hello. They all sat. Kevin related the latest developments to Jason and Nicole. "So, I think we need to move somewhere a bit farther away. Maybe we could…" He didn't get to finish. There was a knock on his door. He opened it and Hugin stepped in.

"Good you are all here. I am afraid that Jason needs to return with me to the store. They were very understanding about the damages caused by the fall and rescue." He smiled at his cover story but everyone sat waiting. "Anyway, the store needs the original renter to come by to sign the paperwork."

Kevin stood. "Okay. I will go with Hugin and Jason. While Jason deals with the paperwork, Hugin will take me to my bike so I can return it. Once I have done that, I will return here. It will probably take me much of the day to get there, get back, and return it to the dealer. Hugin will return to Jason and bring him here. While I am gone, please think about someplace that we might go where Matt will not be able to find us. Questions? No? Okay." Jason, Hugin and Kevin headed out.

Once they were all gone, Nicole asked. "Hungry?"

"Starving."

"Let's order room service." Joana grabbed the menu and they made a list of what they wanted.

XXXXX

Matt saw the white car pull up to the hotel. He also saw the man get out and go inside. He thought the guy looked familiar but he could not pull up any memory of him. *Maybe, since he parked at the hotel and has been in there before, he is a guest there. Maybe I have seen him in the restaurant.* He pushed that thought aside and went back to watching the hotel.

He saw the man come back out and pull around the side of the hotel which Matt couldn't see. A few minutes later, he saw him pull back out and turn onto Hafnarstraeti Street. At the turn, the vehicle was only about ten meters in front of him. He saw another man in the passenger seat. The man was looking away but his profile was clear enough for Matt to recognize him. *He is the guy with the car problem who knocked me out and left me in the woods. That driver guy has to be connected to all of this, or at least, to the car problem guy and that is enough for me to want both of them.*

XXXXX

Nicole and Joana finished their breakfasts and sat talking about random topics, but nothing related to any recent events.

Joana finally asked Nicole. "So, did you guys really find the treasure?"

"Yes. Ingvill did a great job translating the copper sheet so we didn't have a problem getting to it. It really is a valuable find. I am sure that if some of the gold coins or jewelry were sold, there would be a good bit of money involved. But, Jason and I feel that the real value is in the historical significance of it." Nicole looked aside.

Joana reached over and touched Nicole's hand. She smiled. "It's okay. I no longer have any interest in it. It has brought only sadness and trouble for me my whole life. I want to move on."

Nicole smiled too. "Hey, let's walk to the National Museum of Iceland. It is only half a kilometer from here."

"What about Matt? Kevin said that he is out there watching the hotel. How can we get out?"

"There is a back way. It lets out on a side street that can't be seen from the front of the hotel. We can also cover our hair and faces as much as possible to hide our identities."

"I don't know. I feel a little scared without Kevin around. I have beaten up Matt twice but he now has a gun and that worries me."

Nicole smiled. "Wow, you are one tough gal that's for sure. Anyway, he won't do anything even if he does somehow recognize us. He knows we are here, otherwise why would he be watching our hotel? It is a busy road leading to the museum and the museum will probably be crowded."

Joana finally shrugged and said, "Okay. Let's go." Nicole went to her room and Joana into hers. About fifteen minutes later Nicole knocked on her door.

Joana opened it and smiled. "You would think it was winter."

Nicole had on a jacket, a scarf and a stocking cap. She handed Joana another scarf and stocking cap. She already had a jacket that they had bought her the other day. Once Joana had put on the scarf and cap the girls headed out.

They walked down the stairs and opened the side door. Nicole peeked around outside before she led the way out. They turned onto Adalstraeti Street toward the museum, and arrived about ten minutes later and entered.

XXXXX

Matt saw two females walk out to the street from the side of the hotel where the guy picked up the car problem guy. The females were dressed as though it were late fall or winter. They were way over dressed for the weather today. It might be considered chilly but it certainly didn't warrant a scarf and stocking hat. He began to wonder.

XXXXX

Hugin dropped Jason off and headed out to the spot where Kevin left the bike. When he finally arrived, Kevin jumped out and Hugin waited to make sure it started.

Kevin picked up the bike and checked for damage. There were scraps and dents that he would have to pay for but it was otherwise okay. He got on and pushed the start button. It hesitated and died. He tried kick starting it three more times before it revved and continued running.

Hugin waved bye and Kevin gave him a thumbs up. Thirty minutes later Kevin passed Hugin on the way back to Reykjavik.

Jason finished taking care of the rental stuff and wandered around the store waiting for Hugin.

Once Nicole and Joana had gotten into the museum, Nicole quietly told Joana, "I am going to text Kevin to tell him where we are and to come get us when he gets back." Joana nodded. "I am also going to call Jason in case Kevin is out on the highway."

She texted Kevin and waited for a response. After a minute or so and no response, she called Jason's number. It rang and he answered on the second ring. "Hey Nicole. What's going on?"

"Joana and I are at the National Museum of Iceland. I texted Kevin but he might be out on the road. I just wanted someone to know where we are."

"I am done here so I'll take a taxi to you. I should be there in thirty minutes."

"Okay. We'll meet you on the ground floor in the museum café in half an hour."

They ended the call. Nicole turned to Joana. "Jason is coming to meet us here."

XXXXX

Matt was trying to reason out what might be going on. He saw two men come around from the back of the hotel. Then, a short time later, he saw two women come from the same area. That is four people acting somewhat suspicious. There are four people in the group he is following. Except for the driver, who wasn't one of them.

I think the side entrance is where I need to be. He got up, paid his bill, and headed out.

He walked the short distance to the opposite side of the hotel and looked around. Directly opposite the side street was the Hlollabatar restaurant. He went in, ordered a beer, and sat by the nearest window to wait.

XXXXX

Kevin went straight to the bike rental and started the paperwork to return the bike and pay for the damages.

Hugan went to the apartment to dismantle his equipment and cancel his rental.

About the time Kevin got back, Jason and the girls decided that two hours in the museum was enough. They walked back to the hotel but before they left, Jason bought a cap and a pair of sunglasses. He zipped his jacket up to his neck and rolled his collar up. The girls buttoned their jackets, wound their scarfs, and slipped on the stocking caps. They walked back the same way that the girls had come. Shortly, they arrived at the back door, entered, and decided to wait in Kevin's room since it adjoined Joana's room.

Matt had been watching for them, so as soon as they entered he rushed over to the door and entered. He heard them moving up the stairs so he quietly followed them up. He heard the exit door open and close so he rushed up to the next floor. He peeked out just as they all entered a room. Matt noted the room number. He waited a minute or so in the stairwell then entered the hallway.

As he walked to the door, he kept glancing around to see if anyone was around. Once at the door, he pulled the gun from his pocket and held it down at his side toward the back by his butt. He knocked on the door.

"That must be Hugin. Kevin is still too far away. Besides, this is his room and he has a key." Jason opened the door.

Jason flew backwards and landed hard on the floor. Matt quickly moved in and closed the door. He held his gun out and pointed it at Joana. "Well, well. I have you now bitch."

Joana stared at him. Nicole was down on her knees beside Jason holding his head in her lap and trying to stop the blood flowing from his forehead. She glanced at Matt with hatred.

He barely noticed her. He motioned for Joana to move toward Nicole. Joana took two steps to the side and stopped. Matt moved toward the back of the room so that he was half facing the door and half facing Joana and Nicole.

"You people have been nothing but trouble for me. That treasure is mine. It belongs to my family because we are descendants of Arild, the man who killed Ragnvadr. I want the map." Without taking his eyes off of Joana, he told Nicole, "Give me the map."

Nicole told him, "I don't have it on me. It is up in my room."

Matt smiled. "No problem. After I kill Joana and then Jason, we can mosey on up and retrieve it. If you are a good girl about it, then you can live."

Nicole didn't believe that for a minute. She looked back down at Jason, who had started to moan.

Matt stared at Jason and thought about shooting him now just to shut him up. No, he wanted to kill Joana so bad. She had to be first.

He turned to her. Just then the lock clicked on the door and it opened.

Matt started to turn to the door with the gun. Joana yelled, "Matt has a gun!"

Matt quickly brought his attention back to Joana and moved the gun toward her. He suddenly saw a flash and Kevin flew past him onto Joana. He fired.

Kevin fell forward on top of Joana.

Hugin had just exited the elevator when he heard the gunshot. It meant only one thing. Matt was here.

He stood between Kevin and Joana's rooms and listened. He heard Joana crying and saying 'No' over and over. He swung around in front of Kevin's door. He knocked.

Matt waved Nicole over to open the door. She hesitated but he pointed the gun at Jason and she moved to the door. She yanked it open and stood.

She looked down and saw Hugin squatting with a gun aimed into the room. He gave her a slight wave to the side. She moved around behind the door.

Matt looked at the open door then saw too late the gun pointing at him. "What the …?"

Hugin calmly put three bullets in Matt's chest, and who staggered back then fell onto the floor.

Hugin stood and closed the door. He looked at Joana as she scrambled out from under Kevin. "Is he okay?"

"I think so. I'll check." She checked the wound.

Meanwhile, Hugin went to Matt and kicked his gun away then set his own on the bed.

"How is Jason?"

"He is groggy and has a big bump on his head but I think he will be fine."

"Good. Joana, what about Kevin?"

"The bullet hit his shoulder but I can't determine if it is still in there. He needs a hospital."

Hugin turned to Nicole. "Call the front desk and tell them we need the police and medical services."

Nicole moved to the phone at the side of the bed and picked it up.

Hugin went into the bathroom and came out with three small towels. He tossed one to Joana and took the other two to Matt.

He kneeled down next to Matt with his back to Joana. He felt a very weak pulse. Matt wouldn't make it unless the medics arrived soon. He applied one towel to one of the wounds and held the other over Matt's nose and mouth. He applied pressure on both. After twenty or thirty seconds, Matt's body twitched once and was still. Hugin felt for a pulse and found none. He removed the towel from Matt's mouth and placed it on one of his wounds and pressed. Once he had sufficient blood on both towels he slowly stood.

He looked at Joana who was looking back at him. "He didn't make it."

Joana nodded with a slight smirk. "Good." She turned her attention back to Kevin.

They began to hear sirens down on the street.

XXXXX

The police and medics arrived almost simultaneously and began their work in Kevin's room.

They started to question Nicole and Joana since they were closest to the door but Hugin quickly moved to them and suggested that they talk with him first. He explained who everyone was, including Matt. He described the circumstances leading up to the incident and who did the shooting. He pointed to Matt's gun and to his.

Meanwhile, the medics moved Jason and Kevin onto gurneys to transport them to the hospital and allowed Nicole and Joana to accompany them. Two police officers went with them.

Jason was released from the hospital a day later but Kevin was kept for two more days. He didn't require surgery but they wanted to make sure that the wound did not become infected.

Hugin hired a well-known and respected attorney to handle the inquiries into all that had happened over the past several weeks. The lead attorney had an additional staff of five who dealt with the various filings, petitions and other paperwork.

After two months of legal discussions and interviews, Hugin was cleared, and the case was closed and marked as a self-defense shooting.

XXXXX

Three months after the case was closed, Hugin met with Jason, Nicole, Kevin, Joana and Dr. Bergstrom, who demanded that he call her Ingvill from then on. Hugin presented them with a proposal that he and his grandfather had put together.

The proposal was that his grandfather would buy the entire cave find for $500,000 with the approval of the Iceland and Norway governments. The find would then be divided and donated back to museums in Reykjavik, Oslo and York.

The proposal also included payments of $50,000 each to Joana, Kevin, Jason and Nicole for the work they put in to uncover the treasure. Joana had vehemently opposed this saying that she had been the one who almost caused the treasure to not be found at all. All of them began talking at the same time telling her no, it was not true, she should not be blamed, etc.

Finally, Kevin took Joana aside, held her hands and quietly talked to her. After a few minutes, they came back to the group. Joana smiled at them and said okay.

Epilogue – Two Years Later

A Final Vow

The small group was gathered in Lord Wilkinson's spacious library. There was a representative from each of three museums – The Viking Center of York, England, the National Museum of Iceland, and the Historisk Museum in Oslo. There was also a representative from the University of Cincinnati's Department of Archaeology. The other attendees were Kevin Rivers, Joana Wells and his grandson Hugin. However, the meeting could not yet start since three more people were required.

"Please enjoy the refreshments. I am sure we will be able to start soon."

Twenty minutes later, Jason, Nicole and Ingvill came breathless into the room. Jason and Nicole had been waiting for Ingvill's flight, which had been delayed due to some mechanical problem.

Joana saw them first and quickly moved to them. "Hey, you finally made it." She hugged each of them. Kevin was just behind her and did the same.

Hugin moved to his grandfather and whispered that they were ready to start. He pointed to the three newcomers.

Lord Wilkinson moved to the large table and announced that the meeting would begin. Once they were all seated, he began. "Thank you all for coming all the way to my home for this meeting today. The total value of the find has not been completely determined but, in accordance with prior agreements, I am buying the entire find for $500,000 and will then donate all of the items to the three museums represented here today."

"The exceptions are that one object will be selected to be donated to the University of Cincinnati in honor of Dr. James McGuire whose early vision led to this magnificent outcome. Another object will be selected and donated to Serpent Mound Archaeological Site. These selections and the division of the find that will go to each museum will be decided by the committee of one representative from each museum plus Dr. Bergstrom, who will have final authority over any disagreements."

"Additionally, traveling displays of the various objects in the treasure will be scheduled every two years and the first stop will always be at the University of Cincinnati. The remaining stops will be determined by the committee mentioned already."

"Finally, credit for the discovery of the treasure will be permanently assigned to Dr. McGuire, Dr. Bergstrom, Jason Swenson, Nicole Prator, Joana Wells and Hugin Wilkinson."

"Now, please, everyone stay and enjoy the food and drinks in the dining room to your left. Please be sure to introduce yourselves to the four founders of the treasure who are wonderful young people that I am sure you will enjoy meeting."

XXXXX

Ingvill had to return to Oslo the next day but promised to keep in touch will Nicole, Jason, Kevin and Joana.

Nicole and Jason were leaving the following day so the four of them met at Yates Pub on the Ouse River in downtown York. They each ordered Bangers and Mash and a bottle of wine for the table.

"So, what's next for you two?" Kevin asked Jason and Nicole.

"Well," Nicole looked at Jason and then at Kevin and Joana. "We are getting married next year." She waved her hand toward them so they could see her engagement ring. "We definitely want you both to come. Ingvill will be my maid of honor but I want you, Joana, to be one of my bride's maids. Please say you will."

Joana smiled and said, "Of course. I am honored, thank you."

They talked and ate and finished the wine before separating and heading off to their hotels after lots of hugs, handshakes and kisses.

Two days later Kevin and Joana flew back to the states. They had to change flights in Washington, DC for their final leg to Cincinnati, and were sitting in a restaurant near their gate having a sandwich and soft drink.

"Hey, Kevin. I need to use the restroom. I'll be right back." She kissed him and left.

Five minutes later, Kevin looked back toward the restrooms. Ten minutes later he checked his watch and paid the bill. Fifteen minutes later he walked to the restroom and called Joana's name at the door. Several women stared at him as they came out. Two women turned away from going in. Twenty minutes later he was wandering the airport aimlessly. He went to the departure gate then went to the customer service counter to see if she cancelled her ticket, and she had not.

He called the 'watcher' and asked her to find Joana.

XXXXX

Joana felt terrible ditching Kevin but he could not be involved in what she was going to do next.

She had barely made it to her flight to Omaha after skirting past the restroom and rushing to her new flight. She was seated in a middle seat near the rear of the plane. She had bought and carried a roll-a-board suitcase to make sure they didn't get suspicious of someone without luggage. The bag was empty but she didn't care. She wouldn't need anything for what she was going to do.

The flight landed and she walked to the car rental area. She rented a car, tossed her empty bag in the trunk and drove to Bellevue, Nebraska. She hoped that he was still living there. She had never contacted him since she had left.

XXXXX

The 'watcher' contacted Kevin and told him that Joana flew to Omaha and rented a car. She had watched the car on traffic cameras until Joana got off of Highway 75 then she lost the car and Joana.

"What is near that exit?"

She told him that the town of Bellevue is just off the exit and Offutt Air Force base is also right there.

"Do either of them have a connection to Joana's past?"

She told him that she would search and get back to him.

Kevin rushed to the nearest reader board, found the next flight to Omaha, and booked a seat on it. It left in forty-five minutes. This would mean that Joana had an hour and a half head start on him. He called the 'watcher' and told her to book him a rental car and send him a text. She said okay then told him that the only reference she could find for Joana in Bellevue is a school she attended when she was twelve. She had also found an address for someone with the same last name who could be a relative. She passed it on to Kevin.

XXXXX

Joana pulled off the exit and into the parking lot of a restaurant. She needed to think about this. She entered the restaurant which also had a bar area, so she went there and ordered a gin and tonic. She paid her tab, and stared at the television on the wall behind the bar. *He may not even be there or alive for that matter. What am I really going to do if he is there? Why am I even going?*

She mulled over these questions as she sipped her drink. She was half finished with her drink when she rose, left for the parking lot, and her rental car. She got in and sat looking at the passing cars.

She finally drove to his house. She didn't recognize the neighborhood but she immediately knew the house. Again, she sat and stared at the front door. *Am I really going to go inside that filthy place? Do I seriously want to look at his face again after all these years and after all the horror he had heaped on me?*

She took a deep breath, got out of the car but hesitated next to it. She hesitantly walked to the front door, stood a moment then rang the doorbell. She waited. When no one came to the door, she almost left. *No, I have come this far, I will see this through.* She knocked, waited then knocked again. She moved closer to the door and listened. She could hear the faint sound of what was probably a television soap opera show.

She steeled herself and opened the door. She called out a "Hello." No one called back. She called louder.

Finally, a male voice mumbled, "Go away."

Joana moved cautiously to the living room and entered. He was a mess. He was sitting in a wheelchair and the floor was covered with food wrappers and beer bottles. He also smelled as though he hadn't bathed since she last saw him. His back was to her so she walked around to face him.

He slowly looked up at her and seemed to be trying to focus his eyes and mind on what he was seeing.

Joana watched him go through the processing. He hacked several times and spittle dripped down his chin onto his t-shirt, which had probably been white at some point.

He finally seemed to remember who she was. He half smiled and said, "Well, you finally came home honey." He started hacking and coughing.

His voice was barely above a whisper and she hated the sound of it. She especially hated that he called her 'honey'. He had never treated her with sweetness so how could he even think to use the term. She asked. "So, are you dying now?"

"What? I can't hear you. Come closer."

She moved to a position about two feet to the side of his chair. "I asked if you ..."

Quicker than she would have expected him to be, his hand shot out, grabbed her wrist, and pulled her onto his lap face down. *Oh my god. He smells so bad.* She felt his hand on her butt where he began fondling it. He was also trying to reach around to her breasts.

She elbowed his stomach and he pulled back his hands. She rolled off of him and stood clear of his reach. She was breathing rapidly and her heart rate had skyrocketed. She drilled her eyes straight into him. She wanted to kill him so bad. She clenched her fists.

He must have noticed because he asked her. "Do you want to kill me? You do, don't you. I was horrible to you back then. I sold you to my friends. You probably hate me. But, before you do, I want to tell you that you were a really nice piece. Man I enjoyed doing it to you. You got me so horny all the time. All the guys couldn't wait to get their turn on you. You should kill me, you know. I am a horrible human being."

She began to calm. He was begging her to kill him. He was probably in pain and wanted it to be over. He wasn't sorry for what he had done to her. He just wanted to die by her hand.

"So, you are dying, aren't you?"

"Come on kill me. Do it!"

"Nah. I won't give you the satisfaction of an easy death."

She turned and headed for the door.

"You bitch. Bitch. Bitch. Bitch."

She stepped out onto the front stoop and closed the door behind her. Just then a car pulled up. She thought it might be some caregiver for her father. But it wasn't. It was a caregiver, but not for her father. It was Kevin and he cared for her.

She walked quickly to him and intercepted him as he stepped onto the sidewalk. She threw her arms around his neck and kissed him hard on the mouth. He was startled for a moment then he grabbed her tightly and returned the kiss.

They finally stood apart. "Is this your father's house?"

"Yes, and he is dying." She saw his concerned look. "Not by my hand. He is still alive but not for long I suspect. He probably has cancer or something just as bad. He looks horrible, coughs up stuff, and smells like a cesspool. He wanted me to take him out of his misery but I refused."

Kevin relaxed.

"Come on. Let's go. Let's turn in these vehicles and get back to work. I received a text from Hugin and he has a new case for us. It is a hostage rescue of a twelve year old girl."

They got into their rentals and headed off to their new assignment with the Hugin Security and Investigation Company.

Author's Notes:

Viking's in the United States?

There is no archaeological evidence that Vikings settled in the United States. However, my assumption that some may have attempted to explore the area seems reasonable since there is evidence of Viking settlements in eastern Canada.

Mounds and Serpent Mound

Mounds do exit all over the world. I have actually visited them in Korea, Great Britain, Norway, and Ireland. The Serpent Mound does exist in southeast Ohio and it is a fascinating structure. There are many mounds in that area but none, at this point, have been found to contain a chamber and a burial box.

Oslo, Norway

I have made two visits to Oslo to explore museums and sites that are related to the Vikings and to Nordic culture and history. There was an actual battle fought at the site mentioned in the story around the same time in the story. However, the actual combatants and results in the story are my invention.

Reykjavik, Iceland

I visited Iceland and explored their museums and sites in the Reykjavik area. The Hard Rock Café exists and is a fun place to grab a drink and some food. I did not venture out to the mountain mentioned in the story but it is there.

Stockholm, Sweden and The Vasa

I visited Stockholm's many museums and historic sites in the area. The Vasa is a real ship and it is huge, but the design was flawed. It did in fact sink only a short 28 minutes into its sailing and most of those on board were drowned. The tops of the sails were actually still visible after it settled on the bottom of the harbor. The ship was recovered and refloated in 1956 and is preserved in a fantastic museum in Stockholm.

Copenhagen, Denmark and York, England

I visited Copenhagen and York to research the history of Vikings in those areas. There is a great deal of Viking history preserved in a variety of museums and sites in and around York. The invasion mentioned in the story where tens of thousands of the Viking people settled in the York area did happen at the time mentioned.

Archaeology

I have always had an interest in archaeology. I subscribe to two magazines and have been on two archaeological digs in Israel. The concepts in the story are based on my experiences and research. I completed two courses on archaeology at Tel Aviv University while there. They were Archaeology Field Work and Regional History, Geography and Archaeology.

Made in the USA
San Bernardino, CA
27 August 2018